Dragon Ore
Book Three of The Dawning of Power trilogy
By Brian Rathbone

Copyright © 2008 by Brian Rathbone.
White Wolf Press, LLC
Rutherfordton, NC 28139

The Godfist

The Greatland

Prologue

Fields of aquatic vegetation shimmered under clear, blue waters, patches of white sand standing out in bold contrast. The *Stealthy Shark* sliced through calm seas as silent as her name would imply. Standing at the bow, Chase and Fasha watched Istra's eye set the skies afire, and neither dared give voice to their thoughts.

The longer Catrin had been gone, the less Chase liked her plan. Brother Vaughn had been true to his word and, in getting a message to Fasha, had done more than his share to help Chase achieve his goal, but that goal still seemed unattainable. The southern shores of the Greatland stretched on endlessly, and unlike on maps, there were no markings to show where Faulk ended and the Westland began.

"The southern coast of the Westland is less inhabited than that of Faulk," Fasha said. "There are places we can wait for her."

Chase just nodded, silent, unable to maintain much hope. The Greatland was so vast, a person could easily disappear into it, and he feared Catrin and Benjin would do just that.

During their journey, skirting the coastline, they had stopped at small and hidden docks along the way, getting news and supplies. Reports were clear. The Statue of Terhilian found in southern Faulk had been moved to Adderhold by barge, and more recently, another had been found in the Westland. Catrin would have to go to Adderhold. And if she survived that, would she go next to the Westland? Indecision gnawed at Chase. Should he stay with the original plan when his gut told him to go find her? He weighed every possibility in his mind as the coastline slid by.

News of revolts and unrest throughout the Greatland made him wonder if Catrin would ever even get within sight of the statue. It seemed unlikely. Trying to be strong, he committed himself to waiting, just as Catrin had asked him to do. Any other course was just too risky.

In an instant, though, the world changed. A blinding flash of green light backlit the coast, and moments later, a thunderous blast rocked the ship, followed by low, rumbling echoes in the distance.

"May the gods be gentle," Fasha said, her hand over her mouth. Chase swayed on his feet and braced himself on the railing.

"That came from the Westland, didn't it? It was over that way," Chase said, motioning ahead and to the left of their position.

"It did."

"Then the one Catrin set out to destroy?" he asked.

"Will be next."

"I need to get to Adderhold."

Scowling fiercely, Fasha concentrated, and there was a long pause before she nodded firmly and spoke, "I will take you to Madra. Perhaps her wisdom will show us a way."

Chapter 1

The wise old wolf is not wise because he's a wolf, but because he's old.
--Javid Frederick, farmer

* * *

Floating in a haze of semiconsciousness, Catrin wondered if she were dead. Death had claimed her; she knew it had. Her body had failed, unable to cope with the stresses applied by so much power. Yet it did not feel like death; something of life remained. Unable to define it, she searched for what seemed an eternity. Beyond the haze of sleep, something called to her, demanding her attention. It would not be denied, and it found her.

It was an itch.

Refusing to allow rest, it demanded she notice and, at the very least, scratch. Driven by the nagging irritation, she tried to move, and the sensations of her body slowly returned. The painful tingling of flesh left too long without blood ravaged her, and her leaden limbs failed to respond, refused to answer her desperate call for motion. Unable to lift her arms, she struggled to see what bound her and held her fast.

Her eyelids were crusted shut as if they were glued in place. Unwilling to relent, she forced them open. Soft light was like a furious blaze, daring her to see. Still she insisted, and the clouds in her eyes faded enough for her to see the face of an unfamiliar man hovering over her. Fear impaled her.

"Benjin," she tried to say through parched lips, needing his strength more than ever before. But her ears heard only an incoherent mumble, as even her voice refused to do her bidding.

"A moment, m'lady," the stranger said. "Only a moment and he'll be here. He's been by your side for days, but exhaustion overcame him." Another figure darted from the shadows and out of the room before Catrin could see who it was.

6

Her efforts drained the little energy she possessed, but she would not allow herself to succumb, afraid that, if she let herself sleep, she might never wake again. Holding her eyes open by the sheer force of her will, she endured pain with every involuntary blink, but her vision grew clearer, and the fog began to lift from her mind. When Benjin arrived, the concern on his face made her wonder how horrible she must look.

"It's good to see you awake, li'l miss," he said, obviously trying to be cheerful despite her condition.

When Catrin tried to reply, her parched throat ached and she could only cough.

"Get her some water," Benjin said to Morif, who waited in the shadows. He filled a small cup and handed it to Benjin, who held it to Catrin's mouth. She let it pour over her lips, and she rolled it over her tongue before swallowing. Water slid down the back of her throat and tickled, resulting in another fit of coughing, but at least her throat was now moist. She wanted to drain the entire cup, but Benjin gave her only a small amount more before he set the cup aside. "Can you talk?"

"I think," she said, but she had to stop and swallow. "I think I can." Even as she spoke, though, the itching overpowered her. Feeling began to return to her limbs. Her arm moved, unwieldy and slow, and her fingers curled to scratch her side.

Benjin gently took her hand. "You must not scratch no matter how bad it itches."

Catrin looked at her hand. Layers of dead skin, peeled and cracked, encased her like a dried husk, and her blackened fingernails curled back away from the nail beds. Despair shadowed her soul. How could she go on like this? Who had done this to her?

Barabas.

The name was like a sledge landing between her ears. He had done this to her. She had been ready to depart this world, but Barabas somehow sent her back. This was his fault, and she hated him for it. Tears stung her eyes and tickled the sides of her face. She wanted to reach up and soothe it, but she could not. Even if she'd had the will to raise her arm and scratch with her wasted nails, Benjin would stop her, and she hated him for that. "Go away. All of you. Get out."

Benjin frowned, and she thought he would resist, but he nodded slowly. "Rest some more for now, li'l miss. Things'll be better when you next wake."

"Leave me alone," she said, hating herself for it.

* * *

Weeks passed as Catrin recovered. Her fingernails fell off, and eventually she was allowed to rub away the dead skin. Still she itched. Her skin appeared whole, but it was as if the air itself offended the new skin, leaving it blotchy and irritated. Slowly, her strength returned, and when Benjin arrived for one of his daily visits, she actually smiled.

"Would you like to walk?" he asked, and her soul soared. The thought of getting out of bed, standing upright, and walking in the sunlight thrilled her. She was ready--more than ready. Benjin moved to her side and helped her sit up, but her confidence faltered. The world moved unpredictably, swaying from side to side, and her stomach protested.

"Deep breaths. Be calm. Close your eyes if it helps."

It didn't help. Instead she focused on the doorway. Concentrating on the angles, knowing what they should look like, she willed her mind to see it the way it truly was. Gradually it stopped moving, and it felt like a victory when Catrin saw clean, right angles. After a few more deep breaths, she nodded to Benjin; she was ready. He eased her legs over the side, and the cold stone felt good under her feet. She wobbled as she stood, and she leaned on Benjin heavily at times, but she was standing--another victory. They did not walk in the sunlight as she had hoped, but even darkened halls were far better than being confined to bed.

After he'd helped her back into bed, Benjin handed her a small mirror. "Don't be alarmed," he said.

When she mustered the courage to look, she saw a stranger. Her skin was reddish and looked as if it would crack into a thousand pieces if she moved too quickly, but it was her hair that brought tears to her eyes. Still short, the tips looked as her hair always had, but the roots were as white as goose down.

"I look like an old woman."

"It's not so bad," he said, "and it may wear off. You're already looking better. Do you want me to cut it for you?"

"No," Catrin said. The part of her hair that retained its color was a part of her old self, and she refused to let go of it. So many things about her and her world had changed, and she clung to anything that reminded her of her old life; precious little remained, and she cried herself to sleep.

* * *

Each day brought new challenges and new accomplishments. Training herself as she would a horse, Catrin walked a little farther every day, slowly rebuilding her strength and endurance. During this time, she learned of things that happened after the destruction of the statue. Barabas's body had not been found, as if he had disappeared into the statue. Morif and Millie had dragged Catrin and Benjin away from the arena, searching for a place to hide.

People began to rise up against the Zjhon, and most within Adderhold sought to flee, but one man came looking for Catrin: Samda, a Zjhon Master and former servant of Archmaster Belegra.

"He's shown nothing but compassion for you," Millie said. "He's kept us hidden and safe. You can trust him."

Catrin didn't believe a word of it. How could a Zjhon Master want anything other than her death? Yet he could have had them killed or imprisoned and had not. He could have left her to die but had not.

"Why did you come to our aid?" she asked him one day.

"I did what I believed was right, m'lady."

"And when the Zjhon invaded the Godfist, did you believe that was right?"

"At the time, m'lady, I did," Samda replied, his eyes downcast.

"But you no longer believe that?" she asked, and he only shook his head in response. "What changed your mind?"

9

"Many things, m'lady: the explosion of the statue in the Westland, Archmaster Belegra's disregard for human life, and his refusal to admit he'd been wrong. He chose, instead, to make up lies about you, and that I could not abide. But mostly, m'lady, it was you," Samda said, meeting her eyes. She saw no guile there, no deception, only deep regret.

"What about me?"

"At first, it was your presence here when the other statue exploded. I could find no way to explain it. There was only one logical conclusion: we, the Zjhon, had been wrong. We had interpreted the holy writings to say what we wanted them to say. I suspected it many years ago, but I could not discard my beliefs so easily. Can you imagine suddenly realizing that everything your family ever taught you was false? It wasn't easy, but you and Archmaster Belegra convinced me. He threw away lives as if they were of no value, and even as men sought to end your life, you wept for them." Tears filled his eyes.

"I didn't want to believe, even then," Samda continued, "but how could I deny it? I considered fleeing with the rest, but where would I have gone? What would I have done? How could I have lived with myself, knowing so many lives had been lost because of my folly? I could not. I had to find some way to right my wrongs and those committed by the Zjhon empire. I had to help you, and I made my decision. I stopped thinking and started acting. I brought you here so you could heal in safety."

Here turned out to be a complex of caves and tunnels, deep beneath Adderhold.

"There were only a few within Adderhold that know this level of catacombs exist, and of those, I am the only one remaining," Samda said. "The rest have either fled with Belegra and his elite guards or have disappeared."

"What of Belegra? Where do you think he has gone?"

"I believe he seeks the Firstland, m'lady," Samda said. "I was not privy to all his plans, and we did not often discuss the possibility of defeat; it seemed unlikely. But I do know that he'd been studying ancient texts, searching for sources of power. I suppose that is the greatest irony. He speaks of your powers as abominations, yet he seeks those very same powers with relentless ambition, and it seems he has talents of his own--as you have seen for yourself."

"The power to coerce and enslave?" Catrin asked, a fury rising within her. "Yes. I've witnessed it." It was that power that held Prios in thrall and prevented his freedom. The connection between her and Prios was difficult to understand, but she was connected to him nonetheless, and she detested Archmaster Belegra's mistreatment of him. "Who are the robed figures he used to attack me?"

"His cadre, as he calls them. They are from all over the Greatland, ranging from highborn to slave. Before the appointed time of Istra's return, Belegra gave orders: Anyone who manifested powers of any kind was to be brought to him, in shackles if need be. I know not how he learned to coerce them and use their powers, but I fear he seeks even greater and more dangerous arcana within the halls of the ancients."

Catrin wanted to ask about Prios, but she did not yet fully trust Samda, and she decided to keep their connection a secret. "Is the location of the Firstland known?"

"Not to me, m'lady, and if Belegra knew, he'd have kept the knowledge hidden. It's a long-standing Zjhon practice-- keep secrets close and only ever reveal part of the truth. This is how the Godfist was taken by surprise, you see. Hundreds of years ago, when the Zjhon held the only copies of many ancient texts, new copies were created and filled with false information. Rather than remove the sections that told when Istra would return, our ancestors changed the dates--among other things--while preserving the original texts in sacred vaults."

Catrin swayed as the past began to make sense. Benjin had once said that the Vestrana's calculations had been wrong, and now she knew why. Things could have been much different had they known the truth.

"I know not what Belegra will find, if anything. He goes in search of legends and myths, believing he will find Enoch and Ain Giest still alive . . . or maybe even dragons."

"Dragons?"

"Indeed, m'lady, dragons," Samda replied, and he drew a deep breath. "Legends say they were a source of incredible

11

power. Unfortunately, there are very few details in the texts. It seems dragon lore was such common knowledge in those times that it was either not written down or not preserved. We've found vague references but nothing to indicate exactly what kind of power they possessed or how it came to be harnessed by men. The only thing I can say for certain is that, at one point in our history, man and dragon worked together."

Catrin's imagination conjured skies filled with mighty wizards on the backs of dragons. It was both thrilling and terrifying.

"Belegra also seeks knowledge, which is power in itself. In particular, I believe he searches for the locations of the other Statues of Terhilian."

"What?" Catrin asked, agape. "How many statues *are* there?"

"I cannot be sure, but I believe four--possibly five--were buried before they exploded. Of those, two have been found. That would leave the possibility of three unaccounted for."

Three statues--they could be buried just about anywhere, and they could explode at any time, even if left underground. There seemed no way to evade the impending disaster. Frustrated, Catrin changed the subject. "What about the Zjhon armies? Where are they now?"

"I can't say for certain. The siege on Ohmahold has most likely been called off since you are obviously no longer there, and I assume Belegra will join his forces with those of General Dempsy. With the ships that returned from the Godfist, they could sail with a sizable army."

"Still, there would be a considerable force left behind, and they may be coming to retake Adderhold," Benjin added.

"Indeed, and we should not be here when they arrive, but where will we go?" Samda asked, and silence hung in the air.

Catrin was torn. Part of her wanted to go south to meet Chase, as they had planned, but another part wanted to return to Ravenhold, and yet another part wanted to return to Ohmahold. In the back of her mind, though, when she put aside her responsibilities, she wanted most to return to the Godfist. Any road she chose would be perilous; every choice would leave her vulnerable in some way. "South," she said, her mind made up; she would not abandon Chase.

"With an army possibly coming from the north, I'd say that's a wise choice," Benjin said. "With any luck, your cousin will already have transport to Ohmahold arranged."

Samda raised an eyebrow but said nothing.

Millie, though, stood in the corner with her hands on her hips. "You would leave your grandmother to suffer the wrath of the Kytes alone?"

"I can only be in one place at a time. I promised Chase I would meet him. I made no such promise to my grandmother. She'll have to wait for now, but I'll return to Ravenhold when I can," Catrin replied, and Millie pursed her lips.

Morif chuckled.

"What are you laughing at?" Millie asked.

"The girl's got fire. You must grant her that," he replied, smiling. "I like a girl with fire."

Millie just crossed her arms and cast angry glances around the room.

"The more immediate problem is how to get out of Adderhold," Benjin said. "I'd rather not be seen if possible."

"There is a way, but we should leave soon," Samda said. "Do you feel strong enough to travel, li'l miss?"

"I'm ready," she lied.

Through darkened halls, Samda led them, only the light of his lamp guiding the way. Catrin leaned on her staff, her fingers resting in the impressions left by her grip during the destruction of the statue--a silent reminder. Though the staff had been dull and ashen when Benjin returned it to her, its sheen was beginning to return, and the torchlight danced across its surface.

After a meandering trek through the underbelly of Adderhold, Samda stopped at a corner that looked no different from the rest, ran his hands along the wall, and pushed open a hidden door. Inside, a narrow flight of rough-hewn stairs descended into the darkness. A cool breeze carried the smell of the sea, and around a bend in the stair, yellowish moonlight danced across dark water. A small landing jutted into the water, and moored there was a sailing vessel large enough to carry roughly a dozen people.

"Very few know this place exists. I doubt anyone is watching the outlet, but we must be as quiet as possible."

They boarded the boat, retrieved the lines, and using the four rows of oars, paddled toward the moonlight. The opening in the cavern wall was tall and slender. Beyond it stood a ring of towering stones, seemingly barring their path, but as they approached, a narrow channel became visible between two rows of massive stones. There was little room for mistakes, and despite their efforts, they grazed the rocks twice before gaining open water.

A haze blurred the stars and gave the moon a brownish tint, as if the skies were tainted. Still, the light of distant comets bolstered Catrin's strength; energy soaked into her bones and warmed her against the chill wind that descended from the west. The sails snapped taut as they were raised, and with Benjin's help, Samda guided the ship into deep water, far from either shore.

"It's dangerous for us to go out this far in such a small craft, but I think we should get south of Waxenboro, where the lands are much less populated, before we go near shore. We can't go too far, though. South of Mahabrel the Inland Sea becomes much more dangerous and unpredictable. I wouldn't advocate crossing in this boat," Samda said. As if to prove his point, the growing waves tossed them about, nearly capsizing the small craft.

Weakness still caused Catrin to tremble, but she felt much better breathing the salty air. Her body might never be able to do things it had once done, but she was determined to try. Barabas had said her work was not yet done, and she tried to prepare herself for whatever might come next.

After taking a deep breath, Catrin reflexively raised her hand to her hair. She could not feel where the translucent whiteness ended and the remaining color began, but she knew it was there--a crutch. Using her knife, she hacked away the color, shearing the ties to her childhood and embracing the future. No longer could she afford to be a frightened little girl, holding on to relics of the past for the comfort they brought. She needed to face her future with

14

confidence and purpose. As an offering to the sea, she cast her hair into the waves, and with it went one of the shadows that had been haunting her soul. She felt freed and renewed, but these feelings were accompanied by a great weariness. Knowing she needed sleep in order to heal, Catrin calmed her mind and meditated herself to sleep.

* * *

Moving through the darkness, Chase cursed every branch that snapped beneath his boots. Fasha had given him no reason to believe the people here would be hostile, but she hadn't given him any indication that they would be friendly either. All he knew was approximately where to find this woman named Madra and that he could trust her. Fasha had given him directions and even drawn him a map, but he feared he was hopelessly lost, and the thought of finding someone to ask made him feel ill. These people had more reason to fear him than to trust him, and he decided he would keep searching, even if he had to retrace his steps back to the shoreline and begin his journey again.

Just as the thought entered his mind, Chase caught a flash of light through the trees and his hopes soared. Fasha had said that Madra's farm was isolated from the others, like an island within a sea of trees, but he had not thought it could possibly be this deep in the forest. As he cleared the last of the trees and entered a field of tall grass, he stood bathed in pale, yellowish light. Ahead lay lands that seemed to have once been manicured but now were being reclaimed by weeds. Pastures were fenced only in spirit; lines of posts held an occasional slat between them but would keep in no horses or livestock. A feeling of sadness overcame him as he used the tree line for cover, seeing visions of his own homeland, abandoned and neglected. Tears filled his eyes.

When he reached the nearest barn, he was again dismayed by the state of disrepair. Most of the roof had collapsed, and much of what had once been in the hayloft now clogged the aisle as it seemed the ceiling, too, had succumbed to neglect. Staying to the shadows, Chase moved ever closer to the dim light that danced around the edges of a doorframe. Like a distant ray of hope, it drew him forward and banished his fear. When he reached the door, he knocked softly. No answer came. After a moment of trepidation, he pushed open the door. His eyes were met by a contradiction. Inside, sitting alone at a table with nothing but a jar of whiskey and a glass, waited Madra.

A fierce and strong spirit huddled within an aging body. Eyes that spoke of a stone will were rimmed with tears, and a powerful jaw trembled as it tried to hold back the pain. At first, she did not even acknowledge his presence. Instead, she poured another drink. "And who might you be?" she finally asked without looking up.

"My name is Chase," he said when she raised her eyes and met his gaze. He tried to say more, but his knees suddenly felt weak, and his hands began to tremble. He could feel Madra's pain and could think of no words that would be meaningful in the face of such despair.

"I've no patience for halfwits, boy. Go on. Talk. Who sent you?"

"Fasha," he managed to say.

"Let me guess: You came looking for help?"

"Yes, ma'am."

Madra just nodded, bit her lip, and poured her last drink. For a time she simply sat and stared at it. After a few moments, though, she picked it up, stood, and walked outside. Chase followed. Beneath the moon, stars, and comets, Madra stood silent for some time, tears falling to the dusty soil beside her tattered boots. In the end, she raised her glass to the gods: "I beg for help, and you send me those in need. I ask for mercy, and you further test my will. Fine. Have your joke, you thankless jackals. I'll just have to clean up this mess myself!" she said just before she downed her last drink. "Come on, pup. We've work to do."

As he followed Madra back into her home, Chase wondered what he'd gotten himself into.

* * *

When the sun rose, casting a glow across the water, neither shore was visible; only the location of the sun guided them. The winds had taken a southerly turn and grown fierce; their boat cut the waves under full sail, riding the growing swells. With no point of reference, it looked to Catrin as if they were moving slowly, but occasional flotsam appeared in the water and was soon lost in the distance.

"We must get closer to shore before the sea claims us," Benjin shouted to Samda, and they set a westerly course.

By midday, the western coast came into view. The land was mostly forested, and only occasional farmsteads and mills gave any indication of inhabitation. But as the day wore on, the smell of smoke grew heavy on the air, and the setting sun backlit columns of smoke, red and orange, making it appear as if the sky were on fire.

"Perhaps we should move back into deeper water," Benjin said as they neared the coast. The columns of smoke were now close, and acrid clouds rolled over the water. As they passed an isolated farmstead, a band of mounted men appeared, raiding and setting the buildings afire.

"Bandits and thugs," Morif said. "The Zjhon weakened all the lands, and now that they've been routed, anarchy reigns." Samda flushed and kept his eyes downcast. "I mean you no insult, Samda. You've been good to us, but the Zjhon have set the Greatland on a path to destruction." Millie stood, tight-lipped, and cast scathing glances at Morif, but he seemed not to notice as he watched the raiders move on. "There's little food to be had, and too many young folk are dead, with the Zjhon armies, or on the Godfist. If order is not restored, there'll be nothing left to raid by spring."

Catrin watched the razing of the farmstead in horror, seeing visions of her own home destroyed, but she stifled her tears. "Turn back east," she said. "I don't want to land near here." Benjin nodded at her statement.

"The southern waters are far too dangerous," Samda said. "Storms and massive waves strike without warning. It'd be wiser to skirt the western coast and look for a safer place to land," Samda said.

Catrin got a cold feeling in her stomach when she looked at the burning farmstead, and she decided to trust her instincts. "No," she said. "We will risk the crossing."

Chapter 2

Oversight begets disaster.
--Omar Zichter, architect

* * *

An unnatural mist obscured the landscape, green and yellow like a plague, but Catrin recognized her homeland nonetheless. How she had come to be back on the Godfist was lost to her. A part of her seemed to know that she dreamed, but that knowing was overshadowed by fear and foreboding.

Harborton appeared deserted. Not a soul could be found, no birds sang in the trees beyond, and even the leaves were still. As she neared the family farm, though, dark shapes milled about, distorted by the foul mist.

In the barnyard she found her father, Benjin, Uncle Jensen, and even Chase, though she wondered how he had found his way home. Everyone she cared about from her homeland was there, yet no one spoke or even seemed to notice her. Their faces were contorted into masks of fear and rage lit by a feral glow. As one, they moved toward the pasture from which the glow originated, and there, Catrin saw what drew them. The face of Istra stared up from the depths of a gaping wound in the land, and the glow became brighter with every step she took.

She tried to warn them, to tell them to run away, but her voice made no sound, no matter how loudly she tried to scream. Frustration set her soul ablaze as she fought to alert them of the danger, but they would not see--could not hear. Moving inexorably closer, they walked to their deaths, and Catrin was helpless, unable to stop them. Clawing her throat, trying to find her voice, she moved through the cloying mist. With an effort born of love and terror, her scream finally split the air, and every face turned toward her, but before she could warn them, the haze wrapped them in its fetid embrace.

In a flash of ill light, they were gone.

Gentle hands shook Catrin awake. Her eyes burned, and she wiped the sweat from her brow, her mouth tasting of blood.

"It's all right, li'l miss," Benjin said. "I'm here. It was just a dream."

Even in the bright morning light, she could not shake the visions from her mind, and she trembled as she stood. Sucking in a deep breath, she let the damp and salty air drive away the horrors of her dreams. Shading her eyes with her hand, she could see the eastern coast beneath the rising sun.

Prevailing winds continued to drive them, and she estimated they would reach land before noon. Samda brought her a mug of water laced with herbs. "This will help clear your mind," he said.

"Thank you," Catrin said, but she spilled the drink when she spotted a dark and menacing ship approaching. "There's a ship behind us."

"Looks like a mercenary ship," Benjin said, "and I doubt they're friendly. I don't think we can outrun them, even at full sail, but let's raise all we have. Maybe we can make it to shallow water before they catch us." He and Samda moved with purpose to get as much speed as they could. Catrin and the others secured themselves as speed drove the boat into the waves.

After tossing everything that was not precious or essential, the mercenary ship still gained on them, and Catrin knew it would overtake them well before they made land. Benjin and the others seemed to come to the same conclusion and prepared themselves to fight.

Catrin tried to decide what to do. She hadn't used her powers since the destruction of the statue, and she was terrified that they would no longer work or, worse yet, that they would unintentionally hurt those she loved. As her breathing became rapid, she tried to exert control over herself, and she drew deep, steady breaths. It was much like the first time she climbed back onto a horse after having been thrown. Tentatively, she reached for Istra's power. Like breathing, the act of opening herself to the energy felt natural, only, in this case, it felt as if she had spent most of her life holding her breath. The power came reluctantly at first, but then it surged, coming to her in a rush and nearly sweeping her away.

Something within her had changed. It was as if the power she'd felt before had been flowing through a pinhole, and now the dam had burst. With deliberate effort, she pulled herself away from the energy flow. It tempted her with its sweet caress, but she knew she could not give in to its lure or she would be lost. The sudden deprivation of power after such a heady flow made her dizzy, and she swayed where she sat.

As the mercenary ship drew closer, her crew gathered at the bow and hurled insults and jeers across the water. They promised death in a myriad of fashions, and though Catrin knew it was a tactic, she had difficulty avoiding its effects. Her mind invented visions of her death, and she began to sweat. Benjin and the others remained silent, conserving their energy, knowing they would need every reserve to survive.

"They're going to catch us, but they don't want to sink us. They want to rob us. All we have to do is keep them off of us long enough to get to the shallows," Benjin finally said into the silence. "Have no mercy, and don't hesitate. If they drop their guard, take full advantage."

Catrin trembled as the ship drew closer, almost within bow range. The shoreline was so close, she could almost feel the sand beneath her toes, but the water looked plenty deep almost all the way to the white beach, an underwater cliff dropping off into oblivion not far from shore.

Knowing she had to act, Catrin stood on trembling knees and braced herself against the mast. Her staff in hand, she tried to figure out what to do next.

"What are you doing?" Benjin asked. "Get back down. You'll make a good target up there."

"I have to stop them."

"But you aren't fully healed yet. It may not be safe . . ." He trailed off.

"I have to try," Catrin said as she closed her eyes and concentrated. In the past she had used her power to trigger much larger sources of potential energy, but now there was no storm to draw upon, no lightning to call. She would have to rely on Istra's energy alone to assault the ship.

Slowly she opened herself to the source, allowing only a trickle of energy to escape through the mental barrier she maintained between herself and the unmoderated flow of power. A plan began to form in her mind, and though the energy pounded on her barrier, she remained in control.

The air itself carried and conducted energy. As she expanded her senses beyond the bounds of her physical form, she found that she could see, smell, and taste the air around her. Heavy with moisture and teeming with static charge, it became like clay molded by ethereal hands. Pulling the air closer, Catrin gathered it in her cupped palms and packed a continuous flow into a sphere of energy. The air came to her easily, but putting it in the sphere and containing the pressure became increasingly difficult. Drawing more heavily on the energy flow, she reached into her staff and let its comforting energy bolster her.

When she opened her eyes, a translucent ball floated above her palm, its surface always shifting and changing. Raising her palm to her lips, she blew, and the ball of air floated toward the encroaching ship. The farther away it got, the more difficult it was to control and maintain. It was not quite over the bow of the other ship when she had to release it.

A sound like a thunderclap cleaved the air accompanied by a blast of icy wind. At first the mercenaries were stunned, but then arguments broke out. Catrin's attack had been mostly ineffective, but it had convinced some of the mercenaries that this prey was too dangerous to pursue. While they argued, though, the ship moved ever closer.

"Are you all right, li'l miss?"

"I'm fine," she said, putting more of her weight on the mast and trying to steady her quivering knees. "If they do not heed my warning, I'll attack."

Benjin shifted in his seat and looked torn, but he said nothing. The shadow of the mercenary ship was about to close over them, and Catrin drew a deep breath. Just as she began to open herself to the power, men appeared on the mercenary ship with bows. As one, five men drew and aimed at Catrin. In an instant, she drew deeply and let the power flow around her, still drawing more. Her body began to sway from side to side, her arms moving with the rhythm of the power. Arcs of energy trailed behind her staff as it moved, and her hair stood on end. The bowmen did not release, and their arms began to shake from the strain. Slowly, one by one, they lowered their bows.

A shrill cry echoed across the water, and two bodies were thrown over the side of the mercenary ship. Just as the ship moved close enough for the men above to make the jump, it veered away. Catrin released the flow and slumped to the belly of the boat. Though she hated to see anyone die, she had difficulty feeling compassion for the dead captain, and she hoped those who committed the mutiny would remember this day and change their ways.

Just as she began to relax, Millie drew a sharp intake of breath and Benjin cursed. Across the sands came two riders at a full gallop.

"We need to get back to deep water and find another place to land," Benjin said as an army wound its way down a nearby ridge. As the men worked, Catrin watched the riders approach. Wind caught the sails, and the boat began moving away. One of the riders stood in the stirrups and waved his arms, yelling. At first Catrin could not hear what he said, but then the wind shifted and his words drifted to her: "Catrin, wait!"

Benjin heard Chase's call as well, and he smiled broadly as he brought the boat about. Chase reined in his horse, jumped off, and waded to meet them. He looked different-- older. The beginnings of a beard darkened his visage, and Catrin wasn't certain she liked it.

"You look awful," he said as the boat reached shore.

Catrin lowered herself to the sand. "Thanks. You're looking rough yourself. Have you considered shaving?"

"I like it and I'm keeping it."

Catrin laughed and her burdens felt lighter knowing Chase was safe. They walked from the water with their arms

22

around each other. Benjin and Samda rigged the sails on the boat, and they pushed it back out to sea. "I don't want to leave any evidence that we landed here," Benjin said. "Greetings, Chase. You've done well. I look forward to hearing your tale."

"It can't be as good as yours," Chase said with a wink.

A woman with graying hair and eyes like ice stood nearby, holding the two horses. Lines around her eyes gave her a hawkish appearance. Despite all her power, Catrin could get no sense of what the woman was thinking or feeling; she was like a stone.

"Catrin, Benjin, this is Madra. She's the leader of the army you see," Chase said.

"This is the mighty Herald of Istra?" Madra asked. "From the tales I've heard, I expected someone as tall as a bear with eyes of fire."

"Tales are often exaggerated," Catrin responded.

Madra smiled then laughed. "I suppose they are."

Catrin introduced Samda, and she did her best to make him sound like a friend, but Madra and Chase both eyed him with anger and distrust.

Chase pulled Catrin aside while Benjin made the rest of the introductions. "What really happened?"

"To make it all very brief," she said, "I met a druid, who led us through the forests, but the forests caught fire, and then there was a flood. And then I caught a farmer's horse, and he gave us his cross-eyed ox. We sold the ox, and then Millie recognized me and took me to Ravenhold, where I met my grandmother. I can't even tell you the next part. You won't understand."

"Tell me."

"Do you promise not to hate me?"

"Tell me."

"I know who killed our mothers, and I agreed to marry one of their family."

"What?" he said, but their conversation was drawing attention.

"We should discuss this in a more secure location," Madra said. "Let's move inland and make camp."

23

"Take the other horse, Cat," Chase said. "You look like you could use a rest."

Despite her pride, Catrin did not have the energy to decline. She did, however, turn away his offer to give her a boost. She was not that weak.

Lines of soldiers snaked across the sand, and as they drew closer, Catrin saw that they were mostly old men, women, and children--only those the Zjhon armies had left behind. Madra rode ahead to find a suitable place to make camp, and Catrin let Chase lead her horse at a walk while she filled him in on the rest of the details.

"We nearly passed each other," Chase said. "If not for that thunderclap, I would never have known to look for you here. We were heading north, to Adderhold. After the statue exploded, I thought you might not be able to get to me, so I came looking for you."

"I'm grateful fate allowed you to find me. Tell me about Madra and her army. How did you come to travel with them?"

"Fasha brought me to Madra."

"You met Fasha?"

"Yes," Chase said. "She is among the most spirited and brightest people I've ever met. I hope to sail with her again someday. Brother Vaughn took me to the Vestrana in Endland, and they took me to Fasha. We sailed the *Stealthy Shark* to Faulk, but I knew something was wrong when the statue in the Westland exploded, and that's when Fasha took me to Madra. At that time, I don't think even Madra would have guessed that she would be leading an army, but after the statue exploded, the people had had enough. It was Madra who organized them and began the march to Adderhold. I joined them and came in search of you. There were fewer of us in the beginning, but everywhere we go, people join us. In every town it's the same: people are afraid when we arrive, but once we tell them what we are doing, they support us and many join our ranks. But now I don't know what to do. This is not our war, but I'm not sure I can abandon them."

"What does Madra want?" Catrin asked.

"Peace," Chase replied. "The problem is that none of us know how exactly to achieve it."

Catrin understood the problem, having faced the same dilemma herself, but she was no wiser than anyone else. "I wish I knew."

"There is something else I have to tell you. Fasha brought word from the Godfist. I'm sorry, Cat, but someone tried to kill your dad. He was still alive when Fasha left the Godfist, but no one could say if he would survive. Uncle Wendel is strong, though, and I know he still lives. I thought you should know."

Catrin rode in silence, terrified by the thought of someone trying to kill her father and frustrated by not knowing if he still lived. Chase told her more of what happened after she left the Godfist, but she could barely listen. It was just too painful to hear how wrong her plan for peace had gone. She had hoped to unite the people of the Greatland and the Godfist, but her actions had only divided them further.

Beyond a series of steep dunes, the grasslands rolled toward a distant mountain range. Madra and another rider had already staked their horses, and they were pitching tents as Catrin and the others joined with the rest of the army. Walking beside these people, she could hardly consider them an army, and she wondered what good they hoped to accomplish. It was the same question she asked of herself, a question for which she had no answer.

When they arrived at the campsite, Catrin dismounted and began to unsaddle the horse. A woman approached with a currycomb and a bucket of water. "I can care for him, m'lady."

"I'm Catrin. What's your name?"

"Grelda, m'lady."

"You don't need to call me 'm'lady.' I'd enjoy caring for him if it's not an imposition."

"I'll hold 'im for you, m'lady. He likes to kick."

Catrin shook her head and started brushing the gelding's roan coat. Watching his every move, Catrin was ready when he kicked, and she deftly stepped aside. When his coat was brushed, she let him drink. Watching his ears move on each swallow, she pulled the bucket away before he drank too much. The routine gave her peace as it took her back to a simpler time in her life. "Thank you," she said as Grelda led the gelding to the pickets, where only two other horses were tied.

"Madra kept four sound horses hidden from the Zjhon," Chase said. "One went lame on the way here. We don't have enough to do much good except for scouting and occasionally carrying those who need rest. The army moves at a terribly slow pace. Only when Madra has gotten us passage on barges have we made any real progress."

Considering her new circumstances, Catrin began to weigh every option in her mind, but there was no clear choice.

Her thoughts were interrupted, though, when Madra approached. "Now would be a good time to tell us your tale," she said and sat, cross-legged, across from where Catrin stood.

Others gathered, and soon Catrin faced much of the army, who sat silently, waiting for her to speak. Her staff in hand, she spread her arms and opened herself up to a mere trickle of energy to amplify her voice, but the power seemed to have ideas of its own. Inadvertently, she took a step backward, nearly overwhelmed by the rush of raw energy that threatened to wash her away. With a deep breath, she prepared to tell her tale, but before she even spoke, someone in the crowd gasped, and Catrin opened her eyes.

No one moved or spoke up, and Catrin opened herself to the power once again; this time ready for the onslaught. "I am Catrin Volker, daughter of a horse farmer, and the one declared the Herald of Istra," she said, and she recounted her journey, leaving out no details. Gone was the time for secrecy.

For the first time, no one questioned her tale, and no one scoffed at her claims. These people had seen enough already. They believed. It was not from the silence she learned this, but from powerful waves of anxiety that could not be concealed. "I have no desire for conquest. I want only peace, but there are grave dangers facing our world, and I must do what I can to prevent more people from dying.

There are more statues to be found, and Archmaster Belegra's search for weapons of power threatens us all. I do not ask you to join my quest or forward my cause. I ask only that you strive for order and peace, even if you must fight to achieve it. I cannot tell you yet what I will do next, as I've not yet had time to consider all that has changed. I ask you to consider my words and allow me some time."

"You have given us a great deal to consider, and we, too, will need time to evaluate this new information. Until we gather again, please consider yourselves honored guests," Madra said.

Catrin released the stream of power reluctantly, despite her struggle to control it, and it left her yearning for more. Taking a deep breath, she steadied herself, letting the cool evening air caress her. It lulled her and soon she yawned. "I need to rest."

"We don't have any extra tents, but you can sleep in mine," Chase said.

"Thank you, but I think I'd like to sleep under the sky tonight."

"If that's what makes you happy, but if it starts raining, don't come in my tent all wet."

Staring up at the sky from her bedroll, Catrin reveled in the light of the moon, stars, and comets, her fatigue suddenly abated. She counted four comets in the sky, and their energy rejuvenated her.

Within moments, though, the stillness of the night sky was disturbed as what looked like tiny comets streaked across the sky before disappearing. Several people who were looking at the show gasped and exclaimed. Chase came from his tent when he heard the commotion.

"What is it, Cat?"

"I'm not sure. Look to the sky," she said. "It seems harmless, and it's actually quite beautiful."

Chase watched with her for some time as the firestorm raged, but then he stood and stretched. "I should be sleeping," he said as he left for his tent.

Catrin watched longer than she should have, but she was mesmerized and knew she might never witness such an event again. Eventually, she made herself close her eyes. In

27

the quiet of her mind, she heard the faint melody of life, and it lulled her to sleep.

* * *

Madra watched the skies with a mixture of fascination and dread. The world she had known was gone, and in its place was a world where nothing was certain, where entire nations feared a girl who looked as if she might be afraid of her own shadow. Though Madra sensed strength in Catrin, she doubted it would be enough. She, too, had been a gentle flower in her youth, full of hope and optimism, but the world had hardened her. It had taken her optimism and tempered it with cold fear and bitter futility. At times, she thought she might shatter from the stress of it.

Looking across the grass to where Catrin lay, Madra drew a deep breath and did her best to find some shred of hope. For Catrin's sake and her own, she tilted her head back and gazed to the skies. With all her might, she sent her prayers to the gods, hoping that maybe this time they would hear.

Chapter 3

Our eyes are most critical of those who are reflections of ourselves.
--Elinda Wumrick, mother of three

* * *

Distorted echoes of string instruments and cymbals filled the halls of Ravenhold. There was no tune or melody, as if those who played could not hear the notes. Banquet tables were laden with rotting food. Faceless men and women danced without rhythm, as if some unseen force drove them.

Catrin stood at the center of it all in her wedding dress. But when she looked down, it was soiled and torn. Her grandmother beckoned from the head table, but Catrin could not break free from those who danced. Her every step was blocked, and it seemed she was getting farther away. Lissa, looking as Catrin imagined her: like herself but with eyes of ice and fire, stood at her grandmother's side, her slender hand extended to point at Catrin, a silent accusation.

Hands grabbed Catrin's waist and propelled her around the floor, twirling her until she was dizzy. Her legs could no longer hold her, and she fell and fell and fell. When at last she struck cold stone, she looked up to see Carrod Winsiker staring down at her, his lips curled into a sneer. He laughed and the room spun. Every face she saw was twisted in contempt, mocking her. Lissa threw a piece of moldy bread at her, and her grandmother laughed.

Shame and grief overwhelmed Catrin, and she begged for mercy, but they surrounded her, accusing her of abandoning them. Her grandmother came to the fore and opened her mouth to speak, but no sound emerged. Instead, a crimson rose bloomed on her chest, and she dropped to the floor, an arrow protruding from her back. On the balcony stood Catrin's betrothed, engulfed in a nimbus of power. He reached out with fingers of flame and raked the soft flesh of her throat. Crying out in pain, she looked down to see blood soaking her already fouled dress.

When she raised her head again, robed figures threw ropes of fire into the crowd, and those who danced burst into flame, but still they danced. Wicked laughter pounded in her ears, and as a haze of blood clouded her vision, they were gone.

29

"No!" Catrin shouted, grappling with hands that restrained her. She lashed out, desperate with fear.

Benjin frowned down at her. "It was a bad dream. Wake up, li'l miss. You're safe."

Slowly, reality supplanted the image of her dream, and she relaxed. "I'm sorry."

"You've nothing to be ashamed of," he said. "Fate has been unkind to you, and you've not even had time to grieve. Allow yourself to do that, and then, perhaps, the dreams will not be as bad."

"Thank you." People milled about, and several cast Catrin questioning glances.

Madra approached. Everyone in the camp showed deference to her, yet she had a kind word, a pat on the shoulder, or an embrace for each of them. The harsh persona dissolved in those moments, and Catrin saw the real Madra.

"Our dreams bring messages," she said when she reached Catrin. "But they are rarely understood. Give them credence, but do not rely on them for council."

"Thank you, Madra."

"When you've eaten, please join me," Madra said as she walked back to her tent.

Chase brought a half loaf of bread, some smoked fish, and a flask of water. "What do we do from here?" he asked.

Catrin had known this time would come, but she was still not ready to answer. Haunted by her dreams, she tried to find reason, tried to find a course that would not lead to disaster. In a moment of clarity, she firmed her resolve and made a choice. "We go to Ohmahold," she said, but she turned her head when Millie made an annoyed sound in her throat. "On the way, we'll stop at Ravenhold, but we'll only remain there a short time." Millie looked smug but seemed satisfied.

"And after Ohmahold? What then?" Chase asked.

"I'll not remain long in Ohmahold either. I'll fulfill my commitments, and then I'll find a way to get to the Firstland. Belegra poses a serious threat, and I cannot allow him to enslave anyone else. I would go in search of the other statues, but I've no idea how to find them. At least with Belegra I know where he has most likely gone, even if I don't know how to get there."

"Wherever *we* go," Chase said, with a pointed look at Catrin, "*we* are going to need a ship. Fasha was headed for New Moon Bay. Madra knows ways to contact her, as does Brother Vaughn. I guess *we* just need to find a map."

Catrin simply nodded her acknowledgment.

"I think Belegra may have a map, but I doubt you'll find another," Samda said. "I believe it was among his most closely guarded treasures."

"We'll find a way," Chase said with a firm nod. "Let's go. Madra awaits."

On their way to Madra's tent, Catrin saw fear in the eyes of many she passed. Making the mistake of looking one woman in the eye, Catrin felt a wave of terror pour out. Some may seek out the ability to inspire fear in others, but Catrin detested it. It made her feel like a monster.

Madra, at least, showed no signs of fear when they approached. She sat next to the remains of a small fire and motioned for Catrin to sit. Chase and Benjin seemed unsure if they were welcome, but Madra smiled. "Please, all of you, sit with me and let's discuss what lies ahead."

"Thank you, Madra."

"We set out to confront the Zjhon armies and reclaim what is rightfully ours. You're welcome to join us, if you choose. What you've already done has aided us. We're indebted to you for that, but we'll not kneel to you."

"I don't want anyone to kneel to me," Catrin said. "I seek no power or authority. I only want peace. And while I support your goals, I, too, have things I must achieve. I must return to Ravenhold and Ohmahold to fulfill my commitments, but if our paths remain the same for some time, I would welcome a place in your camp."

"Fair enough."

31

Driven by a strong wind, the *Stealthy Shark* knifed through the waves, sending sea spray high into the air. Feeling the cool mist on her cheeks was one of the things Fasha loved most about the sea, and most times, it brought a smile to her face, but on this day, it brought only fear and sadness. Watching Chase as he had waded from the surf, departing her world and entering the world of the land-bound, something inside of her had changed. She could not define what had changed, but nothing in her life had been the same since. Not even the rush of dodging patrol ships brought her any real joy. It was as if all the things that had been important to her suddenly lost their meaning.

Chase's desperate--almost primal--need to save his cousin had affected Fasha more than she had originally realized. Though she knew she belonged at sea, she found herself wanting to meddle in the affairs of the land-bound, something her mother often cautioned against, saying it was a certain path to trouble. Still the thoughts lingered, and Fasha continued to question herself. When sails appeared on the horizon, she had no choice but to concentrate on survival. Her conscience would have to wait.

* * *

Weeks of traveling with Madra's army proved to Catrin that she never wanted to become a soldier. Half of every morning was spent breaking camp, and half the evening was spent making camp. She had to admit that this specific army had problems that no other would. Children ran through the tents in packs, playing and roughhousing. Other, smaller children cried late into the night, every night, making sleep difficult to find. Tempers were short, and patience was in shorter supply than food. When Catrin could take no more, she joined Madra and Benjin by one of the many campfires.

"Soon we'll turn west, toward Adderhold," Madra said.

"We'll go east to Ravenhold," Catrin said. "Thank you for everything you've done for us, and may you find what you seek."

"May the gods be with us all, and may you make your peace--if not for the world, at least for yourself."

"Thank you, Madra. You are kind. I've a favor I must ask of you," Catrin said, and Madra raised an eyebrow. "May I use one of your horses and ride ahead? There're some things I need that may be hard to come by with an army in the area."

"You ask a great deal. We've only three horses, and I cannot afford to lose any of them. I'm sorry. I cannot grant this request. All of them need to be shod, and Hedron says his back hurts too much to do it now."

"Benjin and I can shoe them for you," Catrin said. "I ask nothing in return. It's a small thing we can do to repay the kindness you've shown Chase and the rest of us."

"If you have the skills," Madra said, "I can get you the tools. I'm certain Hedron will appreciate it, as I do."

Catrin and Benjin followed Madra to Hedron's tent. He struggled to stand when they arrived. "Ah, Madra. I'm of no use to you at all now, am I?"

"Nonsense. You'll heal, and then you'll work twice as hard," she said, and they both smiled. "Catrin and Benjin have offered to shoe the horses."

Hedron smiled and shook Benjin's hand. "Well, come then. There's a shoeing kit in the saddlebags. Poor animals are sore in need. Bless you for your kindness."

The shoes were indeed wearing thin, and some were pulling away from the hoof, the nails loose or missing. Catrin held each horse as Benjin did what he could. Some shoes were near to wearing all the way through, and he shook his head. "I'm not sure how long this will last, but they're on better than they were. The filly's shoes are pretty far gone."

"Far better. Far better, indeed," Hedron said. "I'd give her new shoes if we had 'em, but everything is scarce these days."

"Which horse has the best shoes?" Madra asked.

"The chestnut gelding," Benjin said. "Only one of his shoes is wearing thin."

"Take him," Madra said. "Meet us within four days. Don't make me regret this decision," she said. Then she turned her attention to other matters within the camp.

Catrin sought out Millie. "I need gold. Do you have any you would loan me against the gifts I've received?"

"The gold is yours, m'lady. I merely keep it safe. Spend it wisely," she said as she handed Catrin a small but fat purse.

Despite his protests, Catrin persuaded Chase to stay. Leaving her staff in his care, she and Benjin saddled up the chestnut and mounted. "We'll meet you in four days," Benjin said, and Catrin felt the stares on her back as they rode away. The sensation was overwhelmed, though, by the freedom of being on horseback, even if only as a passenger. Synchronizing her movements with the horse, they became almost as one, and she breathed in deeply, enjoying the serenity of the moment.

"What are we after?" Benjin asked.

"I need new clothes, and I'd like to get whatever food we can."

"Clothes?"

"No matter how much power I may have, people look at me and see a peasant and a child. I need clothes that will create a much different impression."

"I suppose you're right," Benjin said, "but this is a dangerous foray. We've no idea what the political climate is in these lands or how people will greet us. They may accept your gold and then slip a knife between your ribs."

Catrin didn't have a response for that. She felt it was a chance she had to take.

They rode through silent wilderness for much of the day, but then more settled lands came into view. Few people worked the fields, but some stood from their labors and stared as Catrin and Benjin rode by. More stares followed as they entered a small town, and Benjin slowed their mount to a walk.

Shop owners hawked wares silently by holding up their finest products and displaying others on outdoor shelves and racks. An elderly woman held up a pair of leather leggings as they passed, and Catrin whispered to Benjin to stop. He reined in and tied the horse off to a nearby post.

The shop owner nodded to Catrin, and only when they were inside the shop did she speak. "Welcome, lady. What have you need of?"

"I need three pairs of leggings, a coat, and shirts," Catrin said while admiring the different designs on display within the shop while Benjin stood at the door, watching the shop and their horse at the same time. "I like this design," Catrin said, looking at a jacket of supple leather with reinforced rawhide patches on the elbows and shoulders, the inside lined with soft cloth. "Can you make the leggings to match this?"

"That I can. Just let me get you measured," the shopkeeper said as she retrieved a long piece of string. With deft and quick movements, she made small knots in the string after each measurement. "I can have those ready in ten or twelve days."

"I need them sooner," Catrin said. "Can you have them done in two days?"

"Impossible. I have work to finish for other customers, and I'd have to work day and night, even if I wasn't already behind. I'm sorry. No."

Catrin nodded and fingered her purse. Pulling out two gold coins, she placed them on the counter. "I need them in two days."

"Yes. Yes. Certainly, m'lady," the shopkeeper said, her eyes going wide. "I'll have them ready. Is there anything else you need?"

"Where might I find a cobbler?"

"My husband's the best in the land, m'lady. Let me get 'im for you," she said and disappeared into the back of the shop. A moment later, a bearded man appeared, looking half asleep, but his wife urged him from behind.

"Mala says you need shoes?"

"Boots. I need a pair of sturdy but comfortable boots. And I need them in two days."

"Can't be done," he said, but Mala cuffed him in the back of the head and whispered in his ear. "Two days, then," he said, rubbing his head. After he measured her feet in equally efficient fashion, Catrin handed him a gold coin.

"Two days."

35

"I wish you'd been less generous with the gold," Benjin said as they rode from town. "We're conspicuous enough as it is."

"We don't have time to wait. I did what I had to do."

"I know, li'l miss. I just have a bad feeling."

"Let's ride to the next town and see if we can find a cooperative food merchant," Catrin said, having bad feelings of her own.

As the sun set, Benjin began looking for suitable campsites, and eventually they settled beneath a grove of oaks. Compared to the chaos of the army encampments, the song of the tree frogs was like a lullaby, and Catrin slept better than she had in weeks.

* * *

In the light of Madra's fire, Chase wondered what would happen next. Here he sat in a strange land, far from his home, yet he found himself tied to these people by bonds of brotherhood and friendship. Their cause was not his, but he felt guilty knowing he would only leave them to their fates. In other circumstances, he would stay with them and help them reclaim their lives, but he knew he could not. It seemed hopeless.

The challenges ahead of Catrin seemed just as insurmountable, and he quailed in the face of them. Once he had felt strong, even powerful. In his sheltered world, back on the Godfist, he had always been certain he would succeed, but now his world seemed impossibly large and equally dangerous, which left him feeling insignificant and powerless. Thinking of his friends and family, he suddenly missed them more than he had ever thought possible. Across the fire, he noticed Madra watching him. Their eyes met, and he could not look away.

"You're a good boy," she said, and Chase could not hide his surprise. "When the gods first sent you to me, I thought you were just another test, but you've proven yourself to me.

You're brave, honest, and hard working. No matter what path you choose, you've as good a chance as any to succeed."

Chase was dumbstruck. He'd never expected to hear such words from Madra. She'd always been gruff yet fair and harsh without being caustic. He'd always thought himself a burden to her and that his efforts had barely made his presence tolerable. Now, looking in her eyes, he saw something entirely different. The rough exterior had been hiding what lay beneath, and through the cracks that she allowed to show, she revealed a bit of herself to him.

"You remind me of my youngest, Medrin. He's a good boy too," she said and her voice cracked.

Chase moved closer and squeezed her hand. "You'll get them back," he said. In the next moment, his perceptions of the world changed once again as one of the strongest people he'd ever met laid her head on his shoulder and cried.

* * *

The sun brought a cheerful summer day to life, and it seemed to Catrin almost as if everything were right in the world. Honey farms and wheat fields dotted the countryside, and soon a larger town came into view. The streets were congested with merchants and beggars alike, both ready to part the unwary from their coin.

Benjin kept to the main thoroughfare and dismounted only when they reached the market proper. Here, guards patrolled and no beggars could be seen. Despite the added measure of safety they brought, Catrin feared the sight of them. Benjin tied their mount to a post in front of a place that sold wagons, not far from a shop that smelled of baking bread.

"Let me have the gold. I'll do the talking," Benjin said, and Catrin handed him the purse. "Good day to you, sir," he said to the wagon merchant.

"That it is," the man replied as Benjin wandered around the lot, inspecting the available wagons. "What can I help you find?"

"I'm not certain I see anything that would suit my needs."

37

"Most of the good ones have gone, and no new ones are being built, friend. You won't find a better selection in all the Greatland during these trying times. Perhaps this fine, single-horse cart would make your burdens lighter?"

"How much?"

"Four silvers."

"Two," Benjin countered.

"Three."

"Three and you include the harness."

"Deal."

Catrin was amazed at how quickly the deal was made. And she saw a look of suspicion cross the merchant's face as Benjin handed him a gold coin, not having anything smaller. The merchant handed Benjin his change in silvers as if each one were an insult. Benjin apologized and slipped the man another silver for his trouble. This brightened the man's expression considerably, but Catrin still sensed distrust.

After unsaddling their mount, Benjin put the harness on him and hooked it to the wagon. When he was done putting the saddle in the wagon, he walked to the baker's shop. Inside, all manner of bread, cake, and biscuit were on display, and bakers were busy taking fresh loaves from massive stone ovens.

"Greetings, friends. What can Amul do for you today?" asked a rotund and flour-covered man from behind the counter.

"I need as many loaves of bread and hard biscuits as you can sell me."

"Well, I certainly couldn't sell you everything since I've my regular customers to think of, and that would take a lot of coin, friend. Have you an army to feed?" the baker asked with a hint of his own suspicion.

"Sometimes it seems that way, friend Amul, but no. How much can you spare?" Benjin asked, and the baker visibly appraised Benjin and Catrin.

"Twenty loaves of bread and twice as many biscuits," the baker said after a moment's contemplation. Benjin paid him handsomely, and they loaded their wagon with haste.

Their purchases were starting to draw attention, and they rushed to escape the scrutiny. Before they left town, though, Benjin made a hurried bargain with a meat merchant, who sold them ten cured hams, and a blacksmith, who sold them a gross of horseshoes and nails. They had spent most of the gold Millie had given Catrin, but she was happy with what they had been able to get.

Fearing they would be followed, Catrin spent most of the ride looking over her shoulder, but no one came. Pulling the wagon was slower than riding, and their horse occasionally struggled with the additional weight, but it was overall a pleasant way to travel. When night arrived, they made camp in a grassy clearing, tied the gelding off to a nearby tree, and took turns sleeping under the stars.

* * *

Watching the night sky, Nat considered his fortune. He'd wasted a lifetime on the Godfist, fighting the preconceived notions of others, always having to prove himself sane. Now, after coming to the Falcon Isles, he found himself transformed from madman to teacher, pariah to mentor, outcast to leader.

The Gunata tribe had been wary of him at first, probably due to bad experiences with others of fewer morals than he. They were a primitive tribe that only in recent decades had come into contact with civilized people. *Civilized*--the word rang falsely in Nat's mind. Civilized: to be civil, benevolent. The term seemed more fitting to describe the unsophisticated Gunata than anyone from the Godfist or the Greatland.

The Gunata did not seem to judge one another or cast aspersions. They lived a simple existence where the tribe mattered more than any individual, yet every person was valued. Nat found it truly refreshing. Still, he had tried to avoid developing feelings for Neenya, but it was a battle he lost. As he had learned bits of her language, and she his, they had become closer, speaking a language only they understood.

During his trips to the mountain, Neenya was always by his side, helping and protecting him. When she told the Gunata of his visions, the elders seemed relieved, as if Nat were filling some crucial role. Nat wasn't certain he understood their reasoning, but they had taken him in, and they treated him as an elder. When Neenya offered herself to him as a wife, the elders approved. Despite the warnings in his head, Nat could not resist.

With the full moon at its zenith, Nat and Neenya stood before the elders.

"Zagut," Chief Umitiri said, and Nat knew that was his signal to kneel. Neenya knelt at his side, her hand in his. Each elder came to them and kissed each of them on the forehead. Chief Umitiri came last. He grasped Nat's head between his thick-fingered hands and looked Nat in the eye. When he kissed Nat's forehead, it felt like a hammer blow, and Nat was thrust into a violent fit as visions overtook him--visions of Catrin standing before a charging bull with hooves of fire.

Chapter 4

In times of rapid change, those who do not adapt, perish.
--Emrold Barnes, historian

* * *

As Catrin approached the leather shop, staying hidden in the shadows, the hair on the back of her neck stood, and a bead of sweat slid down her face. Instincts warned of a trap. Trying to decide if she could trust Mala, she looked at her tattered garments and decided to take the risk. Benjin waited outside town with the wagon, and if she did not return soon, he would come looking for her.

With a deep breath, she entered, and Mala gave a start, her eyes flitting to the back of the shop. "Welcome, m'lady," she said loudly. "I'm just putting a few stitches in the last pair of leggings. Only a moment I'll be. You can try those on for size while you wait."

Catrin pulled the jacket on, and it was a good fit. From the corner of her vision, she saw a figure dart out the back of the shop--the cobbler, she presumed. The boots were ready for her on the counter, and she quickly put them on. The fit was remarkably good, and she complimented his work.

"The man has a gift," Mala said without a hint of a smile, and again she glanced at the back of the shop.

"I cannot wait any longer. I must be going. I'll take those as they are," Catrin said, and she jumped as the cobbler returned. The shopkeeper just continued to sew. The two exchanged a glance, and Catrin nearly bolted.

"Ah, yes. 'Boots. Two days.' I see you've tried 'em on. How do they fit?" the cobbler asked.

"They fit just fine. Thank you. I really must be going now. You can keep that pair if they are not yet finished," Catrin said, grabbing what was ready and turning to leave.

"No. That won't do. Here. These are finished now," the woman said, and she gave Catrin a sack to carry everything in. Catrin thanked her as she backed toward the door. Though there was no visible sign of danger, she ran all the way back to where Benjin waited.

"I'm not certain, but I think someone is coming after us."

"Let's go," Benjin said, and they were soon moving as fast as they could, given their burdens. Heading north and west, they hoped to intercept Madra, but as the sun was sinking low on the horizon, there was no sign of the army.

With a growing gap between themselves and town, Catrin began to feel safer, but she did not relax completely. The snap of a branch in the distance brought her to full attention, and she scanned the nearby trees. Nothing moved.

"I'll watch what lies ahead," Benjin said. "You keep your eyes on the road behind us and the trees. If we're attacked, let the horse go and follow me to the trees. Got it?"

"Got it," she replied, holding on as he urged their horse for more speed.

Just as shadows covered the land, they came, swift as the wind, as if sprung from the abyss. One moment Catrin was watching the trees, the next she was ducking under a whistling blade. Benjin was not as quick, and he cried out. Two shadowy silhouettes passed them and spun around, preparing to make another charge. Catrin quickly turned to Benjin. He was holding his side, and there was blood on his shirt, but his other hand was steady and gripping a sword. He made no move toward the trees. Wishing she'd brought her staff, Catrin opened herself to the power and prepared to fight.

When the riders approached again, Catrin was ready. Using all her senses, she cast out about her, searching for energy sources. The air was filled with raw energy, but most of it was disorganized; positively charged particles simply canceled out nearby negatively charged particles. Catrin knew, though, that she could extend her field of influence and gather like particles to build up a massive charge. Then, just as she could blow out a candle by expelling air from her lungs, she could use the air to conduct her gathered charge. With her hands held high, she hurtled a bolt of energy at one rider. Like lightning, it arced from her fingers and struck with a crack. The charging horse leaped sideways, crashing into Catrin and knocking her from the cart. She hit the ground only a breath before her attacker. He remained mostly still, his leather armor blistered and smoking.

As she pulled herself up, she heard Benjin grunt as he, too, was thrown from the cart. The man she'd unhorsed was getting up, and her use of power had left her trembling. Unsure if she could deliver another blow without passing out, she ran toward him and, doing as she'd seen Benjin teach Chase, delivered a powerful kick to the startled man's jaw. His head jerked sideways, and he crumpled to the ground.

Behind her, Catrin heard hooves approaching at high speed, and she turned to see the other rider bearing back down on Benjin. After dropping his sword, Benjin drew his belt knife and threw. It sailed, end over end, and the handle struck the rider in the face with a solid *thunk*. Benjin unhorsed him as he passed, and he hit the ground with a thud and a sickening crunch. He was dead when Catrin and Benjin reached him. Catrin's kick had left the other man unconscious and bleeding.

"How badly are you hurt?" Catrin asked.

"He nicked me a couple of times, but I'll be fine. I just have to keep my right arm down to stop the bleeding. Can you catch the horses?"

"I think so," Catrin said, her legs still trembling. "What do we do with him?"

"Leave him," Benjin said, wincing. "Catch the horses and get me to the camp. I need stitches, and I can't do this one myself."

The three horses were surprisingly easy to catch, and the two the men had been riding--both fillies--seemed very familiar with one another, giving Catrin no trouble. After tying them to a tree, she gathered what had fallen from the wagon and reloaded it; then she helped Benjin into the seat. With his free hand, he held a lead line that Catrin hooked to the fillies' halters, and Catrin drove the wagon, trying to avoid the many ruts and obstacles along the way.

Eventually, the light of the campfires led them to the army, and they were greeted by the sentries' swords.

"Hold!"

"It's Benjin and Catrin returned and wounded," Benjin barked, and a host of people rushed to assist them. Madra insisted on stitching Benjin's side herself, saying it was worse than he'd made it out to be. Meanwhile, Catrin told their tale to the crowd of expectant faces around her.

The addition of two fine horses to their stock and the wagon full of food were received with wonder, and this act seemed to finally break down the barrier of fear between these people and Catrin. Those who had shied away from her glance some weeks ago now gathered around her.

* * *

"This is taking too long," Jensen said as he watched the second new building take shape. "Half of us are going to freeze t'death if we don't do something."

"That's exactly what the Masters are hoping for, I think," Wendel said. Still weak from his wounds, he was overwhelmed by frustration. If he were fit to walk, he would have already found the underground lake. Now he had to look to Jensen and the others to do most everything for him. He felt of no use at all.

The men from the Greatland proved to be quite skilled; Martik, in particular, had an excellent mind for practical building techniques. His skills were useless, though, without materials. Wendel and many others despised the idea of clear-cutting forestlands; they were simply too precious. Individual trees were being selected and cut down in a way that left the forest intact, but the process consumed equally precious time.

"We may be able to use rock," Martik said.

"Might be able to quarry it," Jensen said, "but moving it'll be tough."

"We have seven horses?" Martik asked.

"Six that are sound," Wendel said.

"I have some ideas about ways to move very heavy things," Martik said. "I could get the rock moved. Perhaps we should settle near a good quarry site?"

"How much weight do you reckon you could move?" Wendel asked.

44

"With six horses and ten men, I could drag a warship up here."

"Come with me," Wendel said. "I have an idea."

* * *

As dawn cast long shadows across the camp, most were just rising, but the sound of pounding hooves brought many to attention. Madra and another rider had been out scouting, and they were racing back. A crowd gathered, and people scrambled to secure Madra's mount as she dismounted before the filly even stopped.

"Mounted troops coming. Northeast. Prepare yourselves," Madra said, and her words spawned a flurry of activity. What had been a sluggish and awakening camp turned to a determined rush. "They looked like the Kytes' men, but I'm not certain."

Not long after, fifty mounted men poured onto the field at a leisurely pace. At their head rode the youngest grandson of Arbuckle Kyte, Catrin's betrothed, and she still didn't know his name. Millie was not far away, and Catrin went to her side. "What's his name?" she whispered into the suspense-filled air.

"You don't know his name? Shame on me. Shame on you. His name is Jharmin Olif Kyte, and he doesn't look happy."

Catrin turned back to him, and when he saw her, a nimbus of power appeared around him, outlining his form in undulating waves of light, like flames. Madra came to Catrin. "We must go meet with him."

"Perhaps it would be better if you went alone," Catrin replied. "He's not fond of me."

"Be that as it may, you must come, unarmed. He knows you're here, and he'll undoubtedly demand an audience with you."

Leaving her staff and knife with Benjin, Catrin walked beside Madra, a sour feeling in her stomach. All the mounted men behind Jharmin were intimidating, but it was Jharmin who posed the greatest threat, despite the fact that he, too, was unarmed. The skin on Catrin's throat itched, as if remembering his fiery touch.

"I had reports of an army on my lands, and now I find the Herald Witch leading a travesty that soils our fields. What makes you think you can cross Lankland without my permission?"

Despite his insults, Catrin chose to remain cordial. "I don't lead this army, and they do not follow me. Our paths are merely the same at the moment."

Jharmin made a noise in his throat and rolled his eyes. "So who *does* lead this mockery of an army?"

"I do. I am Madra of Far Rossing, one of your *former* subjects," Madra said without a hint of courtesy.

"Former?"

"Quite. At one time, your family protected the land and our people, but then you surrendered to the Zjhon. You've been little more than puppets since."

"How dare you speak to me that way, peasant! I should send you back to the hovel you came from," he said, the nimbus around him expanding.

"Please," Catrin said. "There has been enough bloodshed. Now is not the time for fighting. What this land needs is peace and leadership so that it can be rebuilt. A battle today will do nothing but reduce the number of able-bodied people available to do that rebuilding. Would you send your homeland into ruin?"

"Silence, witch. Your evil tongue cannot poison our minds."

"You call her a witch, yet if it were not for her, you would be dead," Madra said.

"Lies and tricks. The Herald Witch makes people believe she's come to save them when all she's done is kill the good people of the Greatland. I don't know exactly how she caused the other statue to explode, but I was in no more danger within Adderhold than I am right now," Jharmin said, looking smug.

"You're an arrogant fool," Madra said as she turned to walk away.

"I want you off my lands by nightfall, and you're never to return--any of you," Jharmin said, his face growing redder as the conflict wore on.

"You'll have to kill us all, then," Madra said. "You can kill your own subjects. I won't stop you. I can only imagine, though, how all those young people in the Zjhon armies will feel when they find out you killed their parents and children."

"Don't mock me, woman. I'm the protector of my people. It is you that poses a threat, and it's my responsibility to protect Lankland from *you.*"

Madra tilted her head back and laughed a harsh, barking laugh. "Kill us, and there'll be fewer left to protect, m'lord. But have it your way. My army goes where I lead it, and I'll leave your lands when I am good and ready. If you wish to fight, then let us be done with it and fight now. What do you say?"

"I say you travel with the Herald Witch, and that makes you my enemy."

"What did I ever do to you?" Catrin asked, no longer able to contain her anger.

"Beside the fact that your family has been killing my family and people for over a hundred years? How about pretending you would marry me just so you could attack Archmaster Belegra."

"I went to Adderhold willing to marry you if that was what it took to save people's lives. You can believe what you want about me and about the statues; I'll not try to change your mind. But do remember that your family has been killing my family for just as long. I know since you killed my mother and both my aunts in a most cowardly fashion," Catrin said, becoming more incensed with each word.

Jharmin appeared genuinely surprised by the accusations and simply stood with his mouth open for a moment. "I don't know what you are talking about."

"That's just how his grandfather wants it," Madra said.

"Silence!" Jharmin said, glaring.

"Jharmin, please," Catrin said, trying desperately to avoid violence. "If you say you knew nothing of their deaths, then I believe you, but you must also understand that I've had no knowledge or involvement in what my family has done here in the Greatland. I grew up on the Godfist. This is all new to me, and I don't know how to fix it, but I'm certain fighting isn't the answer."

Jharmin stood silent, apparently considering her words, but just when he was about to speak, there was a shout from his men. Catrin turned to look where a man pointed. Above the rolling hills, a waving pennant rose, showing Istra and Vestra in their immortal embrace. Soon the standard bearer then the body of the Zjhon army came into view. Row upon row of mounted riders approached, followed by orderly columns of foot soldiers. In the distance the supply wagons were barely visible.

Catrin and Madra looked at Jharmin. "You two had best go prepare yourselves," he said; then he went back to his men.

"What are we going to do?" Catrin asked as she and Madra walked back to camp and the awaiting sea of worried faces. Only the underlying determination on those faces kept Catrin from despairing. These people would die fighting if they had to. Catrin hoped it didn't come to that.

"This is what we came for," Madra said. "Although having the Kytes here makes things more interesting, we'll do what must be done," she said, and she turned to her soldiers. "Stand at attention. Show no fear. If I say attack, attack, but until then, do *nothing*."

The next few moments passed slowly, like the mire of dreams, and Catrin watched events unfold with detached indifference, as if it were not real. It was too strange to be real. She and Madra walked together but apart, Jharmin came from another direction, and a swaggering, older man came from yet another. "State your intentions," he said, his arms crossed over his chest.

"Jharmin Kyte, grandson of Arbuckle--"

"I know who you are. State your intentions."

Jharmin looked shaken, and Catrin was amazed no one else could see the flames that leaped higher around him as his fury grew, but it was obvious they could not.

"I came to investigate reports of an army on my lands," Jharmin said, "and a report that two local guards had been killed," he said, glaring at Catrin. She considered responding but decided to keep her mouth shut.

"I have orders to bring in the Herald Witch," the man said. "We have no need for your services. You're dismissed."

Jharmin's flames soared and danced around him, and his face flushed. "I must insist that you not do battle on these lands. I will remain to see that the people of Lankland are not made to suffer."

"So be it, pup. Stay if you want, but stay out of my way or you might accidentally fall on my sword." Not waiting for a response, he turned to Catrin. "*You* will surrender immediately, otherwise we'll kill you all. *You*," he said, turning to Madra, "will go away."

Madra wasn't looking at him, though, and she did not react to his statement. Instead, she scanned the Zjhon lines. Suddenly she gave a start. "Medrin, Chelby, attend me!" she shouted across the distance. The Zjhon commander turned slowly, and he flushed as two horses separated from his lines.

"Shoot anyone that deserts!" the commander shouted. The two riders continued forward, and Catrin gasped at the twang of a bowstring. One rider ducked under the arrow, and a scuffle broke out in the Zjhon lines. One of the men in Jharmin's army stepped forward and called out another name then another. Behind Catrin, men and women called to their children.

Soon nothing could be heard over the din. More and more riders and those on foot began to leave the Zjhon lines, their loyalty to their families far stronger than their fear of death. The Zjhon commander, who'd not even been courteous enough to give his name, now found himself faced with a flood of defectors. Those still loyal fought to join together and rally, but that number was shrinking rapidly. When the dust settled, Madra's army was by far the largest, with Jharmin's not far behind. The Zjhon commander suddenly found himself faced with superior force.

Jharmin made no move and said nothing; he just stood with his arms crossed over his chest and stared at the Zjhon commander. Catrin knew the danger was not yet averted. A battle between Jharmin's and Madra's armies would lead to

49

horrific casualties, and she had not yet counted the Zjhon out of the equation. When she made up her mind, she could only hope that her actions would not lead to a bloodbath.

Chapter 5

To forget the past is to jeopardize the future.
--Meriaca Jocephus, historian

* * *

"Samda!" Catrin shouted, and everyone turned toward Madra's army, which now looked like a real army. "Approach!"

Samda came swiftly, but his measured stride spoke of confidence. "Lady Catrin," he said when he arrived.

"Traitor," the Zjhon commander spit. Jharmin stared at Samda with distrust.

"I am a traitor to a failed faith. We were wrong, Grevan. Archmaster Belegra is wrong."

"Bah! Lies," Grevan said.

"She has coerced him. He can't be trusted," Jharmin added.

"Mind yourself," Samda said. "Do not forget who presided over your right-to-inherit confirmation." Jharmin flushed and looked at the ground. "And you, Grevan. Who was it that granted you the crest and mark?"

"You'll not intimidate me," Grevan said. "You may have granted me the crest and mark, but it was by Archmaster Belegra's authority. I could execute you now for treason. The Herald Witch will come with me."

"Yes. Yes," Samda said. "You have your orders, Mark Grevan. You can execute me now and take the Herald Witch into custody. What is there to hinder you?" Samda asked with a feral smile. "I can still smell the burning flesh of the last men who attacked her."

"If you feel it is right to follow Archmaster Belegra," Madra said, "then I suggest you follow him into whatever hole he's chosen to hide in."

A tense silence hung in the air. Mark Grevan made no move. "What of you, Jharmin? Where do you stand?"

Jharmin took a moment to consider before he replied. Looking each of the assembled in the eye, he seemed to struggle. "I stand with the people of Lankland," he finally said, "and I believe they have just spoken. You are to remove yourself from my lands and never return."

Mark Grevan said no more. Turning on his heel, he strode away. When he reached what remained of his army, he gave no orders. Instead he mounted, wheeled his horse, and rode back the way he had come. A handful of men followed him, but more chose to go their own way, and they scattered, some alone, some in small bands.

"There will be more," Samda said. "That was but a fraction of the Zjhon's number."

"Thank you, Samda," Catrin said, and Samda bowed before returning to Madra's army. "So, Jharmin, what will it be? Shall we rip each other to ribbons? Or will we rise above this cursed feud?"

It took a moment for Jharmin to respond. The mantle of flames that only Catrin's eyes seemed to be able to perceive dwindled as he seemed to find his calm. When he spoke, his voice conveyed more sadness than anger. "I agree the feud between our families has brought no good to our peoples or us. I declare no peace with you, though, for I've no authority to do so. I will, however, grant you passage across my lands."

"I'll no longer be traveling with Madra and her army, will you grant them passage as well?"

"Madra and her army represent the people of Lankland. I'll not stand in the way of their revenge on the Zjhon. My men will escort them wherever it is they wish to go, and I will escort you personally from my lands."

"Are we in agreement?" Catrin asked, looking at Madra.

"We are," she said.

"We are," Jharmin added.

"Then let it be so," Catrin said. "I must make the arrangements for my party's departure. Lord Kyte, if you would excuse me."

"I'll await you on the hill," he said as he turned to walk away. Catrin and Madra walked back to the waiting army.

"I can now provide horses for you and your companions, so you can ride to Ravenhold," Madra said. "I have my children back, but there are many more sons and daughters out there. This army will go on until all those that live have been returned to their families."

"I wish you blessings and the speed of the gods on your quest, Madra, and I thank you for your generosity. You are a great hero."

When Madra laughed, the humor reached her eyes. She smiled and shook her head. "Look at us. Two great heroes, neither willing to admit it."

* * *

"I insist we stop in the very next town and procure a carriage or a wagon," Millie said. "I'm not built for horseback." Her complaining had started the instant she was told she would ride, and since then it had only grown worse.

Morif rode alongside Catrin and kept his voice low. "If you make her ride all the way to Ravenhold, she'll waddle like a duck for the next moon." Millie shot him a narrow-eyed glance, and he pulled back, chuckling.

"As soon as we can, Millie. As soon as we can," Catrin said, trying not to smile. In truth, much of the terrain they had to cover was not fit for a carriage and would make for a rough wagon ride, but Catrin hoped, for Millie's sake, that they could soon travel by road.

Jharmin and his squad of guards rode at a distance, camping within sight but out of earshot. When they came to a large town, Jharmin rode out to meet Catrin. "On the other side of Mickenton, we can pick up the trade road. I will get us passage down the main thoroughfare, and I don't want anyone wandering off."

"There're things we need from the market," Catrin said.

Jharmin frowned. "What do you need?"

"A carriage and harness."

"I'll have one of my men purchase it for you and deliver it tonight. You may camp here," he said and rode away.

"You'll have your carriage this night," Catrin said to Millie when she returned. "We'll make camp here, and tomorrow we'll be escorted through Mickenton. From there, we travel by road." Her statement brought about many smiles and sighs of relief, not to mention a chuckle from Morif. Millie turned her nose up and walked away.

Jharmin was true to his word, and two of his guards arrived, one with a fine carriage, the other on horseback, carrying an extra saddle. After unhooking his mount, the guard cleaned everything meticulously, and he presented the harness and carriage to Catrin. "Lord Jharmin sends this as a gift."

"Please tell Lord Jharmin that his gift is appreciated," Catrin said. "But I can pay for the carriage."

"I assure you there is no need, m'lady. Lord Jharmin was quite clear on this."

"Thank you, sir."

The guard nodded a stiff bow then returned to his companion, who was tightening saddle straps. As they rode away, Catrin pondered the meaning of Jharmin's gift. She supposed it would be worth it to him if it helped to speed their journey off his lands.

Beyond Mickenton, travel became easier. The trade road was wide and level, and there were many inns along the way. Somehow, Jharmin got word ahead of them, and each night they would come to an empty inn, waiting for them alone. Again, Catrin wondered if this generosity was more insult than gift. If he wanted to keep her company isolated from his people, so be it.

"The day I leave the Greatland will be a joyous day," she said to Benjin one afternoon.

"I understand," he said. "I had hoped never to return, and I'll be happy to leave it behind as well. Under other circumstances, I would say there is great beauty here, but when I look around, I see only conflict and misery, and I tire of it."

By the time they reached the border of Mundleboro, the tension was unbearable. When a rider wearing the Kyte family sigil, the head of a bull, came at speed, everyone in both camps waited expectantly. The foamy sweat around the girth of his saddle spoke of a hard ride, and Catrin feared bad news. She watched, holding her breath, as he dismounted and reported to Jharmin. The change in Jharmin's posture was enough to confirm Catrin's fears; his shoulders slumped, and his head dropped forward. Even from a distance, Catrin could feel his pain.

Moments later one of Jharmin's guards approached. "Lord Arbuckle Kyte has succumbed to age," he said. "Lord Jharmin asks that you leave Lankland on the morrow. He is needed at Wolfhold and will leave this night. Two guards will be left to assure your safe passage back to Mundleboro."

Pain seared Catrin's heart. Compassion for Jharmin overwhelmed her. "Does Jharmin's father live?" Catrin asked Millie.

"No," she said. "He died many years ago in a hunting accident."

"Did my family have anything to do with that *accident?*"

"No. I don't believe so. Your grandfather had his grandfather killed, and then Jharmin's father killed your grandfather. To my knowledge, that was the last killing your family committed."

Catrin was shamed by the tale, and she vowed to put an end to the killing. With her head bowed, she walked toward Jharmin's camp. He was nowhere in sight, but she moved with purpose and intent.

"Hold," a guard said as she neared.

"I request an audience with Lord Kyte."

"A moment, m'lady."

Jharmin emerged from his tent, his eyes red and swollen. "Say what you have to say."

"I came to express my sincere condolences."

His head snapped toward her, and his face flushed, but then he seemed to sense her sincerity. "Thank you for your concern. I doubt your grandmother will feel the same."

"Jharmin," Catrin said, taking his hand in hers. She was surprised when he didn't pull away. "Our families have been horrible to each other, but the time has come to heal this age-old wound. No more can we afford petty squabbles. Let our generation be the one that puts things to right."

Jharmin pulled his hand free slowly and walked toward the horse lines. He walked to his horse, which was kept separate from all the rest, and ran his hands over the glossy coat.

Catrin moved with him, and she scratched at the base of the horse's mane. The colt stretched out his neck and groaned, wiggling his top lip back and forth.

"You know animals," Jharmin said, and Catrin nodded. "Then you understand that it can be difficult to undo a lifetime of training."

"I understand, but I also know our families stand to lose everything in the coming months. I may have grown up on the Godfist, but I really do have the best interest of the Greatland in my heart."

"Go back to your camp," he said with a long sigh. "I'll send word that I will be delayed, and I'll travel to Ravenhold with you. We'll finish this feud one way or another."

His words were clearly a dismissal, but Catrin felt there was a victory in them, a victory for the people of the Greatland.

Millie and Morif left in the carriage with the dawn, hoping to give the Lady Mangst time to prepare for guests. Catrin could only hope her grandmother would understand.

* * *

"Enjoying the wine, Beron?" Master Edling asked.

"Yes," Master Beron replied. "It's quite good."

"And the ham? It's to your liking?"

"Indeed."

"Then you'd best listen to me," Master Edling said. "If Wendel Volker and his Greatlanders have their way, our days of ruling here are over. Gone will be the days of fine eating and drinking. Can you picture yourself working the fields or gutting fish?"

"You've made your point. What is it you want?"

Master Edling smiled. With Beron on his side, he was closer to having a majority vote on the council. Endless deliberation and inconsistent alliances had already proven costly. If he'd had his way, Wendel Volker would already be dead, but others hadn't seen it that way, and his use of Premon Dalls had lost him favor. That would all end now. He was one step closer to regaining his power.

56

"I want you to talk to Jarvis and Humbry. See if you can get them to listen to reason."

Master Beron snorted. "You expect them to listen to me? They don't trust either of us, and they are terrified the Herald will return."

"I'll attend to the Volker girl. You talk to Jarvis and Humbry. I don't care what they believe; I expect you to convince them. Understand?"

"I understand."

* * *

Trying to think of what to say to her grandmother, Catrin clenched her jaw. While she hoped this day would be a new day for Lankland and Mundleboro alike, she knew it had the potential for disaster and ruin, and she could only pray those involved would recognize the uselessness of continued fighting.

Jharmin and his men broke camp and waited for Catrin and her party in a meadow. His guards unfurled his standard, and Catrin got a chill thinking about riding into Ravenhold under the Kyte sigil.

"Your mother would be proud," Benjin said as he helped load her packs and secure them behind her saddle.

"I'm doing my best, but I fear it won't be enough. The hatred between the Mangst and Kyte families has lasted for ages, how can I hope to undo it in a day?"

"You can't," Benjin said. "But you can take the first step. That's often the most difficult one. From there, momentum will carry you along."

In her new clothes, Catrin felt even more out of place. She had hoped to present an imposing image, but she feared she only made herself stand out. The leggings were comfortable but still needed to be broken in. Tossing her leg over her mount proved more difficult than she anticipated, and she suffered the embarrassment of having to try three times before she gained the saddle. With her staff resting in the heel Benjin attached to her stirrup, she rode comfortably.

No one spoke as they approached Ravenhold, but the view of her ancestral home was awe inspiring. Jharmin's face bore no expression, but Chase was clearly stunned by what he saw. He'd seen buildings that physically dominated the land, but Ravenhold seemed to be part of the surroundings, and the landscaping lent to the effect.

Lining the roadway that led to the imposing main entrance, guards stood at attention. Still as stones, they kept their eyes straight ahead, seemingly focused on nothing. Unnerved by the effect, Catrin would almost have preferred leers and catcalls. Atop the central stair, the Lady Mangst emerged, followed by a slip of a girl with fire in her eyes. In the moment Catrin saw her, she resented anyone who had said they looked alike. Lissa had a hard and self-righteous air about her, and the slanted sneer on her face appeared all too natural. Catrin's gut twisted when their eyes met; fury seared the air between them. Her grandmother stood serene and patient, apparently oblivious to the open hostility Lissa radiated.

Jharmin approached with his head high and his chest puffed out, but he managed not to look pompous or arrogant. It was a skill Catrin had to admire. He bowed to the Lady Mangst and Lissa. Catrin bowed as well, and Lissa's fury polluted the air; it washed over Catrin in waves as she straightened, and she tried not to snarl. So much raw emotion was difficult to suppress.

"Lord Kyte," the Lady Mangst said formally. "You are welcome in my home. I am grieved to hear of your grandfather's passing. You have my most sincere condolences."

In Jharmin's eyes and the heady mixture of emotions radiating from him, Catrin sensed a struggle. She assumed he was trying not to let his distrust of the Mangst name despoil this opportunity.

"Lady Mangst, I humbly accept your hospitality and your sentiment," Jharmin said, and he seemed almost sincere.

"Come. Let us feast."

Catrin walked alongside Jharmin. "Thank you," she said.

"It is not for you that I do this," he replied.

"Whatever the reason, I thank you," she said, and though he made no response, she sensed his guard drop just for a moment. It was a short walk to the banquet hall, and

Catrin was amazed by what had been done in such a short time. Arrangements of fresh flowers adorned each table, and liveried servants stood ready with covered trays. Lissa was seated to her grandmother's right, and Jharmin sat to her left. Catrin took the seat next to him, and felt, once again, like an outsider within Ravenhold.

"It has been many years since this house hosted a member of the Kyte family," said the Lady Mangst. "It has been far too long. I welcome you, Jharmin Olif Kyte, and I thank you for the kindness you've shown my granddaughter." Catrin felt Lissa's glare. "You have shown great courage and humility in coming here. I commend you."

"I've postponed my journey home so that we might discuss the future. As Catrin has said, the time for fighting is past."

"Agreed."

"How, Lady Mangst, would you suggest we resolve the differences between our families?"

"Perhaps the Zjhon were right about one thing," the Lady Mangst replied. "Perhaps a marriage between our families is for the best." Lissa's face flushed, and she glared at anyone who met her gaze. "My granddaughter Lissa has reconsidered her refusal to marry. When it was the will of the Zjhon, she found this difficult to accept. Now she sees that it is simply the best thing for our people."

Lissa showed no enthusiasm for the prospect, but she did not voice any objections.

"Ah. So that is why you sent Catrin in her stead?"

"It is."

"Lady Lissa, I've not heard you say this is what you desire. Do you wish to see this marriage through?" he asked, and the Lady Mangst nodded to Lissa.

"Lord Kyte, it would be an honor to join your house," Lissa replied formally.

"I suppose you have no reason to desire me as a husband, but a bitter marriage is not something I seek. If you will not come to me of your own free will, then I suggest we look for some other way to resolve this conflict. Perhaps Catrin would have less aversion to marrying me?"

Catrin opened her mouth, but she could find no words. Lissa, though, did not give her the opportunity. "Forgive me, Lord Kyte. It has been a trying time."

"I understand, Lady Lissa. Catrin tells me you believe my family was responsible for the death of your mother. I cannot guarantee that my family was not involved, but I can tell you that I had no knowledge of such cowardly acts. On behalf of my family, I apologize. I realize this may not mean much to one who had to grow up without a mother, but it is the best I can offer at this time. Perhaps, if you would allow me, I can do more over time."

Lissa was bereft of words.

"Our family owes you apologies as well," said the Lady Mangst. "We've not been innocent of senseless and cowardly deeds. I can assure you that Lissa and Catrin had no knowledge of these doings. I take responsibility for the actions of my late husband and his father. I know they did not treat your family well."

"All this suffering over a feud whose origins are long since forgotten," Jharmin said, shaking his head.

"Not completely forgotten," said the Lady Mangst. "It was the death of your great-great-great-grandmother that started the feud. She was riding with Catrin's great-great-great-grandfather when she was thrown from her horse. She landed on an outcropping of jagged shale, and a sharp edge slit her throat. His explanations were never accepted, and so began the senseless acts of violence. Perhaps now we can leave it in the past."

"Can we do this, Lady Lissa? Will you join with me to right the wrongs of our forefathers?"

A long moment of silence hung between them, but then Lissa drew a deep breath. "Yes, Lord Kyte. I will."

Chapter 6

Beneath the waves exists a bizarre world, full of life.
--Gorksi Veraga, fisherman

* * *

Departure from Ravenhold was bittersweet for Catrin. Despite meeting under less than friendly circumstances, Millie and Morif had been loyal companions, and they had saved her life more than once. Millie dabbed tears from the corners of her eyes as Catrin's party prepared to depart for Ohmahold. Just before Catrin mounted, Millie discreetly pressed a fat purse into her hands. "It's yours, m'lady. May it lessen the burdens of your journey."

"Thank you, Millie. You are a good friend. I'll never forget you."

"You will come back and visit. I insist. If not for me, for your grandmother."

"I make no promises, but I assure you I will try," Catrin said. Lissa avoided her as best she could, but Catrin pulled her aside. "I know you don't like me, but I hope you'll find it in your heart to forgive me. You're my cousin, and I don't want bad feelings between us. Even if you disagree with my actions, or I disagree with yours, we are family."

"You need not remind me of the blood that bonds us. I've spent my life trying to protect the people of Mundleboro, and you walk in as if these lands are rightfully yours. Where were you during the droughts . . . or during the Zjhon invasion? You've no idea what our people have been through, and you had no right to take my place. Go back to your homeland and never return," Lissa said, and she walked away.

"She'll come to understand over time," Jharmin said, seemingly embarrassed by Lissa's behavior.

Catrin's grandmother trembled as she embraced Catrin, and she whispered in her ear. "I am so very proud of you. You deserve the Mangst name more than any of us, and I thank you for what you've done. Come back to us. You'll always have a home here."

"Thank you, Grandma."

As the sun reached its zenith, Benjin mounted and called for the rest to do the same. Samda climbed awkwardly atop his mount with Chase's help, and Catrin cast one final glance at her ancestral home, not knowing if she would ever see it again. In her pocket was a rolled parchment, a writ of passage bearing her grandmother's seal impressed in wax. Within Mundleboro, at least, they would have no reason to fear the local authorities. In the lands beyond, however, the writ would be little more than a piece of parchment, a keepsake.

Following a familiar trail, they rode back toward Ohmahold. A creeping fear gripped Catrin when the toll bridge came into view. Beyond that bridge she no longer had the protection of her homeland. When they reached the top of the span, the toll collectors viewed them with suspicion, but one look at the writ of passage, and they were more than accommodating. The captain of the guard even offered to provide them with an escort through town.

"Thank you, friend," Benjin said. "But that won't be necessary. It's kind of you to offer, though."

When they passed the market, Catrin saw Yusef hawking his livestock, and she wondered what had come of Curly. It had been necessary to sell him, but still she felt guilty.

A few days later, they came to the farmstead where the Tillermans lived, and Catrin asked that they make camp on the outskirts. "There's someone here I need to speak with."

"Are you certain that's wise?" Benjin asked.

"Wise or not. I'm going."

"I'm coming with you."

They rode slowly, trying to not to alarm the locals. Those who saw them went indoors and closed up tight. When they reached the Tillerman farm, it was Jessub who saw them first. "Gramma, Grampa, Cannergy and Elma are back! Look at Elma's clothes and hair and--"

Collette appeared at the cottage door, and she pulled Jessub inside. Rolph emerged from the barn, and he drew a deep breath when he saw them. "I want no harm t'come to my family. If yer angry, punish me. Leave them out of it."

"Be at ease, Rolph. I've not come for revenge. I just had to know why," Catrin said, and Rolph looked relieved but tired. His shoulders seemed to sag under an enormous weight.

"I am sorry. I truly didn't mean ya harm, but I couldn't take Belegra's lies. I couldn't let 'im put other parents through what he put Mother 'n' me through. This came only days after ya left," he said, handing her a wrinkled and worn piece of parchment. On it was a badly faded message, but between the lines was a newer message, a message from Rolph's son Martik.

Father and Mother,

Artus and I are both in good health. I'm so sorry. I tried to keep Fenny safe, but he fell ill during the long voyage to the Godfist. He died before we got here.

The Herald of Istra gave us a choice between freedom and death, and we chose freedom. The Herald gave us time to get to land before she destroyed the Zjhon ships. She could have killed us all but didn't. Her father has granted amnesty to all those who defected, even when his own government would not. Wendel Volker is a good and just man, and I suspect his daughter is no different. She has left the Godfist and is presumed to be traveling to the Greatland. Her name is Catrin Volker, and she is a granddaughter to the Lady Mangst.

Artus and I will come home to you when we can. Until then, know we are safe. Please tell Jessub I miss him, as does Uncle Artus.

All my love,
Martik

"Two o' my sons still live 'cause o' you. I owe ya a great debt. I know I've repaid that debt poorly, and I'm sorry fer that. Ya have my gratitude."

"You need not thank me," Catrin said. "I did what I did because it was the least horrible way I could find to save myself and my homeland. People died as a result of my actions, and that is something I will lament until the end of

63

my days, but it is done. All I want now is for the people of the Greatland and the Godfist alike to be free and safe."

Rolph looked over Catrin's shoulder, and he motioned for Collette and Jessub to come out. "Everything's as it should be," he said as they approached.

"I told ya t'would be," Collette said with a smile. "That man nearly worried 'imself into a sickbed."

"Did ya really get married 'n' fight the Zjhon 'n' destroy the statue 'n'--"

"Jessub, hush," Collette said, but Catrin knelt down in front of the boy.

"I did some very scary and foolish things because I had little choice. I would much rather have spent my time on the farm."

"Not me! I'm gonna be an adventurer when I grow up, 'n' I'm gonna fight bandits 'n' find treasure. You'll see!" Jessub said; then he ran across the barnyard, fighting imaginary foes.

Collette looked at Catrin with tears in her eyes. "I knew I liked ya, soon as we met. I knew ya were a good girl. I can never thank ya enough for sparin' our sons and the other young men. They were only doin' what they were told, and they're such good boys. Ya saved 'em, and yer father's protectin' 'em. Ya'll always be welcome here."

"Thank you--both of you. I must go now. When you get news of my deeds, always know that I'm doing the best I can."

"May the gods bless ya!" Collette called as they rode away, and Catrin actually felt safer knowing she could always go to the Tillerman farm.

"Wait! Elma, *wait!*" Jessub called as they left, and Catrin turned her mount. "I made this for ya," he said, breathing hard.

Catrin opened the folded piece of parchment carefully, for it was worn and tattered around the edges. On it was a faded message, but painted over it in bold strokes was a striking image of a winged woman hovering over a man.

"That's you and my daddy," he said, and the sincerity in his big, brown eyes was like a knife into Catrin's soul.

Climbing down from her horse, she gave Jessub a hug and a kiss on the forehead. "You're a good boy, Jessub."

"Gramma said ya saved my daddy and Uncle Artus. I wish ya coulda saved Uncle Fenny too," he said.

"I'm sorry,"

"Ya did the best ya could," he said with a firm nod. "Good-bye, Elma. Good-bye, Cannergy."

"You did the best you could," Benjin echoed as they rode away.

Catrin tried to hide her tears.

* * *

Wendel watched in amazement as Martik orchestrated a monumental operation. Six horses, ropes, and a dozen men hauled on the massive section of greatoak. At first it had seemed like sacrilege, but the trunks would only lie and rot. Why not make use of them?

Using the trees that were downed to make a trail between the valley and the grove, Martik assembled a rolling monster. Logs were placed in the path before the greatoak, and then they were soaked with water to make them slick. With three horses on each side, they pulled, and amazingly, the leviathan moved.

Now at a place where they had to make a sharp, uphill turn, things were getting tense.

"Keep 'em ropes taut!" Martik shouted, despite the fact that he knew the men were trying to do just that, but the horses had reached a place where the incline was too steep. "Boil me. What made me think I could do this?"

"You're doing just fine," Wendel said. "Breathe deeply for a moment and relax yourself."

Martik stood for a moment, trembling with anxiety, but then he relaxed noticeably.

"Now you're ready to conquer this thing," Wendel said. "Come at it with a clear mind."

Martik nodded and looked thoughtful. "Thank ya," he said.

65

"If it were me," Wendel said, scratching his chin, "I'd unwind the rope around the trunk one time, and that would be enough extra rope to get the horses past the incline."

Martik made an annoyed sound. "Why didn't I think o' that?"

"Sometimes you just have to look at things from a different viewpoint."

* * *

As Catrin, Benjin, and Chase skirted the farmlands, they came to the stone bridge. It now stood well above the swift-running water, which was no longer clogged with debris. Beyond, though, the flood damage was still evident, even if the grass was already beginning to cover it.

As they crossed over a series of hills, Catrin was surprised to recognize parts of the landscape, even as nightmarish as it had been during the flood. If she remembered correctly, they were nearing the area where she and Benjin had climbed the tree, the place where they had lost Barabas. Thinking of him was painful, and she pushed him from her thoughts.

Around a bend, flashes of red and orange were visible. As they crested a rise, a field of flowers awaited. Two hills formed a small valley, and it was covered with vibrant life, the flowers making it look as if it were still afire.

"Pyre-orchids," Benjin said in a whisper. "They're extremely rare and only grow after forest fires, and then only under certain conditions. We must harvest them."

"We don't have time," Catrin said.

"Difficult times are ahead, li'l miss. In those kinds of times, disease can wipe out entire cities. Pyre-orchids can be used to treat almost every known plague. We cannot afford to miss this opportunity."

"Then let's do what needs doing and move on."

Harvesting the orchids proved as easy as removing the flower from the stem, and they soon had the flowers bundled together and divided up between them. Beyond the burned-out forests of Astor were lands that Catrin dreaded. She doubted she could find the place they had exited the

66

ancient mines, and even if she could, they would have to wait for the full moon to get past the daggerfish, which left them little choice but to travel through populated lands.

At the first town they reached, Benjin spotted signs of the Vestrana at a local inn. "I'm going to go in and talk to the innkeeper," he said. "I'd like to get rooms for the night but only if we can remain discreet. Stay here and try not to draw attention to yourselves." He slipped into the inn.

Waiting for him to return, Catrin held her breath. Despite signs of the Vestrana, she feared a trap. When Benjin appeared at the back corner of the inn, she drew a deep breath. With a wave, he told them to join him, and they led the horses to the back of the inn, where two stable boys waited. Benjin gave each stable boy a copper and asked that they stack the bales of orchids somewhere dry. They looked at him strangely, but he tossed them each another copper and they were eager to help.

The innkeeper was an older, bearded man with a broad, vein-streaked nose. His name was Orman, and his smile was infectious. "Welcome to the Brendton Inn, friends. The food's hot and the beds clean. If you'll follow me, there's a private room this way. I'll bring your dinner there."

"Does he know who we are?" Catrin asked when Orman left.

"I think he suspects, but he gave all the right signs. We should be safe in his care," Benjin said.

But Catrin still had doubts. Too many things were no longer certain or safe. When Orman returned with food, she wondered if it might be poisoned but decided she could not live the rest of her life in fear. With trembling hands, she grabbed a stuffed pepper. It was delicious.

Orman returned to clear the plates and brought a tray of mugs and a jug of dandelion wine. "Secret family recipe," he said. He poured wine for each of them and handed out the mugs. When he handed Catrin her mug, their eyes locked. His brief stare commanded her attention without being overt. Wrapping her hand around the mug, she realized there was a piece of parchment cleverly wrapped around half the mug so it was concealed in her grip. Toward the top, she felt a wax seal.

Uncertainty festered in Catrin's belly, but she just thanked Orman for the wine. He left as if nothing had occurred, closing the door behind himself. The secrecy employed in delivering the message demanded she read it in private, but her curiosity would not be quelled. With a quick glance, she saw the image of a hummingbird impressed into the wax. Excitement charged through her. "I need to collect my thoughts," she said. "I'm going to meditate for a while."

The others spoke softly as Catrin settled herself into a corner with her back to them. The seal broke away easily, and she opened the parchment with a mixture of hope and dread.

Birds roost where dandelions hide.

Frustrated, Catrin tried to understand what the message meant. The hummingbird seal would almost certainly belong to Brother Vaughn, and the mention of birds solidified that deduction. The taste of dandelion wine was still on her tongue, and Orman had said it was a secret recipe, but she struggled to find meaning in *Birds roost.*

The message was a warning, of that she was certain, and she guessed it wasn't safe to go to Ohmahold. Birds. Messages. The realization slammed into her consciousness. Orman would send a message by bird. Could it really be so simple? "I think Brother Vaughn wants us to wait here for him," she said when she returned to the table.

"Did you get that from your meditation or did you just decide you like this place?" Chase asked.

"A cryptic message was delivered to me, and I'm not certain, but I think it's a warning," she said, still feeling compelled to keep the message secret. Sharing it would reveal Orman as the messenger, and she sensed that would be against his wishes. Perhaps he feared Samda. "I think Brother Vaughn wants to meet us here."

"Would you care to share the message?" Chase asked. "Maybe we could help interpret it."

"No. The message was intended for me alone, and I cannot share it. I'm sorry."

Chase raised an eyebrow but did not press her further. Benjin looked her in the eye and seemed satisfied by what he saw.

"I don't think it's safe to stay here long. There are more people looking for you than just Brother Vaughn. There may be other messages being exchanged this very moment," Samda said.

"I agree," Chase added, and when he met her eyes, Catrin saw his determination and knew he was going to fight her.

"Come with me," she said, and he walked to the corner with her. She could feel the stares on her back, but she could think of no other way to convince her companions without offending Samda and still respect Orman's privacy.

When she showed Chase the message, he looked uncertain at first, but then he seemed to see the hidden meanings. "I think Cat's right. I say we wait here, at least for a few days," he said when they returned to the table.

"We need to get a better understanding of the layout of the inn and its surroundings," Benjin said. "I don't want to be trapped here. We'll pair up and keep watch on the streets. If someone is trying to trap us, we'll need as much warning as possible."

* * *

Despite what were mostly pleasant days in a comfortable setting, Catrin paced the floor, unable to stem her anxiety. Every horse or wagon that passed was suspect, and even when in her room, she could not stifle her worry. Having stayed abed longer than the others, she tried to calm her mind. When the door to her room suddenly flew open, she nearly leaped from her skin. No one entered, but then two grinning faces peeked in. Only her happiness to see them could overcome the overwhelming desire to wring their necks.

"Strom! Osbourne! How did you get here?"

"We came with Brother Vaughn." At the mention of his name, he came to the door, grinning as wide as the rest.

"Greetings, Catrin. I was confident you would understand my message, but I must admit it's a relief to find you here. There are many things we need to discuss."

Chase charged up the stairs from the common room, having heard the commotion. "Who goes there?" he challenged. "By the gods, how'd you get in here? Forget it. I don't care." He ran to embrace Strom, Osbourne, and Brother Vaughn. "I'll go get Benjin and Samda."

"Who?" Brother Vaughn asked, his visage going stony.

"Samda was a Zjhon Master, but his beliefs have changed. He's been helping us," Catrin said.

"I know who he is. A detestable man if I ever met one. We can get you out of here without him ever knowing. Chase, can you try to get Benjin to come alone?"

"Wait," Catrin said. "I don't want to leave Samda. He saved my life, just as you did. I could no more leave him behind in such a way than I could you."

Brother Vaughn seemed torn, but then he tightened his jaw and nodded. "Let us talk where we can be comfortable and drink a bit of Orman's dandelion wine, then."

In his excitement, Chase darted ahead to apprise Benjin, taking the stairs two at a time. Catrin walked beside Brother Vaughn. "I respect your opinion, and I'm sorry for disagreeing with you."

"People *can* change, but they rarely do. I will trust your judgment, but it will take some time before I will trust his."

"I can ask no more than that," she said as they entered the private dining hall. Food and wine were waiting when they arrived, which made Catrin slightly uncomfortable, not liking when others anticipated her moves.

Benjin still wore a shocked expression when he arrived. Chase followed. Then came Samda, who wore a mixture of guilt and pride like a cloak. Catrin watched the looks exchanged between Brother Vaughn and Samda. There was no kindness between them, but they both managed to remain civil.

"How did you get in here?" Benjin asked. "We've been watching every entrance."

"Orman's a crafty fellow," Brother Vaughn said. "Full of surprises, he is. I'll not spoil his fun by revealing his methods." Strom and Osbourne nodded in agreement.

"I suppose the important question is: What do you plan to do next?" Brother Vaughn asked.

"I'm going after Belegra," Catrin said. "I believe he goes in search of the Firstland."

"I've gotten reports that give your suspicion credence, but I must ask how you plan to find the Firstland."

"I don't know, but I must find a way."

Brother Vaughn paced the floor in deep thought but stopped suddenly in front of Samda. Their noses almost touching, he growled. "You know why I loathe you. You know what you did. Catrin has accepted you, and I have chosen to honor her decision, but if you reveal any of what I say to anyone or if you betray her, I'll find you, and you will die slowly."

Catrin held her breath, shocked by the venom that poured from Brother Vaughn.

"What the Zjhon did was wrong--I know--but nothing can bring those shepherds back, no matter how much I will it to be so. I'll not betray you or Catrin."

"Be true to your word, and you have nothing to fear," Brother Vaughn said, and he turned back to the group, his visage once again peaceful. "There has been great change in the Cathuran order since the Zjhon killed Mother Gwendolin." He paused to glare at Samda, who seemed truly surprised and confused. "Long-standing beliefs are being challenged, and the order is divided. I could not remain while they squabble amongst themselves. I made my choice, and I started searching for you. When the bird came, Strom, Osbourne, and I made good our escape before the balance of power shifted."

"You left the order?" Catrin asked, shocked.

"In a sense, yes. There have been times in the past when the order dispersed to find truth, and I am on such a quest. The library you found contains thousands of volumes, and it'll take generations to glean all that we can from them, but I did make some discoveries before I departed Ohmahold. You were correct when you translated *Om'Sa* to mean *men leave*. The book you found chronicles the departure of the first men from the Firstland.

"They fled the Gholgi, who we now know were large, reptilian creatures that somehow betrayed the first men. The picture is still very cloudy, as I have only tapped the smallest

71

part of the knowledge that was hidden. If only we had more time," he said with a sigh. "I found no maps to indicate where the Firstland is, but I did find something rather intriguing: a reference to a powerful staff known as the Staff of Life, and your staff matches the description, except yours has no stones in the eyes of the serpent, if I recall correctly."

"Your memory is correct," Catrin said. "But Benjin had the noonstones mounted in the eyes. The serpent, I believe, is a dragon. If I draw heavily on the staff, the eyes shine and the wings become visible." After retrieving the staff from her room, Catrin showed him.

"Amazing. The wings were not described, but perhaps they were unknown at the time. Otherwise, thanks to Benjin's uncanny intuition, the staff looks exactly as it was described." He drew a sharp intake of breath when he saw the handprints embedded in the staff's flesh. "By the gods! How did that happen?"

Catrin told the tale, and those who hadn't heard it stood in shock. Samda seemed confused. "Those are not noonstones," he said, pointing to the eyes of the serpent.

"What?" Catrin asked.

"I've seen noonstone; it's as black as night. Those, I believe, are something even more rare--dragon ore. I thought you knew."

"Where did you see this black stone?" Brother Vaughn asked.

"It was one of Belegra's treasures. He showed it to me once as a way to convince me he was right, to show he had the favor of the gods," Samda replied, looking haunted. "He said that once he uncovered its secrets, he would be able to save the world. I believed him then."

No one spoke for a moment, and even Brother Vaughn seemed to recognize Samda's pain. An idea began to form in Catrin's mind, but she kept it to herself. For the moment, it really didn't matter; she understood how to use the stones she had, whatever they were called.

Samda suddenly cocked his head to one side, "Do you hear that?"

72

Chase hurried to the window and pulled the shutter slowly open. "We've got to go. Now! Zjhon riders, coming fast."

A moment later Orman charged through the door, his face bright red. "Get your things and get upstairs."

Chapter 7

Beyond the civilized lands exist wild places, inhabited by creatures both curious and deadly.
--Rianna Goresh, trapper

* * *

It didn't take long for the group to gather their belongings since none of them had allowed themselves to get comfortable. At the end of the upstairs hall, Orman waited. He took them through a door that led to another stairwell. "Watch your heads," he said as he climbed.

The roof sloped down on both sides, and the attic ceiling was not high enough for even Catrin to stand straight. Orman opened a massive wooden chest that sat in a corner and took out the old blankets that filled it. After fighting with it for a tense moment, he removed the bottom of the chest, revealing a hidden shaft with a ladder descending in to the darkness.

"Down ya go," he said.

Strom went down first since he knew the way, and he lit a torch that waited below.

"I need you to send a message," Brother Vaughn said to Orman before he left. "I need a ship where foxes roost. You know who to contact."

Orman nodded.

Catrin waited until only she, Benjin, and Orman remained in the attic. "Thank you for all you've done. Good-bye, Orman," she said as Benjin urged her into the shaft.

The tunnel below was dark and cold and smelled like nothing else. Walls of rough stone and dirt cut a meandering course, but the tunnel was relatively short. At the end, another ladder led to a hatch that was already open. Looking down were the faces of the two stable boys, and their visible anxiety demanded haste.

"Thanks, Wilmer, Jidan; you've done well," Brother Vaughn said as he climbed from the tunnel.

Catrin followed and emerged in the feed room behind the stables. In the pasturelands beyond, their horses waited, saddled and loaded.

"By the gods, are those pyre-orchids?" Brother Vaughn asked.

"Yes," Catrin said. "We found them on our way, and Benjin insisted we harvest them."

"Bless him, but we won't have the time to dry them properly. They'll surely mold, and I cannot let such a treasure go to waste. Is Mirta still the healer in these parts?" he asked Wilmer, who nodded, mute. "Take these to her. It's very important. She'll know what to do. Understand?"

The boys nodded and quickly unloaded the pyre-orchids. Brother Vaughn went to one of the bundles and removed a single orchid. After marveling at its beauty for a brief moment, he carefully tore the delicate petals off, one by one, and pressed them into a book he retrieved from his pack.

After reaching into her purse, Catrin tossed each boy a gold coin then waved good-bye. The boys talked excitedly about how they would spend their new fortune.

Whether by design or luck, the evergreen trees lining the pasture gave them perfect cover during their escape; Catrin suspected it was by design. Riding double, they had to move more slowly, but they still managed to cover a lot of ground before nightfall. No pursuers revealed themselves, but that didn't mean they weren't there, waiting for an opportunity to strike. Constantly alert, Catrin scanned the trees around her as they moved through lightly forested foothills.

"We'll be heading north and west through the forest for most of the way," Brother Vaughn said.

"Where are we going?" Chase asked.

"To my ancestral home. It was abandoned generations ago, but I know the way."

The northern forests were untouched by fire, and Catrin reveled in the glory of the undisturbed land. Concentrating as hard as she could, she tried to hear the dryads. The song she heard was so soft, she wondered if she were imagining it, but its incredible beauty and complexity argued otherwise.

When they camped for the night, she went to her bedroll early and spent hours listening to the song of nature. The next day brought warm, gentle breezes that stirred the turning leaves. Many succumbed to the call of the wind and drifted to the forest floor below, and the group rode through a rain of color.

With all the movement, it was difficult to remain watchful, but Catrin spotted a dark shape moving through the trees ahead, and she held up her fist to call a halt. In a moment, she knew it was already too late for stealth. The dark shape stopped, and a low whistle split the air.

"They've seen us," Benjin said, and the pounding of hooves gave additional proof. "There's no time to run. Arm yourselves."

Catrin pulled her staff from the stirrup. Mounted men, in gear similar to that of the elite troops they had encountered in the past, charged through the trees. Benjin and the others formed a protective ring around Catrin. Chase, Strom, and Osbourne dismounted, so passengers would not hinder those who rode.

Chase made first contact with the enemy when he stepped from behind a tree and used a fallen branch to unhorse one of the Zjhon. Torn from the sight by a rider bearing down on those who surrounded her, Catrin wished she had a bow. Instead, she drew her belt knife and threw. It struck the soldier's helmet but did little besides distract him. The distraction was enough for Benjin, though, and he landed a killing strike.

More riders circled and scored hits of their own. Samda was pulled from his horse, and only Osbourne's intervention kept him from being killed. In saving Samda, though, Osbourne turned his back on another rider. Samda's shout warned him, and he ducked just in time, getting only a slice across his face.

Samda grabbed a handful of dirt and threw it into the eyes of the rider's mount as he charged past. Blinded, the horse fought his rider, and they went down when the horse tripped on a rotting stump. Chase appeared a moment later on a Zjhon horse, which matched strides with the horse beside him. Shouting a battle cry, he leaped from the saddle

76

and grappled with the other man, pulling him to the ground, but the soldier's boot caught in the stirrup, and his mount dragged him. Chase held on for a moment but then let the panicking horse finish off the soldier.

Riders passed so quickly and in so many directions, Catrin could not keep track of where all the attackers were. Three men rode in close and occupied Benjin, Chase, and Brother Vaughn. Catrin winced at every blow they took. Unwilling to sit idly by while her companions fought, she opened herself to the power. Like drawing a deep breath before diving into the water, she inhaled the energy and held it within herself until she felt she might explode. The sound of hoofbeats from behind said she would have her chance to fight.

Turning just as the soldier closed the gap, Catrin held her staff high and prepared to unleash her stored energy. He pulled his sword back for a mighty swing, and time seemed to slow as it arced back toward her, slicing the air and singing the song of death. Before it reached her, though, Samda shouted her name, and time seemed to accelerate. Catrin opened her mouth to shout, but she had not even formed the words when Samda jumped between her and the blade.

He crumpled to the ground soundlessly, the soldier's sword protruding from his chest, and Catrin was so shocked that she failed to deliver her own attack. Deprived of his sword, the soldier punched Catrin in the face as he rode by and unhorsed her. She tried to brace herself but still hit the ground hard. Her horse pranced around her, and she had to roll to keep from being trampled.

Chase pulled her from the ground. "We're in trouble," he said, but then he had to defend himself as the attack raged on.

In a desperate attempt to protect her party, Catrin drew, once again, on the energy around her but could not focus, and the energy refused to do her bidding. After a desperate effort, the floodgates opened, and the river of power washed over her, unchecked. Sucking in deep breaths, she struggled to keep her footing lest she be swept away.

Three riders wheeled in unison and weaved through the trees as they charged. One flew from his saddle when Strom released the branch he'd been holding back; it struck the soldier across his nose with a crunch. Osbourne released the branch he'd been holding but to little effect; the leaves just raked against his target's face.

When Brother Vaughn ran with astonishing speed toward the momentarily stunned soldier's charging mount, Catrin shouted, but he did not hear. The thought of seeing him run down tore at her heart, but to her surprise, he sprang at the horse's head and latched onto the bridle. Using his weight, he brought the animal's head down until he touched the ground; then he rolled clear. The horse, carried by its momentum, flipped forward and sent its rider crashing into a nearby tree. The horse pulled itself from the ground and disappeared into the trees.

The last soldier continued forward, and Benjin rode to meet him. Overwhelmed with power, Catrin tried desperately to find a way to release it. The song of the dryads grew stronger in her mind, and she could feel their presence as they bolstered and guided her. With a terrified shriek, she cast out her energy, trying to connect it with the soldier. Just as his sword arced toward Benjin, a visible tendril of energy reached out to him. With a blinding light and a sharp crack, her energy connected with him and flowed violently between them.

The soldier was thrown from his horse and landed, smoking, on the ground. Benjin moved in to finish him off. Catrin, though, felt as if she had been the one struck, and she crumpled to the ground. Chase arrived at her side. "Are you hurt?" he asked.

"No. I don't think so. Samda?"

"I'm sorry, Cat. He's gone."

Lowering her head to cry, Catrin vented her impotent rage and sorrow. Nothing she could do would bring him back, but that didn't lessen her anguish, guilt, or her poignant sense of loss, which had become all too familiar. Only the need to tend to the wounded kept depression from claiming her.

Benjin had several deep wounds, and Catrin helped Brother Vaughn close and bandage them as best he could. Chase walked with a limp, and Osbourne's face was covered in drying blood, but at least the bleeding had stopped. Using a damp cloth, Catrin wiped the blood from his eyes.

"I tried to save him, Cat. I tried so hard. I'm sorry I failed."

"You did the best you could do, and you helped save all of us that live. Samda gave his life for me, and there was nothing any of us could've done to stop him," she said.

"He kept his word," Brother Vaughn said as he pulled a blanket over Samda. "It may not make up for everything he did, but Samda died an honorable death. People can indeed change. I underestimated him."

Still wary, they gathered the Zjhon horses still in the area, giving each of them their own mount. Making better time, they rode in somber silence. Samda's body, tied to the saddle of a Zjhon horse, was a painful reminder of the dangers they faced and the losses they had suffered.

When they reached a field dotted with small mounds that were laid out in an orderly fashion, Brother Vaughn stopped, motioned for everyone else to remain where they were, and walked into the field. For a few moments, he stood silent, but then he turned back to them, "Here lie my ancestors. Samda has earned the right to lie with them."

Though he had once been an enemy, he had also been a friend and protector. With hearts encumbered by grief, sadness, and regret, they laid Samda to rest. Before they left the burial mounds behind, Catrin found an acorn and planted it near where Samda lay, so that, from his death, new life could spring.

* * *

Mirta bent over little Becka, wiping the sweat from her forehead. Becka breathed shallow, ragged breaths, and Mirta could do nothing to help her. Becka was among the first, but it would spread, and Mirta began to cry, certain what she saw was the beginning of a plague.

As she wiped her tears, the bell rang, and she moved to the front of her shop, most of which was serving as a temporary sick house. When she saw two young boys, her heart sank. Would they, too, succumb?

"Miss Mirta?" one boy said meekly. "We have something for you, but it's kind of big. Where d'ya want it?"

"I don't have time for tricks today, boys," Mirta said. "I'm not expecting anything, and I don't have any room. If you're not sick, then run along."

"But, Miss Mirta, won't you at least look? The man said you'd want it. I can't remember what he called it. Fire lily? No, that wasn't it."

"Pyre-orchid?" Mirta asked, astonished, but her feet were already taking her through the door. There, on a simple wood cart, sat enough pyre-orchids to treat half the Greatland, but they were starting to rot. "Thank the gods! You must help me get this inside right now. You're Orman's boys, aren't ya?"

"Yes, ma'am. I'm Wilmer and this is my brother, Jidan."

"Good," Mirta said. "Your father won't mind me borrowing you for the day. Once we have them unloaded, I'll send one of you back with a message for him."

"Yes, ma'am," Wilmer said.

* * *

"There isn't much left," Brother Vaughn said as they rode into a secluded valley clogged with underbrush. Here and there, though, evidence of what had once been a glorious home could still be found. Fluted columns and crumbling walls struggled for existence as the land reclaimed them. "Be watchful. There are unmarked wells and other dangers beneath the growth."

Beyond the valley waited the sea, and the waves called to Catrin like an old friend. Her time aboard the *Slippery Eel* had been an experience she would never forget, and though she would never have called herself a sailor, a part of her was at home on the seas.

"A ship should meet us here soon," Brother Vaughn said. "Until then, we wait." When they reached an area relatively free of underbrush, he led them to a rough archway at the base of the mountains. Beyond the archway was a natural chamber large enough to hold them and their mounts. "This cavern was once used for storage, but it

80

should serve us well. There is a river nearby where we can fish."

His mention of fish reminded everyone of their hunger. Brother Vaughn led Catrin, Chase, and Strom to a likely fishing hole. They did their best to fish without the proper gear, but their efforts yielded only two small fish before nightfall. On the walk back, though, Brother Vaughn gathered tubers and roots he said would make for a fine stew. It was not the best meal any of them had ever eaten, but it greatly improved the mood.

Chase constructed a wall of branches to cover the archway, and they huddled around a low fire as the evening chill set in.

"I must thank you again, Catrin," Brother Vaughn said, "for having the courage to locate the library at Ohmahold. The treasures within have provided inspiration for every member of the order, and I look forward to sharing much of what I've learned with the farmers and craftsmen of the world. Gustad has examined some of the weapons and armor and claims to have learned more about metalworking in one day than he had his whole life."

"You should see the swords, Cat," Strom said. "The metal shimmers and Gustad said one sword had been folded more than a thousand times. Milo let us look at it with his lenses, and you could actually see it!" Strom said.

"Yeah, and those new lenses came from things Milo found in the library," Osbourne added.

"I'm glad," Catrin said. "Did you find anything to help me?"

"I assembled a team of trusted colleagues," Brother Vaughn said. "We found as much as we could. It was distressingly little, and much of it was difficult to understand, but I'll do my best to help you. We found a text written in the oldest form of High Script, and then we found a more recent copy that had been translated. Using this text, we have been able to translate much more of *Om'Sa*.

"As I told you before, the first men fled the Firstland because they were losing the war against the Gholgi. Before the war, we believe man used the Gholgi much as we use horses for transportation. The references we've found

81

indicate that they were intelligent creatures, and they learned fast. When they had gained a certain level of understanding, they revolted. The tales of the carnage are horrifying."

"You don't think the Gholgi are still there, do you? I mean, if they are, won't they just kill Belegra and his men?" Osbourne asked.

"We don't know. I'd never heard of them before translating *Om'Sa*, but I must assume they still exist."

"Hopefully, if any are still there when we get there, they will have forgotten what the first men taught them. Maybe they'll be afraid of us," Osbourne said.

"I'm not sure what to hope for," Catrin said.

"Many of the things we learned are of no consequence here," Brother Vaughn continued. "But Sister Annora found some things that might be helpful. Though I'm not certain I'll get it right, I'll try one with you," Brother Vaughn said, looking at Catrin.

"What do you need me to do?"

"If everyone else could remain quiet for a few moments, please. Catrin, I want you to stare straight ahead and remember exactly what you see, every detail. Then I want you to close your eyes and picture exactly what you saw."

"I see it."

"Now open your eyes. Does it look any different?"

"No. Is it supposed to look different?" she asked, but he did not answer.

"I want you to close your eyes again, and picture exactly what you saw. Do you see it?"

"I do."

"Now I want you to keep your eyes closed, and open *this one*," he said, and he smacked her hard on the forehead. Catrin sat back from the surprise and the impact, her eyes still squeezed shut, but it was as if someone had thrown open the shutters; a world of energy was revealed to her. She could see everything around her with her eyes shut, but it all looked very different. Rather than seeing colors or texture, she saw ever-moving patterns of energy both intricate and beautiful.

Around each person's wounds, she saw disturbances in the energy fields and areas where nothing moved at all.

Oddly she saw a subtle but similar disturbance around Brother Vaughn's ears and head.

"Do you have trouble hearing?"

"Yes. Sometimes I do. At times I get a terrible ringing in my ears. How can you tell?"

"I see disturbances in your energy field."

"It worked?"

"Yes. It worked," Catrin said, and as she opened her eyes, her new vision overlaid what her eyes saw. Though initially disorienting, the combined senses gave her a much clearer picture of her companions' health. When Benjin turned, she saw the injury in his shoulder that pained him so much, old as it was. The more she looked with her new senses, the more natural they became, until she could no longer imagine life without them. Colors were richer and more vivid. Scents on the breeze told stories, and even the caress of that wind felt more personal.

"I'm so very happy," Brother Vaughn said, beaming. "I didn't think it was going to do anything, and then I would've looked quite the fool, smacking you in the forehead and all. Do you see anything else? Is there anything else you can do with your new sight?"

"I can see the disturbances caused by all of your wounds, and I can sense your overall well-being much more acutely now, but I'm not certain there is anything I can do with it besides maybe identify illnesses."

"Give it time," Benjin said. "Some use will present itself."

"Well said," Brother Vaughn added.

"Is there anything else you could teach her?" Osbourne asked, excited by their success.

"There were two more things we could try. Do you feel up to trying something else?"

"I do."

"Are you gonna smack her again?" Strom asked. "I'd like to see that again."

Catrin stuck her tongue out at him and closed her eyes.

"I want you to put your ear to the ground and tell me what you hear. Cover your other ear if that helps."

Catrin did as he instructed. "I think I hear my own heartbeat and a hollow echo."

"Now I want you to listen for words," Brother Vaughn said. "Do you hear a song or melody?"

"I have heard songs of nature, but I don't hear anything like that now. No."

"Try asking a question."

"Ask the ground a question?" Strom snorted, but Chase shushed him.

"Will a ship come for us?" Catrin asked. There was no response, nothing at all. "I don't hear anything."

"Ah well, I suppose it was worth a try," Brother Vaughn said, clearly disappointed.

"What else can you try?" Osbourne asked, his enthusiasm unabated. "C'mon, Cat, you're good at this kind of thing. You can do it."

"The last exercise was said to be the one least often achieved, but I am willing to try if Catrin is."

"I can try one more."

"We have to go outside for this one. Pick any tree that calls out to you."

"Trees call out to people?" Strom asked; Osbourne elbowed him in the ribs.

Catrin ignored him and walked through the trees, listening for the slightest contact. With her new vision, she saw energy fields around the trees and just about everything else. A nearby tree showed signs of disease, its leaves riddled with spots; most had already fallen off. "This one."

"Put your arms around it and pull yourself close. Don't turn your head to the side; look straight into the tree and press your nose and lips against the bark."

"You want her to hug and kiss a tree?"

"Shut up, Strom!" everyone else said in unison.

Catrin didn't let it bother her, she would do almost anything to increase her powers, and that realization was exhilarating as well as frightening. Approaching the tree, she reached out her arms and embraced it. Pressing her face against the jagged bark, she waited. Nothing happened.

84

"I don't feel anything," she said, her voice muffled against the bark of the tree. Disappointment coursed through her.

"I'm sorry. That's all the ancient druid text said to do. I don't know anything else to try."

"This, too, was worth trying," she said, still hugging the tree. "Thank you, Brother Vaughn. Thank you, tree." Just as she was about to pull away, she heard a faint melody. Pressing her face harder against the tree, it grew louder and clearer. Harder she pressed and louder it grew.

"Catrin?" she heard someone ask, but she ignored him and everything else her ears heard; she listened, instead, with her heart. The melody grew louder and took on more intensity. The bark her face was pressed against began to feel warm and soft, and slowly her face slid forward, into the tree. It was a bizarre sensation, but she did not feel threatened; instead she felt like an honored guest.

Before her third eye, a figure materialized. Childlike in build, the figure had a beautiful face, full of wisdom and the serenity of ages. "Greetings, heart of the land."

"Greetings, tree mother," Catrin replied, unsure where the words had come from. Like the echoes of a distant past, she felt as if she had done this before; it felt natural and right.

"It has been so long since your kind has spoken to us. I suppose we stopped listening."

"The knowledge was lost," Catrin said. "It was only recently rediscovered."

"Speaking to you makes me weary. I am so very tired."

"I see a disturbance in your energy. Can I help you?"

"Thank you, heart of the land. You are kind, but it has been so long, I don't remember how. I've forgotten the old songs. But I'll try."

Wrapping Catrin in a warm embrace, the dryad began to sing. Her energy flowed against Catrin's, and slowly they began to merge. From deep in Catrin's mind, a new melody came, playing harmony to that of the dryad. Together they sang until their energy vibrated and undulated. Like dark spots in the dryad's aura, the disturbances swirled and coalesced, but the melody seemed to vibrate them apart, and

Catrin began to focus on them. Some she took into herself, trying to make order from chaos. A feeling of nausea and weariness overwhelmed her, and she thought she might lose consciousness.

"You are tired, heart of the land. You must go now, but I thank you. I send you away with a gift. Live well, heart of the land. Live well."

In the next moment, Catrin was back in her body and the bark was biting into her flesh. She pulled away and steadied herself; her legs wobbled and shook. "I don't know your name. Please, tell me your name," she said, and in the back of her mind she heard a voice whisper: *Shirlafawna.*

"Are you well? Catrin! Talk to me!" Chase said.

"I'm fine. I'm just tired," she said, but then she gasped. From behind each tree peeked a dryad in their physical forms, and they greeted Catrin as friends. Shirlafawna had given her a glorious gift indeed. Looking at Shirlafawna's tree, Catrin sensed the energy field recovering even if her eyes still saw disease; her senses showed a return to health; the physical would follow. Somehow, *that* she knew. Despite her exhilaration, she was truly weary, and she returned to the cavern to rest.

Chapter 8

Without forgetfulness, forgiveness is incomplete.
--Amelia Kudara, maidservant

* * *

"Do you see that?" Brother Vaughn asked as they walked back from the river.

"I see it," Catrin said as a strange shape flew overhead; it was unlike any bird she'd ever seen.

"The winged foxes are found only here. My uncle brought me here when I was a boy, knowing how much I loved anything that flew, and these were his gift to me. A marvel unlike any other, unique to my homeland."

"They're beautiful," Chase said as another fox leaped an impossible distance between two trees, using its winglike membranes to sail through the air. It was then that Catrin recalled what Brother Vaughn had said about needing a ship where foxes roost, and now she understood his meaning.

Nearby, a violet hummingbird floated around some bushes, looking for one last drink before his migration. Catrin watched him with all her vision, mesmerized by his beauty. He seemed to sense her scrutiny and boldly flew in front of her, weaving back and forth before her face. For a moment she was connected to him, and she lent him energy for the long journey. Extending her hand, she offered a perch, and to everyone's surprise, he landed on her finger, chirped, and momentarily stuck out his translucent, strawlike tongue.

After a brief rest, the bird chirped and seemed to wish them farewell before leaping into the air. He turned and flew straight as an arrow, and Catrin could still sense him long after he was lost from sight, the sensation growing fainter as the distance between them grew.

"That was one of the most remarkable things I've ever seen," Brother Vaughn said. "I've coaxed them with sugar water, but never have I seen one land on a person."

"He sensed me watching him, I think," Catrin said. "When he came to look at me, I offered him a place to rest, and then I lent him energy for his journey."

"Truly astounding," Brother Vaughn said.

When they returned to the cavern, Catrin no longer had to wonder who the intended recipient of Brother Vaughn's message was, for Nora, Kenward, and Fasha Trell waited within, already talking with Benjin. Though Catrin had never met Fasha before, there was no question who she was; the family resemblance was remarkable.

"Good. You've returned," Nora said with a nod. "We've no time to waste. There're still soldiers in these parts, and I want no part of fighting on land."

The greetings were made in haste as everyone scrambled to gather the gear. Catrin felt as if a strong wind were sweeping her away as they marched toward the coast. At the bottom of a rocky ridge, two ships waited in a small cove: the *Slippery Eel* and the *Stealthy Shark*.

"When I got Brother Vaughn's message, I knew it was time we did something more," Nora said. "Duty calls us to help in the name of the Vestrana. For many lifetimes the Vestrana has been a useful tool--a convenience--but now it must serve its true purpose. We must help the Herald achieve victory over the madness. I don't need a seer to tell me it's so."

"Thank you, Captain Trell. All of you have my thanks," Catrin said.

"Are you joking?" Kenward said. "Do you think I'd miss the greatest adventure of all? Not me."

Nora smacked him on the back of the head. "You'll behave yourself and follow orders, fool boy."

"Yes, Mother," he said, but then he glanced at Fasha and they grinned at each other.

Nora rolled her eyes. "They'll be the death of me yet," she said. "The real question is how to get to the Firstland. We could spend a lifetime wandering the seas and not find it. What do we know?"

"I've never found anything to prove it," Brother Vaughn said, "but I've always believed the Firstland lies to the south. If we could find the Keys of Terhilian, we would have a much better idea. The old texts say in the great carving of the Terhilian Lovers, the man points to the Firstland and the woman to the Greatland."

"I've always thought the Firstland was to the east," Kenward said. "Past the mountain island and the great shallows."

Fasha scoffed and rolled her eyes.

Nora just shook her head. "I was thinking north, beyond the ice seas. Anyone want to offer up west?" she asked, throwing her hands up in frustration, but an idea began to form in Catrin's mind.

"When hummingbirds migrate, do they make stops along the way?" she asked Brother Vaughn, and Kenward cast her a curious glance.

"If I'm correct, they make the journey in a single flight, as hard as that is to believe. Why do you ask?"

"When we first met, you said you thought the violet hummingbirds migrated to the Godfist, but I'm certain they do not. If they do not migrate to the Godfist, then perhaps they travel to the Firstland."

"How can you be certain? You've not been to every part of the Godfist. Maybe they all go to the eastern or southern coasts," Chase said.

"I'm nearly certain. I can still sense the hummingbird that landed on my finger," Catrin said, and now Nora and Fasha gave her astonished looks. "He grows faint as he gets farther away, but he's that way," she said, pointing, her eyes closed.

"East!" Kenward said, and he did a happy dance that clearly disgusted Fasha.

"I'd say southeast," she said, her arms crossed over her chest.

"Maybe a little south," Kenward conceded, but his grin did not fade.

"I've nothing better to go by. South and east it is," Nora said as they reached the shoreline.

* * *

In a wagon loaded with jars of powdered pyre-orchid, Mirta rode through town, trying to avoid the roadways that were still clogged with snow. On the main thoroughfare, the snow was mostly cleared, and she had to guide her mare around only occasional patches of ice. Along the way, she stopped to see Becka, who was now fully recovered. The spread of illness had been staunched, here at least, but Mirta knew many others throughout the Greatland were at risk. Orman wouldn't tell her who had sent the precious flowers, but Mirta had her suspicions. Wilmer and Jidan weren't talking, and Mirta had to admire their ability to keep a secret. She supposed it was a family trait.

What really mattered was that the gift not be wasted. It had taken time to dry and prepare the powder, then months making sure that the sick were truly cured. Now she knew she could wait no more. In the harshness of winter, there would be many in need. For them, Mirta was leaving her home, her loved ones, what seemed her entire life. Suisa could tend to those she left behind; she was a skilled woman with a kindly manner. Still, Mirta's heart ached as she released herself from responsibility to home and opened herself to responsibility to everyone.

With a wave to the crowd that had gathered to see her off, despite the cold, Mirta chirruped and slapped the leather lines across her mare's rump.

* * *

As the seasons passed, a new sort of normality set in, Rolph Tillerman did as he and his ancestors always had: he worked the land. His efforts provided food for his family and for others around him, but lately his labors seemed almost a waste of time, a poor attempt at keeping starvation at bay. Jessub was a growing boy, but he was not ready to take his place as the man of the farm, and Rolph began to question how much longer he would be able to hold up under the physical strains of his labors. His father had always

90

said that farming was the work of a young man; teaching that young man to farm was the job of his father. Martik. If only he were here to raise Jessub, to teach him all the lessons he would need to survive, then things would be better.

"I'm just too old," Rolph said to himself as the pain in his back escalated from a dull ache to a sharp, stabbing pain. Forced to admit he could no more, Rolph held a hand to his back and walked slowly to the cottage where Collette waited, her hands on her hips.

"Didn' I tell ya no' to work yerself t'death?" she asked. "Better to git a little done each day, I says, an' then a little more the next. That's what I says, an' look at ya. Come on now. Git in here and let me git a look at ya. Foolish old man."

As Rolph settled himself in the most comfortable position he could, he stayed quiet while his wife lovingly massaged his aching muscles and lectured him about being more careful and listening to her. Rolph closed his eyes and let himself relax. At least some things in his world remained the same. That realization gave him hope. Somehow he would find a way to make things right.

A moment later, though, Jessub charged into the cottage, the door slamming behind him, which was something he'd been scolded about far too many times. Covered in mud, cuts, and scrapes, he looked the part of a scamp, especially with the broad grin on his face. "Gramma, Grampa," he said, "look what I caught!" He held up a small, lizardlike animal that still squirmed in his hand.

"I don't care what it is," Collette said, immediately shuffling the boy back outside. "I want it out o' my house, and yer not t'come back in 'til yer stripped and washed. Understood?"

"Yes, Gramma," he said, and though his eyes were cast downward for a moment, in the next he was running back to the mud hole, presumably in search of more salamanders. "That boy'll be the death o' me yet."

Rolph just shook his head and sighed.

Staring at the endless waves, Catrin wondered if she would ever see land again. Having long since lost contact with the hummingbird, she was no longer so certain of their course, and they had seen nothing for months--no fish, no birds, nothing but deep water.

Kenward stood nearby watching the *Stealthy Shark* as she slowed and turned. "What is that woman up to this time?" he said, but then came the mirror flashes, and he cursed. "Prepare to board the *Shark*. She's wounded and we must capture the crew."

Catrin sighed. Nora never stopped. Rather than simply sail, the entire trip was transformed into a training exercise. Each drill brought new challenges, and Catrin was certain this one would as well. The races and some of the maneuvers had been exciting and even fun, but boardings were brutal. Only practice weapons were used, but they left everyone bruised and welted, not to mention exhausted.

"They've beaten us back twice already," Kenward said. "And they've taken us twice. No mistakes. No mercy. If my mother or sister leave an opening, take it, or they will humiliate you. Trust me on this. Leave them welted and bruised at the end of this day, and there'll be more racing than boarding for the next week."

The crew readied themselves, rallied by his words. Catrin felt her heart pounding, and she gathered her will, wanting to avenge Kenward's losses and her own. His eye was still blackened from a punch his own mother had landed. Strom had already "killed" Catrin by sneaking up on her and hitting her across the back with the flat of his sword. Benjin had forced her to submit twice without ever hitting her. Holding her corner of the boarding net, she waited for Kenward's command, ready to fight.

At ramming speed, he sailed without wavering.

* * *

"What's that boilin' maniac doing?" Fasha shouted.
"Raise the--"

"Hold!" Nora said. "Not yet. Stand ready to be boarded.
Take no prisoners," she added with a pointed glance at
Benjin.

"He's gonna sink both of us," Fasha said but remained
at her post. The *Slippery Eel* charged through the waves as
Kenward used every trick he knew to get speed. The crew
moved without hesitation, despite what were obviously
ludicrous orders. "How does he get his crew to go along
with his crazy ideas?"

"They believe in him," Nora said. "Fools and dreamers
they may be, but somehow they make it work."

"Kenward will come for mother and me," Fasha said.
"He'll be seeking revenge. I'm certain of it."

"Chase and Catrin will come for me . . . together I
think," Benjin said.

"Do you think our plan is gonna work?" Strom asked.

"They'll never see it coming," Fasha said. Nora
remained silent, anxiously watching the *Slippery Eel*'s daring
approach. "Stand ready to repel!" she said as the *Eel*
executed a turn that left it coming toward the *Shark*
sideways, driving a wall of water before it. "Brace
yourselves!"

Atop the *Eel*'s wake, the *Shark* heaved and rolled, her
decks thrown far from the *Eel*'s.

"Hold!" Kenward's shout carried above the roaring
water. As the *Shark* rolled on the receding wave, it came
back closer to the *Eel*. Sliding down in the water, her decks
dropped below the *Eel*'s. "Now!" came Kenward's
command.

Howling like animals, his crew attacked. Catrin and
Chase moved toward Benjin, who looked up to see if
Osbourne and Strom were in place. Taking a deep breath, he
bent his knees. Fasha bounced lightly on the balls of her feet,
swaying back and forth like a panther waiting to strike. She
gave him a nod. The bait was ready, the trap set.

93

* * *

Catrin gained the *Shark*'s deck before anyone else and ran, growling, at Benjin. His eyes met hers, daring her to take him. Chase caught up to her and charged alongside. Kenward roared like a madman as he charged Fasha and Nora. "Now!" he yelled only an instant before Benjin did the same.

Using all the quickness and agility she possessed, Catrin turned sharply and rolled. Rising up, she used her momentum to hurl her sword at Strom. Chase executed a similar maneuver, though all Catrin saw was a blur of limbs beside her. With a loud crack, Catrin's sword landed across the backs of Strom's hands, making him lose his grip on the net he held. Chase's sword struck Osbourne so violently, he fell from the rigging, cursing. Their net fell harmlessly to the deck, their trap sprung.

Kenward caught Benjin off his guard and smacked him across the chest with the flat of his blade. Fasha went down in a heap under Bryn, who dropped from the rigging. "Dead!" he yelled. Nora watched it all with an air of detachment, but that changed when Catrin slid across the deck into the backs of her knees. Grabbing Chase's sword as she passed it, Catrin rolled herself in position to stab Nora. "Dead!" she shouted.

"Dead!"

"Dead!" came the call across the deck, and nearly two-thirds of the *Shark*'s crew was down.

"Advantage Kenward," Nora said as Catrin helped her rise. Kenward smiled as he helped his sister from the deck.

"Good fight, Sis."

"Good fight."

"You're a madman, Kenward," Nora said, "but somehow you inspire those around you to equal madness. I'd never have expected Catrin to take me down, nor Bryn Fasha, but you gave them heart and courage. I'm proud of you and your crew. Now get your ship away from the *Shark* before you sink us all."

Fasha made a disgusted sound in her throat and rolled her eyes.

"Aw, now don't be sore because you lost, Sis."

"Next time," she said. "No mercy. No prisoners."

"Next time," he said, grinning. "Thanks, Mom. See you soon!"

"Fool boy."

* * *

Victory greatly improved the mood aboard the *Slippery Eel,* and Kenward gathered everyone at the prow. "The words my mother said today were neither trivial nor easily earned. Today you made my mother proud of me, and I thank you for that," he said, a catch in his voice and a tear in his eye. "You made me proud, and you gave Fasha and my mother reason to respect and fear you. You're actually starting to frighten me a little."

Laughter helped ease the tension, and Catrin began to see the wisdom of Nora's drills. Rather than letting the crews consider the unlikelihood of finding the Firstland or worry over the shortage of food, she kept them busy, honing their skills, while developing teamwork and camaraderie.

Everyone turned when, across the water, sounds of celebration came from the *Stealthy Shark.* "Seafloor ahead!" the lookout called an instant later. "Land ho!"

Still distant on the horizon, a dark smudge rose above the waterline. Like a bastion of hope, it drew them on. Ahead, dark water suddenly changed to azure, and sandy, white bottom came into view. Mirror flashes flew between the ships, and Kenward paced impatiently. "Drop anchor."

"What?" Chase asked. "Why are we stopping?"

"Mother fears the shallows. She says we'll run aground if we enter now. These are tidal waters, and she wants to wait for the full moon."

"That'll be weeks from now," Chase said, dismayed.

"True, but there should be an abundance of sea life along the shelf. We'll fish and eat whatever we can catch. We can't load our holds; that would only put us lower in the water and increase the risk of running aground. We'll have to do that when we reach the other side."

"How far across is it?" Catrin asked.

"I wish I knew; that would make convincing Mother to move on much easier, but not knowing, I can't argue her logic. Waiting for the full moon will give us the greatest chance of survival. If we were to get caught by receding tides, we could get stuck, at the very least, but more likely, we'd be sunk. For now, we wait."

"I bet we can catch more fish than they can," Chase said, grinning. Kenward grinned back and used his mirror to issue the challenge.

"We'll eat good tonight," Chase whispered to Catrin with a wink.

* * *

In the darkness, Prios climbed. With no light to guide him, he could rely only on the senses his power provided. Climbing without sight, that most primal sense, was disorienting and more terrifying than anything he had ever imagined. The only consolation was that he could not perceive the heights from which he perilously hung.

On his back was an empty pack, meant only to secure his goal. He had no food or water to sustain him, and Prios knew that he could waste no time. Each moment his death became more likely, and he bit his lip as he continued to climb.

When at last he reached an opening in the face of the mountain, Prios was overcome by a sense of foreboding. The hairs on his arms and neck stood straight, and sweat began to seep into his eyes. Within the mountain, he sensed massive life, both vibrant and deadly. His life now hung on an assumption. If these beasts were not truly dormant at night, then he would most likely be dead within moments.

Before he lost his courage, he took a step into the massive stone chamber. Though he could not see its vastness, he could *feel* it. Pockets of life could be felt all around, but one in particular drew Prios closer. No attack came, but he wondered if he was simply being toyed with, being made to believe he could succeed in such an audacious theft only to be torn to shreds before he could make good his escape.

When he reached an area where the life force around him was divided into many smaller entities, he tried to ignore the fact that he sensed one massive entity behind all the smaller ones. Prios froze and remained as still as a stone, his hair, once again, standing on end. Overwhelmed by the sensation that something was watching him, waiting for him to make his fatal mistake, he waited and prayed.

Unable to bear the suspense any longer, he reached out and laid his hands on a warm and smooth shell. Perhaps it was his imagination that caused the shadows to shift and swirl, but it caused him to pause for a moment, and as he did, his senses perceived something. Amid all the small life forces around him, one stood out. Though it emitted no light, Prios could feel the power. A smile formed on his lips, as he realized that this was his opportunity to give Archmaster Belegra exactly what he had asked for and, at the same time, give him something that may be beyond his ability to control.

As soon as his hands touched the shell, he felt the shadows move again, and he could no longer deny his fear. With the speed of desperation, he put the egg in his pack and secured it on his back before running back to the cavern entrance. Without his sight, he was unprepared for such speed, and a protruding piece of rock sent him sprawling, nearly sending him tumbling into the open air. With only a hand's width of stone ledge behind him, Prios checked to be certain the egg was still whole. It could have been a freak wind, but he thought he felt hot breath on his neck, and he needed no urging to begin his descent. With his eyes squeezed shut, he lowered himself over the ledge and waited for powerful jaws to close around him.

Pressed against his back, the egg in his pack shifted, and Prios sensed awareness. As he moved to the next toehold, a name floated into his mind like something from a dream: Kyrien.

* * *

Having eaten more types of seafood than she had ever imagined existed, from armored skate to monstrous crabs-- they seemed to catch some of everything--Catrin longed for a steak or a piece of bacon. Grubb identified some fish that were unsafe to eat and a few more he wasn't certain about; those were thrown back. It seemed a harmless practice at first, but staying in one place surrounded by bleeding fish turned out to be a mistake.

Dorsal fins the size of mainsails jutted from the water and circled the ship. Catrin and Chase stood at the gunwales, watching the terrifying display. Deep booms reverberated through the ships as the massive predators inspected them by bumping into them. Jarred by the impacts, Catrin watched in horror as dark shadows glided through the water with amazing speed and grace. She prayed they would go away.

Seabirds, also drawn by the chance for an easy meal, gathered around what remained of the discarded fish. In a moment that would forever be burned into Catrin's memory, one of the giant sharks leaped from the water, jaws agape, and took a mouthful of seabirds with it before crashing back into the water with a mighty impact. Seeing the agility of such large and dangerous creatures made Catrin feel small and vulnerable, yet she could not look away, held in thrall by their terrifying beauty.

With such danger in the waters, fishing efforts were curtailed. After moving to deeper water, both crews spent time simply resting and hoping the sharks did not return.

* * *

Along with the full moon came more than a dozen comets, their combined light creating a dreamlike landscape. Uncertainty gnawed at both crews as they entered the shallows, not knowing if they would ever escape.

Even when she was not on duty, Catrin kept watch; underwater hills and barely submerged islands threatened them at every moment. When the way ahead became too

98

difficult to gauge, men were sent out in boats to check the depth and find safe passage. Using a weight tied to a long length of rope, they quickly made measurements. Markings on the rope indicated the safe level, and too many times that marker was near the surface.

Despite the danger, they had to concentrate on their task, for wondrous sights abounded, threatening to draw the attention of those on watch. During Catrin's off-duty watches, she occasionally let herself become absorbed in the beauty of the strange place. Colorful fish darted around equally colorful reefs. Flights of manta rays, each wider than the ships were long, glided through the water, looking as if they were flying.

As they moved farther into the shallows, small islands dotted the horizon, providing additional navigational challenges. The mountain was still distant, but it became ever more intimidating as it grew closer.

It was shocking to see life take hold in such a bizarre place, but there were islands covered with trees and bushes, and the waters around them teemed with creatures. The trees' branches harbored birds, snakes, frogs, and even crabs. Snakes moved from island to island, skimming the surface with their serpentine movements.

Beyond a cluster of islands, they reached a place where no land broke the surface and the waters became a bit deeper. Here grew trees like nothing any of them had ever seen before. Stiltlike root systems extended to the seafloor and kept the trunks above water. Encased in delicate crystals, the bark and leaves danced in the light. Given the robust green color of the leaves and their strong energy fields, Catrin guessed this was a normal condition rather than some bizarre ailment.

"Are those what I think they are?" Brother Vaughn asked Kenward.

"I'm not sure what kind of trees they are, but they certainly are remarkable."

Fasha brought the *Stealthy Shark* in close, and Benjin shouted across the distance, "Could those really be saltbark trees I see?"

"I think you're right," Brother Vaughn shouted back. "Saltbark is a precious remedy told of only in legend," he said to Kenward. "Can we send a boat in to investigate?"

"We can't afford to waste any time," Kenward said. "If you go, you must not fall behind. Any delay could cost us our lives. Are you certain a few leaves are worth the risk?"

"It was said to cure ailments with no other known remedy. It can cure blindness in some cases; it can be used to treat poisonous snakebites, jellyfish and ray stings, and I'm certain there are other things I've forgotten."

"It's your skin you'll be risking. I'll not stand in your way."

After a brief discussion with Benjin, Brother Vaughn asked that they lower a boat. "We can pick up Benjin since he is most interested in the trees, and we'll harvest what we can as quickly as we can. You'll not have to wait on us," he promised. Kenward assigned crewmembers to man the oars, and Catrin stepped in front of him.

"I'm going," she said.

"Too dangerous."

"I'm going." He tried to speak a couple of times, but then seemed to reconsider, and he stepped aside, allowing her to climb down. Brother Vaughn came next, loaded with empty sacks. Bryn and Farsy manned the oars. Catrin released her oars from the locks and tried to match their strokes. Soon they skimmed across the relatively still waters. Benjin boarded with excitement in his eyes, and they worked together to get out in front of both ships.

"We can harvest until the *Eel* reaches us, and then we'll need to get back. No sense taking unnecessary chances," Benjin said.

Feeling as if she were in another world, Catrin watched the surreal landscape slide by. Saltbark trees, most widely spaced, seemed to prefer isolation, but not far in the distance stood a cluster of trees separated by only narrow channels.

Benjin guided them toward it. "Be careful. We've no idea what might be hiding within the branches. All we need are the leaves. Try not to pick any area bare."

When they reached the first tree, Catrin could hardly believe her eyes. Each deep green leaf was encased in a delicate frosting of nearly identical crystals. Reaching out, she pinched a stem, and the leaf came off easily in her hand. Holding it up to the light, it cast rainbows across her palm. Knowing they had only a limited time to harvest, she got busy picking leaves.

Despite Benjin's warnings, she became careless in her haste and yanked her hand back with a sudden intake of breath when a coiled snake hissed from behind the foliage. Their wariness renewed, they moved from tree to tree, crabs scattering as they approached. A small lizard fell into the boat, and Catrin climbed as far atop the gunwales as she could. Benjin used a gloved hand to return it to the trees, and only then did Catrin return to her seat.

Casting a sidelong glance at the ships, Benjin declared it time they return.

"Wait," Catrin said, seeing a flash of movement within the trees. "Did you see that?"

"I didn't see anything," Benjin said, and everyone else shook their heads. Still Catrin watched the trees and jumped when a green-haired dryad peeked around her tree. Coated in the same sparkling crystals, her hair gleamed. Her eyes shone with life and curiosity. Longingly, the dryad stretched her hands out toward Catrin, who wished she could ask them to turn back.

"Is something wrong, li'l miss?"

"No," she said, unsure why she was reluctant to share what she had seen. It just seemed too private, and she would respect the dryad she longed to embrace.

Chapter 9

On the final day, a scourge of wind and fire shall descend from the skies, and all creation shall be laid low.
--Fisidecles, the Mad Prophet

* * *

Watching the increasingly shallow waters that surrounded them, Catrin's eyes were drawn to the mountain that now dominated the horizon. Clouds filled the air around it, and its energy seemed almost threatening. As it drew ever closer, the scenery began to change. Evidence of a long-forgotten civilization surrounded them. Rectangular forms, clearly the remains of buildings, dotted the area, and jars littered the seafloor, some of which were whole.

The crews watched in silence, awed by the sights. A monolithic hand reached from the sand, the sword it held broken and worn. Nearby were the remains of a ship. Only the skeleton remained, laid out neatly and standing out in stark contrast to the white sand. The forefoot and stem were well preserved, however, and were fashioned to resemble a dragon in flight. The sight of the dragon, seemingly flying underwater, thrilled Catrin, despite the dangers the ancient shipwreck warned of.

A large island came into view. It was covered with trees that were laden with color, flowers weighing down their branches. Here Catrin saw a beautiful but distressing sight: violet hummingbirds by the hundreds, forming clouds of iridescent light that danced through the trees. If the birds ended their migration here, that meant Catrin's idea of following them to the Firstland had been founded on a mistake. She had gambled and lost. Now they were months from the Greatland and faced with the possibility of getting stuck there.

Twice the *Slippery Eel* dragged along the seafloor, dangerously close to running aground, but Kenward did not want to completely empty the hold yet, not knowing how much farther the shallows continued. The *Stealthy Shark* rode higher in the water, but they, too, had come close to disaster,

caught between shallow water and the ruins of an ancient
fortress, but her crew managed to avoid the dangers.

"Have mercy!" the lookout called. "Look at that!"

A ring of stone pillars, each the size of a greatoak, stood
in a circle. There would be twenty-four in all, if not for the
two that had fallen and now lay across the shallows ahead,
creating a formidable barrier. Each column had a face carved
on it, and they were visages of madness and despair.

"We're gonna have to sail around it," Kenward said.

"Zjhon warship grounded to the south, sir. Looks like
it's been abandoned," Bryn called out from the rigging.

"They didn't make it," Kenward said. "I hope we have
better luck than they did."

The sight of the ship gave Catrin heart; this was no
ancient shipwreck. Perhaps they were going the right way
after all. Still, there would be no way to tell which way to go
beyond the shallows. Kenward had once told her that ships
leave no footprints, and now she understood the hard truth
of his words.

After furious debate between the ships, they split up to
survey the area, hoping to find a safe channel to sail through.
Kenward turned the *Eel* north, sailing perpendicular to the
fallen columns. Pieces of other columns, which had
obviously been much taller at one time, littered the area, and
they had to move slowly. The farther north they sailed,
though, the fouler the air became, filled with a noxious odor.

Beyond the fallen columns were luminous rifts in the
seafloor; the gas they spewed churned the waters violently,
and a foul haze hung over the water.

"It's not safe to sail over gas bubbles," Kenward said.
"Ships have sunk in water filled with bubbles. When there is
so much gas in the water, it disturbs the buoyancy that keeps
us afloat. If even part of the ship enters those waters, she
could be torn apart. We'll have to go back."

Not long after they turned around came a dreadful
series of flashes--a distress call. The *Stealthy Shark* was
grounded.

"They made it past the Zjhon warship, but the currents
pulled them into sand. They are trying to pull themselves
free using the anchor and windlass, but it doesn't look good.

The only blessing is that they are on a sand bar. If we can pull her free, she shouldn't take much damage. We just have to get to the other side. Mother wants me to come south now and tow them backwards, but I disagree. We're going to try and make the other side, and then we'll pull them forward."

"Are you sure you want to disobey your mother?" Catrin asked, imagining the fight it would cause.

"My mother knows that sometimes you must follow your instincts to survive. My instincts are telling me to get through first. Besides, if I fail, she'll have a long swim before she can scold me."

Setting a course for the columns that still stood, Kenward scanned the water along with everyone else. They found several gaps between fallen chunks of column, but they led nowhere.

"There!" Bryn called. "Look, sir, to the north. See the gap?"

"Send a boat to check the depth, and see if the water beyond is deep enough as well."

Men scrambled to comply, knowing that time was running out for the *Shark*.

The gap proved wide enough for the *Eel* to slip through unscathed, which was obviously not the case for the Zjhon ships that had preceded them. Rub marks and even bits of wood clung to the columns.

"They came this way. That's for certain," Bryn said, and Kenward nodded his agreement, clearly deep in thought.

As they sailed within the columns, Catrin was overwhelmed by the similarities to the Grove of the Elders, and even though it was covered in water, she could feel the power of the land beneath her. Here, too, she guessed, was a place where the power of the land was most concentrated. Drinking it in, she let the natural energy flow around her and bolster her.

The seafloor rose in a gentle dome that crested at the center of the columns. Unable to cut straight through, Kenward guided the ship in an arc, following the columns as guides. Once past the fallen columns, he turned north. As they passed through two of the tallest columns that remained standing, Catrin felt as if she were leaving one world and entering another. Departure from the intense energy field left her swaying on her feet.

Cutting a meandering course, they reached waters not far from where the *Stealthy Shark* waited, eerily still in the water. Gathered at the stern, the crew were taking turns at the windlass. As soon as they spotted the *Eel,* a flurry of flashes came.

"She's not happy," Kenward said with a grin. "We'll see what song she sings when I pull them out. Fasha might just walk the plank on her own." When they had gotten as close to the *Shark* as they safely could, he turned to his crew. "Get a boat dropped and take a heavy line to the *Shark*."

Once the rope was firmly secured to each ship, Kenward raised the sails. For a time, nothing happened, but then both ships began to slide forward a finger's width at a time until the *Shark* slipped free.

The waters ahead were deeper, and the level of tension decreased greatly, but still they were wary of unforeseen obstacles. In the shadow of the giant mountain, which was now so close that Catrin felt she could reach out and touch it, the foul smell they had experienced earlier became strong once again, and pockets of bubbles suddenly erupted in the waters around them. Careful to avoid the roiling waters, they lost time finding a clear path.

Cheers rose from both ships, though, when the lookouts spotted the end of the shallows, and Catrin climbed the rigging to see the dark waters for herself. Beyond a ragged line of white sand, it beckoned and threatened. Unexplored waters awaited.

When the ships gained deep water, the order to fish immediately followed. Knowing they might need more food than the ships could hold to survive the voyage, they made use of every bit of space and packed it with food. Both ships sat low in the water by nightfall.

"I must admit," Kenward said. "I feel as if I have survived the dragon's claws only to land in his teeth. Do you have any idea of what way we should go now?"

"I don't," Catrin said, wishing she could do something. Then a desperate idea came to her, and she wondered if it could work. "Brother Vaughn, may I discuss something that happened in the Inner Sanctuary with violating confidence?"

"These circumstances warrant flexibility. Speak freely."

"Were you one of those who chanted during my time in the viewing chamber?"

"Yes. I was."

"Do you know both sides of the harmony?"

"Actually, I do. I learned only one part at first, but when you did not return, we had to be creative, and I ended up learning the other part as well. What are you thinking?"

"Could you teach the crew how to perform the chant?"

"I suppose I could," Brother Vaughn said, thoughtful. "I don't know if it will work without the stone chair . . . or the special chambers. I don't know."

"We could try," Catrin said firmly.

"We could try," he conceded. "But I'm still not certain it will be safe."

After gathering the off-duty members of both crews, Brother Vaughn instructed them on the chants. He taught them both parts as a precaution. Catrin, though, did not attend the sessions, afraid knowing the individual parts too well would somehow affect her ability to perceive it as a whole rather than the sum of its parts.

"Are you certain you want to try this, li'l miss? We almost lost you under the best of conditions. Trying from out here could be deadly."

"I can think of no other way to find the Firstland. We could sail for the rest of our lives and not find it. I will at least make an attempt."

"I suppose you're right."

* * *

Rolph Tillerman packed the last few items into the wagon that would take him away from his home, away from the place where he, his father, and his grandfather had been born and raised. Most of the items packed were for practical reasons, but a few were purely for sentimental purposes--he simply could not leave his entire past behind. Collette did what she could to hide her tears, but he could feel her pain as if it were his own. She had married him here and raised their children here.

Only Jessub seemed excited about the prospect of their journey, and at times, it seemed only his enthusiasm kept Rolph and Collette moving. Under any other circumstances, they would have stayed, but the choice had been taken from them. Hampered by injuries and his advancing age, Rolph had been unable to plant enough crops to keep them fed, and when it looked as if most of what he planted would succumb to pests and disease, he knew what he had to do. Others, too, could no longer afford to remain, and what had once been a thriving community now looked to be in its final days. Rolph knew that the others would help him if they could, but no one was in a position to do anything beyond survive, and it seemed they would need a great deal of luck to do that. Luck seemed one of the many things that were in short supply, and Rolph would not risk Collette's or Jessub's life on it. Instead, he would take an equally daunting risk, and he wondered if he were making a mistake.

Jessub appeared from behind the barn, dirty and scraped as usual.

"Come on, Jessub," Collette said. "We've got to go now, an' look at ya. Yer a boilin' mess, and you've torn yer last good pair o' breeches. Git up here this instant!"

"I'm comin', Gramma," Jessub said, his smile never wavering. "I just had to git my knife from the loft."

Rolph shook his head. He'd been hesitant to give the boy a knife for fear that he'd lop off his own thumbs just to see what it felt like. In all his years, he'd never seen a boy as inquisitive and rambunctious as Jessub, save maybe himself at that age. With one final look at his home and a squeeze on the shoulder from Collette, he chirruped and smacked the lines on Elmheart's rump. A new journey had begun.

* * *

In the deckhouse, they gathered. Hastily constructed partitions divided the room only in spirit. Facing the open door, Catrin looked out at the blue sky; clouds like salmon scales forecasted wind, but she was determined. Three times already Brother Vaughn had found reasons not to proceed, but she could wait no more.

"Now is the time. Please begin," she pleaded.

"Are you certain, li'l miss?"

"I am."

At first, the disjointed chanting seemed nothing like what she had experienced at Ohmahold, but then the two groups found synchronicity, and the harmony meshed. Wooden containers used as drums provided the bass. The vibrations were not as deep, but they resonated within the deckhouse.

Closing her eyes, Catrin rode the vibration and drew a trickle of energy, when she opened her eyes, she flew into the blue sky, free of her mortal shroud. In a moment of sheer bliss, she rolled and danced on the wind, lighter than a feather.

Determined not to waste the opportunity, she flew across the water, faster than the wind, casting her senses in every direction, drawing more and more power as a result. In a trancelike state, she flew, searching for land with all her senses. Then, in a moment of clarity, she realized that all she had to do was search for life and she would most likely find land.

At first, all she found were large, fast-moving sea creatures, but then she began to sense rivers of life flowing toward one place. When she moved over one of these shimmering rivers, she saw schools of migrating fish. Farther ahead, she found land. Tiny at first, it grew so quickly that Catrin could hardly believe her speed. What had first appeared to be one landmass was really a series of many small islands. On one, carved into the face of a massive cliff, was a familiar but foreign image: a man and a woman sharing an embrace. Except these figures were nothing like Istra and Vestra; they had large, round eyes and broad noses. They wore strange clothing and even stranger headdresses.

Despite the embrace, one of the man's arms was extended, pointing . . . to the Firstland; the woman pointed back to the Greatland. Exhilarated, Catrin prepared to return, but when she turned around, she made a terrifying discovery. Unlike her trip from the viewing chamber, no trail of energy extended back to her body.

Trying to gauge the direction from which she had come, she realized how dire her situation really was. If she was off by even the slightest amount, given the distance she had covered, she would have very little chance of finding the ships.

Desperation gripped her as she made her best guess and applied her will to speed. Only the chance of spotting the giant mountain or the shallows kept her from losing all hope. Homogenous waves slid past, only occasional whitecaps breaking the monotony. Unable to accurately judge her speed, she had to be ever watchful, lest she fly right past them.

Weariness set in, and she could no longer extend her senses because it took all her energy just to continue moving. The waves moved ever slower past until she moved no faster than a ship, and she began to lose hope.

You must come.

The intense feeling brought Catrin from her stupor. Rather than words in her mind, this was more like overwhelming emotion, pouring into her, bolstering her, and she began moving a little faster. Still, she struggled to remain focused, feeling as if she were diffusing, like a drop of extract in water.

Do not despair.

Again, Catrin realized she was losing concentration. It would be so easy to just fall asleep, to let herself dissolve away, to become one with all creation.

I need you. You must free me. You must.

The emotional intrusions annoyed her, disturbing her rest. She was so tired and wanted only to sleep a while longer. A wave of desperate need washed over her, overwhelming her, and she was flooded with the hope that someone *would* come. Someone *would* end the agony and despair. *Someone.*

Catrin. Catrin. Catrin.

When her eyes opened, it was a shock. Her body demanded breath, and she sucked in air. Her limbs would not respond, and when she saw Benjin take her hand, it did not look like her own; her skin was ashen with a bluish tint. For the moment, breathing was paramount.

* * *

"This is crazy," Gustad said as Milo stood his shoulders, scraping bat droppings from the walls of a massive shaft that was filled with bats. Nearly fifty miles south of Ohmahold, they had covered the entire distance underground, never leaving the ancient mine complex. Several times Gustad had feared they were hopelessly lost, but they did manage to find the place indicated on their map.

"The ancient text says this stuff is what we need," Milo said. "This is the only way I know how to get it. You wouldn't consider keeping a bat as a pet, would you?"

"Not a chance," Gustad said, the very thought giving him a chill. "Hurry up. You're not light on the shoulders, you know." With his hands holding Milo's legs, Gustad stood with his knees slightly bent, trying to hold on to Milo's constantly shifting weight without hurting his back.

"I'm almost done," Milo said. "I need more light."

"I can't hold you and the torch," Gustad said.

"Let go of my leg and hand me the torch. I'll only be a moment more."

Gustad squatted down and grabbed the torch from where he had propped it. Standing back up was slow and difficult, but Milo used a toehold to support much of his weight. Still, Gustad was breathing hard when he handed Milo the torch.

Bits of rock and bat dung fell from the air as Milo worked, and Gustad wiped his face with one hand, holding Milo steady with the other. Pain seared his shoulder as Milo stood on his toes to reach something.

"There's a great big spot . . . just out of reach," Milo said, his effort to stretch clear in his voice. Shifting his weight, he slipped, sending sparks and bits of still-burning torch all around. Blowing and using his free hand, Gustad wiped the embers away from his face. An ember on Milo's robe started to smolder, but he could not reach it. He opened his mouth to say something, but a shout of pain was all the came out as Milo put most of his weight on one foot, creating tremendous pressure on Gustad's shoulder.

A moment later, Milo must have realized he was on fire, for he leaped from Gustad's shoulders and stamped out his robes, at times only a hand's width from the ledge, beyond which lay the gaping shaft that dropped an unknowable distance into the darkness.

"These droppings had better be worth it," Gustad said, rubbing his sore shoulders.

* * *

Leaning on the gunwale, Catrin pointed. "That way," she said. "There we will find the Keys of Terhilian, and the Terhilian Lovers will show us the way. But if I remember correctly, the man pointed . . . that way."

Kenward looked to where she pointed. "South and then southwest. I don't suppose we should risk trying to cut straight to the Firstland. Better to sail to the keys and then let the Terhilian Lovers point the way. If we knew how far the keys were from the Firstland, we could chance it, but since we don't know, I suppose we'll have to go the long way."

After a series of mirror flashes, it seemed Nora and Fasha agreed. Orders were given to fish. "We'll fill the holds again if we can. The winds are growing stronger, which'll make that more difficult, but you know your jobs. Let's fish."

Catrin attacked her tasks and helped others finish theirs. Once the trawl tubs, nets, and pots were dropped, there was little to do except wait.

"I'm glad we'll be leaving here soon," Kenward said as he joined Catrin, both staring at the shallows behind them. "That mountain gives me the crawls."

Catrin wondered if he might be more sensitive to energy patterns than he knew, for, to her, the mountain's angry energy field raged like an inferno. Like a pot of boiling water with the lid left on, its intensity grew. "I agree," she said.

"Let's see if we've caught anything. The sooner we're done, the sooner we leave." Kenward issued orders and demanded speed from his crew. Everyone moved with determination and purpose, knowing that following orders was the surest way to stay alive. The wind continued to hinder their efforts; the fish just seemed to stop biting, but still they caught a host of crabs. Catrin joined those who boiled and cleaned the crabs, trying to get them into some preserved form.

The *Stealthy Shark* had better luck in the deeper water and loaded their hold with tuna and small sharks. The big sharks did not show themselves on this side of the shallows, which made Catrin feel a great deal safer.

The crew retrieved their gear and made for the waters near the *Shark*. Kenward was stubborn, but he was not foolish enough to deny that Fasha had found the better fishing ground. Fasha's messages indicated that her hold was full, but they would continue fishing until the *Eel's* hold was filled. Kenward swallowed his pride and gratefully accepted what was sent from the *Shark*. The combined effort filled the hold in a relatively short time, and there seemed a collective sigh of relief when they set sail for the Keys of Terhilian.

"I can't say exactly how far the keys are," Catrin said later that day. "It's difficult to gauge, but I would say three months."

"At least we're not sailing blind," Kenward said. "Your abilities amaze me. It's a pity they're so dangerous to use. I feared you would never return from your journey. How do you do it? Is it like flying?"

"It's hard to explain, but I'd say it's better than flying because you don't have to worry about falling. I just make up my mind which way to go, and the world moves beneath me, as if I'm not moving at all. Tell me. What do you see when you look at the mountain?"

He raised an eyebrow but then concentrated on the mountain for a long time. "Pressure," he said finally. "Inevitability. I can't explain it."

"I think, Kenward, you've more talent than you know. I, too, see the 'pressure,' as you put it. I wonder if you don't have some abilities with Istra's power."

Kenward stood, stunned, his mouth hanging open. "You really think so?"

"Let's find out. Say nothing," she said. "Chase, would you come here a moment?"

"Let me finish this first," Chase said, helping Farsy load pine boxes back into the hold. He came over when they were done. "What do you need?"

"Look at the mountain, and tell me what you see."

"I see a mountain. It's big. What's this all about?"

"Do you see anything unusual about it?"

"C'mon, Cat," he said, but then he saw how serious she was; with her eyes she pleaded. Sighing, he turned and looked again. Catrin watched him intently and jumped when he gave a start.

"Gods have mercy," he said. "I thought you were nuts, but the mountain is breathing--flexing. It just moved!" His shout got everyone's attention, and both crews watched in horror as the colossal and seemingly permanent mountain jumped and split. With the ferocity of the gods, the top blew apart and a column of fire leaped into the sky. Nearly half of what remained slid sideways and dropped into the sea with an inconceivably violent impact. Black clouds filled the air and rolled across the sea as if the world were ending. No one moved at first, but then the reality of the situation set in.

"Turn us about!" Kenward barked. "Set a course back for the mountain!" For a moment, the crew hesitated, unsure they had heard correctly. "Now!" he shouted, and no one argued. Too many times he had proven his wisdom and skill, which was needed now more than ever before. Frantically, he signaled the *Shark* then started cursing when the response came. "They'll run before the wave and clouds, but I don't think we have enough time. The wave will overwhelm us. Have I judged wrongly?"

"What wave?" Catrin asked, and Kenward pointed. In fascinated horror, Catrin watched the seas rise to an impossible height, nearly as tall as the mountain had been, and the wall of water raced toward them like the shadow of death.

"I trust your instincts," Catrin said. "Do what you think is best."

Anguish was clear on Kenward's face as the *Stealthy Shark* disappeared in the diminishing light, heading in the opposite direction. Before the wave reached them, dense ash began to fall from the sky, coating everything. Unlike the ashes from a fire, it was heavy and gritty. Like black snow, it fell and accumulated, weighing them down.

"Keep the decks clear of ash," Kenward demanded. "If we take on too much, it'll either sink or capsize us." His words inspired haste, and despite the encroaching darkness, the crew struggled against an irrepressible tide of ash.

The pressure in the air suddenly changed, and Catrin drew a deep breath through the cloth she had wrapped around her face. Kenward howled like a madman as the wave overtook them. Sailing straight into it at full speed, they began to climb, and soon they were pointing straight into the sky, staring at a roiling mass of ash and fire streaked with red lightning.

Groaning as she flexed against the tremendous forces, the ship slowed. Holding on, Catrin cried out as Farsy and another man tumbled from the rigging and into the dark waters below. Finally cresting the wave, the *Slippery Eel* seemed to drop from the sky.

* * *

Benjin watched, helpless, as the *Slippery Eel* was lost from sight. Death would come no matter which course they chose, he thought. He would have preferred to stay together, but Nora and Fasha stood firm and stayed their course, away from the eruption. Powerless and impotent, he cursed fate and waited for the inevitable.

Rising up to blot out the sky, the wave came, roaring as it displaced the wind. Tying himself to a cleat that protruded from the deck, Benjin stood facing the stern, staring up at the roiling sky, only rope and harness keeping him from falling into the water below. Feeling more as if he were on the face of a cliff than the deck of a ship, he closed his eyes and held on as tight as he could.

Overwhelmed by the speed and height of the wave, the *Stealthy Shark* rolled forward, tumbling end over end along the crest like a piece of driftwood in the surf. Above the roar could be heard the snapping of wood. The rigging was torn

114

away first along with the masts, but then the seas claimed the deckhouse, steerage, and most of the gunwales, tearing them away is if they were made of parchment.

When Benjin once again felt air on his face, he sucked a deep breath and prepared to be plunged beneath the water again, but what remained of the *Shark* stayed upright and raced down the trailing edge of the swell. Looking around, he saw Fasha still moored to a cleat. Like him, she had chosen to tie herself off to a part of the deck itself. The choice had saved their lives, but they were alone; no one else remained.

Fasha looked up after untying herself. "I've lost the *Shark*."

Chapter 10

Life is fragile and can be quelled in uncountable ways.
--Brachias Pall, assassin

* * *

Momentarily weightless, Catrin hung, suspended in air, until her feet touched the deck once again. The *Slippery Eel* slammed into the trailing edge of the wave and raced back toward the relatively calm waters behind it. More waves came but none as big as the first.

"Men overboard!" Catrin shouted. Not far away, she spotted someone in the water. Determined to help, she tied an oar from one of the boats to the end of a rope and cast it toward him. For several tense moments, Catrin watched Farsy try to reach the oar, fighting the waves. Kenward slowed the ship, and Farsy grasped Catrin's line.

Chase came to her aid, and they pulled him in, wrapping him in blankets once he was on deck. The crew searched the water for the other man, but he was lost. After a headcount, they found it was Nimsy, a man who'd always been kind to Catrin, and she wept in mourning, tears streaking her soot-stained face as she continued to shovel ash from the deck.

"Have mercy! The finger of the gods!" someone shouted, and Catrin looked to the rigging, following the stares. There she saw a terrifying sight. Orange and red flames licked the rigging without consuming or even scorching it. Fingers of liquid light crawled over the mast and crow's nest, reaching toward the sky. Sheets of translucent flame enveloped the sails and danced over them, seemingly without touching them, as if it were only the specter of fire. It was almost like what she had seen in the Pinook harbor but visible to all.

The energy of the ash storm intensified, reaching out to them, and Catrin feared they would be struck by ghastly red lightning. When the crew began praying and casting offerings into the sea, she joined them by offering a lock of her hair. Perhaps if she gave something of herself, she thought, the gods would show mercy.

Shouts on the other side of the deck got her attention, and a crowd gathered there as Nimsy was miraculously pulled from the water. Could the gods have heard their prayers? Unsure what to believe, Catrin cut a much larger lock of her hair and cast it into the waves, knowing it could do no harm.

Turning slowly, the *Slippery Eel* came about and made for the waters where the *Stealthy Shark* had last been seen. The ash cloud blotted out the sky from above, and more ash rolled steadily across the water toward them.

"Take cover in the deckhouse!" Kenward ordered, and the crew rushed to comply, seeing what looked like the breath of a demon bearing down on them. "Hold your breath and cover yourselves," he shouted just before the remains of the pyroclastic cloud washed over the *Slippery Eel,* engulfing her in a rolling maelstrom of ash and fire. When it passed, shouts and coughing were all that could be heard. Covered in ash and burns, the crew put out the fires and gave every effort, but the ash accumulated faster than they could remove it, slowly pulling them under.

Like a blessing from the gods, a strong wind descended from the north and drove the ash before it, dispersing it. While it made the problem worse for a while, eventually the air began to clear and the sun was visible behind a foul and gauzy haze. Ash still fell, but the intensity was greatly dissipated as the wind diffused the ash and spread it over a larger area. Fire still belched from what remained of the mountain, but even that began to subside.

Tears filled Catrin's eyes as the first of the debris appeared. Seeing only small bits at the start, she prayed the *Stealthy Shark* had survived, but then large chunks began to appear, scattered across the waves. Kenward watched with his jaw clenched, and Catrin could almost see his heart breaking. She held her breath, waiting for something to wake her from this nightmare.

"Survivors to port!" the lookout shouted, and Catrin ran to see who it was. On a floating section of sail and rigging were Strom, Osbourne, Nora, and three of Fasha's crewman. Elated, Catrin help lower the boarding net while men cast out lines for them to grab on to.

Osbourne reached the deck first and asked for help preparing a litter. "Nora's hurt bad," he said. "We're gonna need help getting her aboard."

Kenward and his crew moved with determination that bordered on panic. Soon, though, the crewman secured Nora to the litter and she was raised to the deck. Barely conscious, she apprised Kenward on her condition and how her wounds were to be treated. Even as they set broken bones and closed gaping wounds, she continued to give orders through clenched teeth.

"Find Fasha," she said before her eyes closed. Kenward stood over her, willing her chest to rise and fall.

"Do what you can to find the rest," Catrin said. "I'll come for you if her condition changes."

"Bless you," he said as he turned back to his crew. "Get boats in the water! I want everyone found. Now!" As soon as the boats were in the water, he moved the *Eel* away, looking for anyone in the distance.

Nora was taken to Kenward's cabin and made as comfortable as possible. She drifted in and out of consciousness, mumbling incoherently. Catrin sat at her side, trying to remember what she had learned from past attempts at healing. Perhaps she was fooling herself, she thought, but her efforts seemed to calm Nora and sent her into a peaceful sleep. After a time, Catrin felt she had done what she could do, and she went in search of Kenward to apprise him of her condition. He stood at the wheel, his eyes filled with tears. They had found more debris but no more survivors. As daylight began to fade, he turned the *Eel* back to retrieve the boats.

Cheers carried across the water as three more of Fasha's crew were pulled into the boats. Catrin and Kenward stood side by side, trying to deny the harsh reality. Benjin, Fasha, and most of her crew were lost. The *Stealthy Shark* was no more.

"I'm so sorry," Kenward said as his shoulders began to shake. His poignant anguish washed over Catrin, mixed with her own, and drove a wedge into her soul. Impotent rage gnawed at her very being, and she felt as if she would erupt, just as the mountain had.

Kenward continued the search for three days, but it was Nora who demanded they move on. "If they were going to be found, it would've happened by now. We must accept it, Son. They're gone."

* * *

Nat waited on a mossy rock near the spring where Neenya swam. This place was special to her, and she brought him here only when she was feeling especially happy. Her smile drew him closer, and he marveled at the way the light danced in her eyes.

It had been a long time since he last visited the mountaintop; he always seemed to be busy with one task or another. Life was pleasant here, and he could easily forget his worries. Trips to the mountain brought only pain and grief. Most of the time, he didn't even understand his visions. What good came from them? Secretly, he'd been working on mental exercises that he hoped would suppress the visions. It shamed him, but a peaceful life with Neenya seemed worth it.

As he bent down to kiss her, though, he felt a warm sensation on his lips, and he wiped them with the back of his hand, which came away covered in blood. Neenya's scream faded as the world shifted.

Atop an unbelievably tall wave ran a white panther; on its back rode Catrin, her colorless hair pulled back by the wind. The staff she held came alive, its eyes gleaming as it spread its wings and flew. The white cat reared, but the water pulled at his legs, and he tumbled into the leading edge of the crashing wave. In an instant Catrin and her cat were gone.

Still the water came, and Nat, standing on the highest mount, watched the seas rise until the water lapped at his feet.

"Neenya," Nat said when the vision released him. "We must hurry."

* * *

Pulling hard on the too light load, Mark Vedregon cursed the monsters that continually ruined his nets. They

119

had caught enough fish to feed his men for a week, but as had happened so many times before, *something* cut the nets before they reached the surface. More of the reptile beasts, he suspected--Gholgi, Belegra had called them. Powerful and crafty, they were proving to be capable foes. Hindering their fishing efforts was only one of the ways the beasts harried Mark Vedregon and his men, slowly wearing them down.

"Nets were cut again, sir. Shall we repair 'em?"

"Not now. We can do that when we get back to shore. Drop the trawl tubs. Maybe we'll get lucky and hook some of those boiling beasts in the process."

"Aye, sir."

"Even if we could catch enough to feed us," Second Richt said, "Archmaster Belegra will take it to feed his pet." His moody gaze scanned the seas, but then he stopped. Pointing out to sea, he stood mute and trembling, unable to make himself speak. Mark Vedregon gave frantic orders, and the crew moved with haste, despite knowing it was already too late. The sea would claim them.

* * *

Miss Mariss walked the avenues, passing faces both familiar and strange. So many things had changed, and yet many were still the same. When she reached the docks, Amnar greeted her with his usual toothless grin.

"Hallo, missus," he said. "I set a nice mackerel aside fer ya and a few toadfish. The currents run strange these days; I'd have more for ya if I could."

"I appreciate what you have, Amnar. We make do with what we can get these days," she said, moving on to where Lendra and her new mate, Bavil, waited.

"The pots were heavy today, Miss Mariss. We've blue crab, shedders, and wall-climbers for you."

"Thank you," she said, dropping a silver into Lendra's palm. Looking beyond the docks, Miss Mariss wondered how Strom, Catrin, and the others fared, but a curious sight drew her attention. Children playing on the beach ran out to grab stranded fish and crabs as the bay began to rapidly

120

recede. Faster that the swiftest tide, the water rushed away from land, as if there were a great hole in the seafloor.

For a time she was mesmerized by the sight, as were others, but then the realization set in and her mind could conceive only one explanation. "Get away from the water! Make for high ground," she shouted. "The seas are coming! The seas are coming!"

* * *

At the helm of the *Slippery Eel*, Kenward gripped the wheel as if it were his only link to sanity. Sadness, more powerful than anything he'd ever imagined, threatened to cripple his mind and body. Tears sprang to his eyes without warning, as feelings of loss manifested as physical pain. He felt as if his heart were truly broken.

Using a short staff as a cane, Nora limped to his side, but he said nothing; he just continued to stare out at the endless horizon.

"I miss her too," she said.

Those words were more than Kenward could bear, and he began to cry. "I'm so sorry," he said, and he gave the wheel over to Bryn. Unable to even lift his eyes to meet hers, he walked to his mother and wrapped her in a tight hug as he wept.

"It wasn't your doing, Son. You are not to blame."

"I was supposed to save her," he said, feeling as if his chest might explode. "Why couldn't I save her?"

"I don't know. I'm sorry, Son. I miss her too," Nora said. Together they cried. In a rare display, they stood, holding each other. Crewmen came, one by one, each with a kind word or a pat on the shoulder. Silently and together, the ship mourned.

To Kenward, the loss seemed surreal, and he kept expecting to wake up, for all this to have been but a dream. Nothing seemed as it should. Colors were dull, and sounds that might once have been beautiful were now harsh and somehow disrespectful. The world without Fasha seemed a poorer place. She had been a second half of him, always there to counter him, a constant challenge to his wits. His mother had intended to hand the *Trader's Wind* down to Fasha; he was certain of it. That thought led him to another crushing realization: His pain was but a small fraction of what his mother must be experiencing. "I know I can never take Fasha's place," he said, "but I'll try harder."

"Nonsense," Nora said. "You're doing just fine. Fasha is my daughter, and nothing could ever replace her, but I would be just as lost without you."

Kenward raised his eyes, surprised by what he heard.

Nora laughed. "A fool boy you may be, but you're *my* fool boy."

* * *

By the dim light of her lamp, Nora lay in her hammock, caressing the walls of Kenward's ship with her fingertips, her mind elsewhere. She was proud of Kenward for allowing himself to grieve, and she was proud of herself. She'd been taught to conceal her feelings from the crew, to always present a confident front. While the tactic had worked well during her career, Kenward had taught her something. His crew exuded something that surpassed loyalty. They followed him not because he commanded them, but because they *cared* about him; some might say they loved him.

It explained the one thing that Fasha had always questioned: How did he get his crew to obey his reckless orders? Nora could see Fasha as she had been in those moments, her arms crossed over her chest and fire in her eyes. From her pocket, she pulled a gold locket that filled her palm. Inside were things that would be valuable to only a mother: the dried, crumbling remains of a sea daisy and a tiny coral fan. Kenward had given her the sea daisy when he was five summers, and the coral had come from a small, unnamed island they had found when avoiding a massive storm. After the storm had passed, Fasha, who was ten at the time, spent an afternoon swimming around the colorful reefs. When she came back to the ship, she was so excited to show Nora what she'd found. Fasha's smile and laughter were forever ingrained in her memory.

Flipping the locket closed, Nora sighed. Somehow, she would keep Kenward safe.

* * *

When the Keys of Terhilian finally came into view, they looked little like what Catrin recalled. What had been white beaches lined by thick forest were now fields of mud and debris as far as could be seen. She sighed in relief when they came to the Terhilian Lovers, which had withstood the fury of the sea.

Kenward set a course, following the megalithic statue's pointing finger. "Let's get there and be done with this," he said. "I've no more taste for adventure. I'll happily take a quiet life of trading."

"It took you long enough to figure that out, fool boy," Nora said, leaning on her short staff. Her bones were still knitting, but she insisted on watching over the crew. Catrin agreed with Kenward, wanting nothing more to do with adventure. What she would have once thought of as glorious and exciting now tasted of death and despair. Too many had died, and Catrin could find no justification, no end worth those means.

The possibility of any of them surviving this journey grew smaller with every day, and Catrin knew she would probably never leave the Firstland, assuming they found it. If she did, though, she promised herself she would go home. Dead or alive, that was where her father was, and she was determined to find her way back to him.

From the beginning, her journey had been costly, but the loss of Benjin was more than she could bear. Only the love she had for those still around her kept her from throwing herself into the sea. Chase stood by her side and put his arm around her. "Do you want to talk about it?"

"No."

"You can't keep it all inside, Cat; it'll eat its way out eventually."

"Then let it," she said, feeling foolish. "Talking won't bring them back, and I doubt it'll make me feel any better. Why bother?"

"I miss him too," Chase said, and his simple admission uncorked the wellspring of emotion she could no longer keep inside.

Her jaw quivered and her shoulders shook, but she did not want to cry. To cry was to be a victim, to lament her losses and accept them, but she didn't want to accept them; that was simply too painful. She wanted someone to blame, someone to *punish*.

"I need exercise," she said. "Will you spar with me?"

"Will you talk to me afterward and tell me how you are really feeling?" Chase asked.

"If I must."

"You must," he said, getting practice swords from storage. He tossed one to Catrin but was unprepared for her sudden attack.

"So that's how you want it?" he asked, lying on his back and rubbing the lump that was growing on the back of his head. Rolling backward, he got back to his feet and readied himself for her next attack.

Pent-up rage drove Catrin. In front of her, she saw not Chase, but the source of all her problems, and she attacked without thought or mercy. Moving by sheer instinct, she fought as she had never fought before, and Chase fell before her attacks.

"That's enough for me," he said, limping and rubbing his bruises. "Find someone else to beat up." He walked away, looking hurt.

Catrin was not yet done venting her anger, but no one else would spar with her, having seen how poorly Chase had fared against her raging attacks.

Unwilling to keep her anger inside any longer, she searched the dry hold and found a sack of dried reeds. After hanging it from the rigging, she attacked, her practice sword slicing the air, pounding the sack mercilessly. Even after reducing the sack to shreds, though, she did not feel any better.

Her heart pounding, she climbed atop the bowsprit. "Why do you hate me so much?" she screamed at the sky, challenging the gods themselves. "What have I done to deserve such evil and malice?"

124

Crew members stopped what they were doing, and Bryn readied a harness in case she fell from her dangerous perch, but Catrin barely noticed them. "Come, Istra. Come, Vestra. Right here . . . right now. Let us end this. If you wish me to suffer, then come down here and fight me yourselves. Cowards! I don't fear you, and I spit on your names. I cast your own hate back at you. What do you say to that?"

As if to answer her, lightning split the air and thunder rolled across the water. Gusting winds threatened to knock her from the bowsprit, but she remained there, challenging the gods to a duel. Only when Chase grabbed her ankles did she see the world around her again. Dark clouds moved in swiftly from the west, and stinging rain began to fall.

"Cowards!" she shouted one last time, shaking her fist in the air, before she let Chase guide her back to the deck.

"Cripes, Cat. You're scaring the crew. Calm down."

Shaking, Catrin took deep breaths and tried to do as he said. When the rage passed, though, exhaustion took its place, and she let Chase carry her to her cabin.

"It'll all work out somehow, Cat. Even if we have to take on the gods themselves, somehow we'll make it right. I promise," he said as he pulled a blanket over her, and she fell into a dreamless sleep.

* * *

"Not too much now," Milo said as he leaned in over Gustad's shoulder.

"I know. I know," Gustad said as he mixed water with the materials listed in the ancient text. Since Milo had found a recipe for what had been called *fire powder,* he had focused on nothing else. Gustad had tried to talk him out of experimenting with the formula a dozen times, fearing it was too dangerous, but Milo would not be dissuaded. His hands more steady than Milo's, Gustad gently rolled the mixture and kneaded it until it was uniform.

"That looks about right to me," Milo said. "Let's take it outside and test it."

"Just a moment," Gustad said. "Let me clean up all this mess." Despite his efforts, a mixture of different ingredients covered the worktable, and a fine dust hung in the air. "Could you get me some water?"

"You and your cleanliness," Milo said. "We can clean up when we get back from testing this. Now let's go." Reaching his hand out to the metal bowl that held the snakelike pieces of fire powder clay, a tiny blue arc of static leaped between his finger and the bowl. It was enough to ignite the dust in the air and produced a mighty thump. The initial explosion threw Milo and Gustad back, which was a blessing since the ignited dust engulfed the fire powder snakes. Two larger explosions followed, creating a mighty cloud of noxious smoke.

From beneath the remains of a crumbled worktable, Gustad crawled. His hair smoking and his face blackened, he glared at Milo.

"I told you it would work," Milo said, grinning, and Gustad just shook his head.

* * *

"Birds ahead, sir," Bryn called from the crow's nest.

"Land can't be too far," Kenward said. "Double the watch. Keep your eyes open for outcroppings and reefs. I want no surprises."

Catrin, her gaze focused on the waves, looking for any sign of obstacles, was terrified to see a huge, dark shape dart beneath the ship and emerge on the other side, its movements graceful and serpentine. More came, seemingly drawn by curiosity if not hunger. None broke the surface, leaving Catrin and the crew to guess at their true nature.

"Never seen the likes of that," Kenward said. "They haven't attacked yet, but remain watchful nonetheless. Bring out the spears from the hold; we may need to fend them off yet." His words inspired fear in the crew as they watched the dark shapes moving beneath them, taunting them, staying just deep enough to remain ambiguous.

"Rocks to port," Bryn called, and Kenward guided the ship clear of the danger. "Land, sir! I see land!"

Excitement ran through the crew as a large landmass came into view, but for Catrin it was a moment of dread.

Here she was, the Firstland, a place of legend and the place where some said the first men and women were born. It was a place abandoned--surrendered--by her ancestors. As it stretched across the horizon, Catrin was overwhelmed by anxiety, suddenly convinced she would die on the Firstland. In the past she had believed, deep down, that she would survive, that someday she and her loved ones would all get home safely, but Benjin was gone. Too many others were already dead. What reason did she have to believe she wouldn't be next? She found no reassurance, and her guts churned.

The shores had been devastated far worse than the Keys of Terhilian. High into the mountainous terrain, the twisted mass of mud and severed life dominated the landscape. Birds clouded the skies over the mass of rotted vegetation. Though most of the carcasses had been picked clean, leaving only bleached bones as evidence of their existence, land-based scavengers searched for an easy meal. Even from afar, the smell was overpowering, and Kenward ordered more sail.

"We'll need to find a part of the coast that was not affected by the wave. The waters here are far too clogged with debris to be safe, and no one wants to travel through that mess," he said. For nearly half a day, they saw nothing but destruction, but then they reached an area dominated by towering rock formations that jutted from the sea and sheltered a large bay.

"Look!" Chase called, pointing. Two peaks, close together, cradled what remained of a Zjhon warship. Seeing the ship high above them was disconcerting, and Catrin was filled with a mixture of hope and dread. Surely no one had survived, she thought. Maybe Archmaster Belegra was already dead, and they could just go home. No matter how much she wanted to believe it, she knew it wasn't true. Her death awaited. Like a looming premonition, the feeling had grown stronger every day that Benjin was gone. Even bright skies could not chase away the cloud of darkness that followed her, surrounding her. Despite the nagging despair, she drew a deep breath and turned to face the wind, determined to do the best she could.

Beyond a gap in the wall, pristine, unmolested shoreline was visible. Black beaches skirted heavily forested and mountainous terrain. Along the shores, creatures both varied and bizarre covered the landscape. Huge animals that looked like bloated seals crowded together on jutting rock formations. Others like wild boars, only with skin like marbled leather and the size of horses, roamed in packs. Saltwater crocodiles as long as the *Slippery Eel* rested in shallow waters, often with only their eyes above water.

In a horrifying display, a whale, black as night, thrust itself from the water and onto a rocky outcropping, grabbing one of the bloated seals and tossing it into the air. Others of its ilk moved in and assisted with the kill, giving Catrin her first glimpse of predators working as a team. Her father and Benjin had told her about wolves hunting in packs, but it was shocking to witness such calculated and communal brutality, something she had thought only humans were capable of.

Painfully aware of her own carnal nature, inherent and blood given, she wondered if it could be overcome or if, deep down, they were all just predators waiting for their next kill. Thinking of Barabas and Mother Gwendolin along with other kind-hearted folks she had met on her journey, she knew it could suppressed, and she gained even more respect for those who did it so well, seemingly without effort.

Across the bay, jagged peaks rose on either side of a wide river valley, and even from the distance the sights there were awe inspiring.

"The Valley of Victors," Brother Vaughn said in little more than a whisper. "I had always thought the old tales exaggerated, but here it is before me. The old tales failed to express its true majesty. I am humbled."

"Looks like a good way to get inland," Kenward said.

"That should be the Perintong River," Brother Vaughn said. "Beyond the Valley of Victors and the Eternal Guardians should be the ancient city of Ri. That's where Belegra would go. I'm nearly certain of it."

Catrin nodded, filled with dread. "Take me as far upriver as you can, please," she said, and Kenward gave the orders.

Trembling, Catrin gripped her staff, trying to master her fears. Even the landscape challenged her courage. Steep walls lined the river valley, and every inch was covered with some kind of carving, but it was the carvings of armed men, monstrous and proud, that demanded Catrin's attention. Even worn by the ravages of time, enough detail remained to convey the ferocity of these men, for men they all were. Not a single female image was to be found, which Catrin found even more disturbing.

Winds, funneled by the massive valley, drove the *Slippery Eel* upriver, against the sluggish current. Around a bend came the most imposing sight yet. Crouched down, one on either side of the river, waited a pair of megalithic stone warriors, each with one arm in the water and the other held in the air, gripping swords that crossed overhead.

The features of one were nearly indistinguishable, but the other delivered an imposing glare. Half his face was missing, yet he seemed to stare into Catrin's soul and find her wanting.

"The Eternal Guardians," Brother Vaughn said, and Catrin knew their image would haunt her dreams.

Chapter 11

To enslave that which is free is to invite your own betrayal.
--Barabas, druid

* * *

Beyond the guardians, the valley walls closed in. The river narrowed, and the current became swift and turbulent. Ahead, fallen monuments obstructed the river, evidenced by the mighty but broken hand that jutted from the swirling water.

"Can't go around that," Kenward said. "What will you do, Catrin? Now that we are here, what will you do?"

"I must find Belegra, even if that means searching the Firstland from end to end," she said. She could not turn back, not after having come so far and having lost so many. She had to complete this journey in honor of those who had given their lives toward that end.

Dark shapes moved within the trees along the shores, and strange, raucous calls rose above the roar of the water. Eyes appeared in the water near the ship, and the crew jumped when an impact left the ship thrumming.

"I can't keep the *Eel* here," Kenward said. "I'm going to have to keep much of the crew aboard and return to the harbor, but that leaves only a handful of people to accompany you. I don't know what to do."

"You know exactly what to do, fool boy. You just don't *want* to do it, so you refuse accept it. Do what must be done."

"Thank you, Mother. You are correct; I know. If you are to reach Ri, Catrin, I suggest you take a landing party to shore a short ways back downriver, where the waters are calmer. We'll sail back to the harbor and prepare for the long journey home. When you've achieved your goal, come back to your boat. Light a signal fire--the more smoke, the better-- and we'll come for you. There are mirrors in your packs; use those if you can't get a fire lit. I'm sorry I can offer no more."

"Well said, my son."

Uncertainty festered in Catrin's belly. Daunted by the thought of exploring the Firstland with only five people, she set her jaw, her determination bolstered by the commitment of those who stood around her: Chase, Strom, Osbourne, and Brother Vaughn. All stood ready to disembark, and Catrin sensed no fear from them, only the drive to do what must be done.

The land slid by quickly, and Kenward selected what he considered an ideal place for them to disembark. The current was sluggish, and reddish, gritty sand formed a bare shoreline. Beyond, the forest claimed every scrap of land in its emerald grip. When faced with the question of which bank to land on, Catrin let her instincts decide: east. She wasn't certain why. She had no visions or overpowering emotion; it just felt right.

"May the gods bless you on your journey," Kenward said. "We'll wait sixty days. If you do not return, we must sail."

"If you've seen no signal in thirty days, leave. Don't wait for us if it puts your lives in danger," Catrin said, a tear in her eye and a catch in her voice.

"You'll be back in less than thirty, but we'll wait sixty," Nora said with a sharp nod, and Kenward smiled. Catrin wished she shared Nora's confidence. "Your packs are loaded, and we're ready to drop your boat. Travel well and return safe."

Catrin and the others climbed into the suspended boat, and the crew lowered them to the water. The parting was surreal; she found it difficult to believe that she was about to step onto fabled soil abandoned by man more than three thousand years past. Only lightly armed, she doubted her party was prepared for the trials ahead. This place harbored creatures they had never seen before and knew nothing about. Anything that moved was suspect.

Once ashore, they dragged their boat to some nearby trees and covered it with branches, aware that even this task could be deadly if carried out carelessly. Picking through the branches, they found snakes, frogs, and colorful lizards in abundance. Even with great care, there were a few tense moments.

131

Moving deeper into the forest seemed suicide from what Catrin had already seen; her mind imagined every creature as a deadly and poisonous foe. Given that she had no way to tell which were dangerous and which were benign, it was a healthy outlook, even if unpleasant.

Sailing with the current, the *Slippery Eel* was soon lost from sight. Any feeling of security Catrin had fled with the *Eel*, but she led the group as best she could, slowly picking their way into a foreign and unknown land. Using short swords, they cut through obstacles at a crawling pace, but sunlight could be seen on the forest floor ahead, and the group moved with determination.

When they broke free of the tangled mass of vines and thorns, they entered a strange twilight, where the vegetation took on surprising shapes. Despite the dense growth, the outlines of ancient structures could still be seen, and occasional walls still stood, covered completely in growth and looking as if they had occurred naturally.

Chase pulled the vines back from a column, revealing the fine detail that was previously hidden. Gracefully fluted and tapered, they were a marvelous testament to the ancients' stonework and building skills. Farther on, they discovered a field of man-shaped growths that harbored ancient sculptures of men with ideal physiques, their muscle definition conveyed with tremendous detail.

No one spoke as they moved among the eerie shapes, and Catrin couldn't shake the fear that they would all suddenly spring to life and attack. When they reached the far end of the field, they found a low, stone wall. Beyond it was a relatively clear space and another, similar wall. Between, the land was flat and, for a short distance, unobstructed: a road.

"If this is a road, it should lead to Ri, shouldn't it?" Chase asked.

"Your reasoning is sound. We should follow the road," Brother Vaughn said.

Catrin could give no reason for her fear of the road, only that she felt sick whenever she looked at it. Perhaps, she thought, it was because of what she would find at its end.

Knowing it made sense to follow the road, she reluctantly agreed.

The rest of the day was spent picking through the less dense foliage that was reclaiming the ancient roadway, but their progress was significantly faster than when traveling through the forest. In some places, larger structures remained mostly standing, and in one case, an elaborate entrance decorated the side of a mountain. Catrin was tempted to explore it, but her gut told her she had not yet reached her destination and she resisted the urge.

"How do you know Belegra isn't in there?" Chase asked.

"It just doesn't feel right," was the only answer Catrin could provide, but it seemed to satisfy him. Crowded between the river and the valley walls were a continuous supply of distractions, enticing places that could hold treasures beyond their reckoning, and only the will to achieve their goal kept them from straying.

When they came to a place where the road was blocked with massive stones and the trees and vines that covered them, they found evidence of a fight, and it looked as if many Zjhon soldiers had died. Pieces of armor and torn bits of uniforms littered the ground, but a nearby mound told of survivors; someone had buried the dead.

Evidence of those Catrin sought should have been welcome, but it only increased her uneasiness; the knowledge of another, unknown foe had everyone on edge, and they moved slowly, scanning the trees for danger.

When darkness claimed the land, they had to stop. They made a hasty camp with a small fire. Beyond the meager light of their fire, Catrin could see little in the darkness. The leaves above blocked the small amount of light the night sky gave through thick clouds.

Shadows moved around them, detectable by only the minute change in the shade of darkness. It was the smell that brought Catrin to full alert. Musky and overpowering, the odor suddenly filled the air. Before she could even open her mouth to give warning, the trees exploded with activity. Even though the attackers had the element of surprise, they did not find the camp sleeping. Wary and afraid, most had been lying awake in their bedrolls, and they sprang to action.

Gathering around Catrin, her Guardians sought to defend her from a foe they had not yet clearly seen. Catrin reached to the sky, searching for distant comets by feeling for their energy. Pale blue light washed over the camp as ropes of liquid lightning arced between her fingers, reaching toward the sky. In that light, the Gholgi were made even more terrifying, looking otherworldly.

With skin like moving granite, they resembled bears with long, feral jaws lined with gleaming teeth. Most of the time moving on all fours, they stood nearly as tall as Catrin, but when confronted, they stood on their hind legs and towered over her and her Guardians.

Their movements were not of a full-on attack, though; instead they charged through the group, splitting them up, trying to separate their intended prey from the pack. Strom and Osbourne took to the trees when they were nearly run down, and one of the Gholgi went down when Strom swung from the branches and kicked it hard in the face. The beast's head snapped to one side, and it crumpled to the ground.

Brother Vaughn rolled away from a charging Gholgi, but when he stood, another swept his legs out from under him.

Issuing her own roar, Catrin unleashed her attack. Streaks of energy struck multiple Gholgi, stunning some and knocking others down, but one still came. Only Chase remained by Catrin's side as she swayed on her feet, and he stepped forward to meet the approaching Gholgi. The beast roared--a sound like distant thunder--and stood on its hind legs. Chase charged in, his sword leveled at the beast's abdomen, even as Catrin drew on every power source available to her. The Gholgi used its height to level a massive blow at Chase's head before Catrin could react. Chase ducked away from the blow but was sent spinning and landed in a heap.

Three Gholgi got between Catrin and her Guardians, and they changed their tactics. Now they had her separated, and they drove her into the forest. Osbourne swung down from a branch, trying to reproduce Strom's kick, and did succeed in blinding one of the Gholgi with his heels before he fell from the tree. Brother Vaughn and Chase tried to reach Catrin, but the Gholgi repelled them.

Followed by two of the beasts, Catrin fled as fast as she could through the dense foliage. Like a sentient being, the forest hindered her every movement, tangling her in its web, trying to devour her. Growing louder as they came, the Gholgi gained on her, and she knew she could not outrun them; she had to turn and fight.

Trying to draw more energy while at a full run proved to be impossible, and she searched for the best place to make her stand. Ahead, where the land rose steeply, two Gholgi stepped into her path, making the choice for her. Moving together, they tried to herd Catrin back into the trees, but as soon as she stopped, she drew deeply and lashed out. Twin beams of energy split the air, and Catrin clenched her teeth, ready for the backlash of her attack. When it came, it was less than she'd expected, and she hoped that just being prepared for the repercussion could somehow lessen it. The Gholgi were momentarily stunned, and Catrin ran for higher ground, away from the forest.

She had taken only three good strides before the Gholgi resumed their hunt with what seemed a renewed sense of urgency. Grunts and growls passed between them, sounding to Catrin as if they were speaking a guttural language. Driven by fear, she climbed, hoping the Gholgi were not skilled climbers. Ahead lay a rocky vale, and if only she could reach it, she would be safe. It was an irrational thought, but it inspired her to even greater speed. Exhaustion threatened to overcome her; her vision blurred and the world took on a yellow haze, but she drew a deep breath and climbed.

Beyond one last boulder waited rich grasses that promised a soft bed. Littered with chunks of granite and bathed in moonlight, the vale looked as if some god had split a mountain into bits and sprinkled them along the valley floor. Reaching up to grab the top of the boulder, Catrin cried out as a Gholgi clutched her leg, pulling her backward, its claws biting through her leggings and into her flesh.

In the moment before she knew she would succumb, the attack suddenly stopped; the Gholgi released its grip and was gone. Exhausted and losing blood, Catrin could make no sense of what had just happened, and she concentrated on simply reaching the vale. In a dreamlike state, she crawled across the grasses to one of the boulders.

Leaning against the rock was more comfortable than she had expected, and she was grateful for a place to rest; she felt safe. Cutting her leggings away from the wounds on her leg, she winced. From deep gashes, some nearly to the bone, seeped her precious blood. If she did not stop the bleeding, she would die, but her meager efforts did not staunch the flow.

Weariness began to overtake her and she thought it might be nice to lie down on the grass and sleep, but a nagging voice in the back of her mind reminded her that sleep meant death. She was not ready to die yet; her work was not yet done.

Pulling her eyes open, she realized she was already lying down, the grass pressing against her face. After pushing herself back into a sitting position, she drew a deep breath, and her head spun.

Draw on the life around you.

She didn't know from where the message came, but it was a welcome one, full of hope and compassion. Opening herself up, she allowed the life around her to flow into her, and she was surprised by the power of it. Looking down, she saw blood still running from her wounds, and she knew the additional energy would not be enough to save her. She had to find a way to stop the bleeding.

Despite the warnings, she thought of Enoch Giest and how he had healed himself. The lines of all those he taught to heal themselves had been doomed. Knowing the effects, Catrin concluded it was worth the risk as long as she did not have children or teach anyone else how to do it. Of course, that was assuming she could figure it out herself in the limited time she had left.

Using the last of her strength, she reached out to the comets and drew a trickle of power. Combined with the life energy she still felt flowing around her, she attained clear thought. She knew what her body had to do to heal itself. All she had to do was get a message through the barrier between her conscious and subconscious minds without shattering it in the process.

Somehow, instinctively, she knew where to find the barrier, and she visualized it as a wall of stone and mortar in her mind. Not wanting to take down the entire wall, she chipped away at the mortar around a single stone. With her trusty, old belt knife, which still existed in her memory, she broke away the mortar, and light began to stream through from the other side, blindingly bright and filled with colors Catrin had never before seen.

Determined, she wiggled the stone until it started moving a little more with each swing. Then it broke free with a suddenness that left her reeling. Radiant light poured through the hole, and Catrin approached it with apprehension. Beyond lay an unknown reality, the part of her that truly understood how her body worked yet was somehow blind to her immediate need. She knew her body could create a clot to stop the bleeding and fill the wounds with scar tissue, but it did not seem to realize the imminent need, for her blood still flowed.

Applying her will, she pressed her face to the wall and shouted into the hole, "Stop the bleeding. Heal my leg." She sensed something akin to acknowledgment and pulled her face away. With the stone still in her hand, she brought it back up to the hole, but before she could slide it into place, she looked through and saw a stunningly beautiful face staring back with an equally awestruck expression.

Thrilled and terrified, Catrin stared for a moment, memorizing every detail, every curve and highlight, but then from somewhere came a warning, little more than a sense of danger. Closing her eyes, Catrin shoved the stone back into place. Only then did she realize the damage she had done: None of the mortar remained. Light streamed around the stone. Then the stone wiggled.

It had never occurred to Catrin that her subconscious might want to communicate with her just as badly, but when the stone suddenly fell from its hole, she scrambled to replace it, trying to remember how mortar was made. Perhaps, she thought, if she could think of how to make mortar, she could conjure up some to fill in around the brick. It seemed strange to think of making mortar in her mind for what was only her visual representation of something, but it felt very real to her.

Stuffing the stone back into the hole, she tried her best to imagine up some mortar, and she cheered when she finally succeeded. Just as she reached up to apply her mortar, though, her heart leaped; the stone slowly moved away from her and fell through to the other side.

Light poured through, and Catrin's curiosity soared, but the warnings returned, and she slammed her hands, full of mortar, over the hole. In her mind, she stayed there, guarding her meager barrier and hoping her mental wall would not come tumbling down. Sleep overcame her, and her dreams were filled with visions of Enoch and Ain Giest laughing at her.

* * *

Stretching himself between a branch and a rock outcropping, Chase prayed he didn't slip. Keeping himself from looking down was difficult; it was an almost morbid fascination, wondering if the fall below would kill him or just leave him broken and wounded.

With a grunt, he thrust himself across the divide and dug his fingers into the first impression he could find. Slamming his body against the stone, he used his knees and toes to keep his grip. When he gained the top of the outcropping, he leaned against the cliff wall behind him, regaining his breath, and looked down.

Losing himself in the vertigo, he let his mind go where it would. Visions of the Gholgi attack were etched in his memory. Osbourne and Brother Vaughn had both been hurt, and he'd sent Strom back to the ship with them, for protection. It had seemed like a good idea at the time, but now he was alone and had no idea of how to find Catrin, if she still lived. Unwilling to believe her dead, he pressed on, staying to the higher reaches to avoid most of the wildlife, though he wondered if the climbing was any less dangerous than what waited below.

Nightfall brought overwhelming despair since it meant he would not find Catrin this day; she was lost to him. Tears dripped from his nose, and he wiped them away angrily. They were not defeated yet. Catrin still lived, he told himself, and he made himself believe it.

Chapter 12

In the deepest shadows, fire, both terrible and magnificent, can spring to life.
--Casicus Mod, coal miner

* * *

Encumbered by the basket of fish he carried, Prios climbed the loose rocks with great care. Belegra had ordered everything he caught saved, but Prios filled his stomach while away from the archmaster's watchful eyes. These days they seemed to see only what they wanted to see, and Prios was determined to take every advantage.

Catrin was near; he could feel her presence. Despite Belegra's madness, he could not risk reaching out to her. The last time he had, Belegra had fallen on him, demanding to know what he'd been doing, full of suspicion and rage. Prios had endured the beating and stuck to his original tale: he'd been searching for their foes, keeping watch for danger. Belegra had not believed him, but other matters distracted him, and Prios lived in fear of the moment Belegra remembered his treachery.

Staring up at the heights, he prepared himself to play the role of faithful slave, though it sickened him more each time. Soon he would be free, all this but a memory. Reaching the ancient stone stair, which provided sure footing, Prios barely looked where he was going.

Waiting inside the gaping cavern, Belegra paced, impatience clear in his posture. "Is that all you've brought back? That is barely enough for half a day. When Vedregon returns, I'll have you flogged for your failure!"

Prios did not bother to tell him that Mark Vedregon was dead, along with all the other soldiers and the rest of the cadre. Those who had not been killed by the Gholgi or disease where taken by the sea. Prios had tried to tell Belegra the truth, but he refused to hear; instead, Belegra always claimed he would have Prios beaten or tortured when the soldiers returned.

Taking the basket of fish to the hole in the cavern wall, Prios prepared to feed Kyrien.

"He's too weak to come to you. Get in there and feed him," Belegra said. His eyes wild with fervor, he licked his lips.

Prios could not help feeling that Belegra wanted Kyrien to eat him instead of the fish. Leaving the basket right under the hole, he straddled it and pulled himself into the foul-smelling chamber. The hole was barely large enough to admit the basket, but he yanked it through. Kyrien cowered in the back of the chamber, his green-flecked gold eyes fixed on Prios, following his every movement.

Dumping the basket not far from Kyrien's head, Prios backed away. Kyrien sniffed the fish and snorted, then smacked Prios with his tail.

"Clean up while you're in there," Belegra said.

Prios did as he was told, despite every instinct telling him to flee the crowded cell. Kyrien hated him, and Prios feared the beast would rip him to shreds if he ever overcame his fear of Belegra. For now, Kyrien simply cowered in the back of his cell, and when the sun was high, he wailed.

* * *

Filled with horror, Catrin awoke, still leaning against the mass of granite. When she tried to rise, her body was sluggish. Slowly, she felt the blood returning to her limbs, and she stood. Echoing through the vale was a haunting call; like the cries of a wounded animal, it was filled with despair and, at times, an odd glimmer of hope. Hearing it made Catrin want to cry.

In a sudden rush, memories of the previous day overwhelmed her, and she looked down at her leg. Her leggings were tattered and missing the section she had cut away. Beneath were scabbed gashes where her open wounds had been. The flesh around them was pink and smooth, but she could move without a great deal of pain, and she wondered if her memories could be real. Had she truly healed herself?

141

Closing her eyes, she located her center then the wall that stood between her conscious and subconscious minds. No matter how hard she tried, she could not make the wall whole again. Always one stone was missing, and the mortar that filled the hole was riddled with cracks and fissures that allowed the brilliant light to pour through. With a deep breath, she made herself open her eyes. She was still alive, and she chose to treat every new moment as a gift. She should be dead--she knew it, and now she needed to make the best of what she had.

The keening wails continued, and Catrin firmed her resolve. She would find the poor creature and ends its misery. Even as the thought entered her mind, Catrin sensed a shift in the energy around her, and the vale was transformed. No more were the grasses littered with boulders; in their places stood dragons. Tall and proud, they surrounded her.

In awestruck fascination, Catrin watched the only remaining boulder, the one she had slept against, unfold itself. Granite-colored skin shifted and moved and began to take on a greenish hue, as if reflecting the grasses around it. A massive head on a serpentine neck moved in front of Catrin's face and oscillated back and forth in a hypnotic motion.

Free him.

Overwhelming compulsion came with the raw emotion of the message. It was not like the way Belegra controlled his cadre, it was more like a melding of intentions. The strength of the desire blended with Catrin's own desire, and her will to accomplish the task became one with the dragon she faced.

Raising itself up to its full height, standing on its two powerful legs, the majestic dragon spread its wings and moved its head back down to Catrin. With a touch more gentle than she would have imagined possible, it pushed her with its rock-hard maw.

Go.

The command was palpable, but Catrin refused to leave just yet. She remembered the sensations she had felt the night before and the messages she had perceived. Looking

142

the dragon in the eye, Catrin drew herself up with all the courage she could muster. "Thank you," she said. "All of you."

The dragons all raised a keening wail to match that of the one she heard from above, and Catrin left them behind, determined to succeed. Following the sound proved difficult in a place where the echoes had a life of their own, but she moved with purpose, using her staff to provide stability in rough places.

As she drew nearer, sound overwhelmed her other senses, and for a time, she moved without seeing, only the call guiding her. Looking up, she saw the side of a mountain covered with winding stairs and crumbling roadways. At seemingly random intervals, grand entranceways dotted the rock face. The wails came from one such entranceway, high above where she stood. Squinting, she followed the stair with her eyes. From the high entranceways down to the winding terrace where all the stairways originated, she traced it. When she reached what she thought was the correct stair, it showed no evidence of recent use, and Catrin climbed with little confidence, not knowing if she were taking the right path.

Despite places where the stair was nearly perfectly preserved, there were places it barely existed. In one such place, Catrin came to a gap. Below was a sheer drop to the vale floor. Driven beyond reason by her desire to end this quest, she leaped across the divide. As she soared through the air, her arms windmilled. The heel of her staff struck rock before she landed. The impact sent her spinning, and she nearly lost her grip on the staff. Off balance, she struck the rock hard, driving the wind from her lungs. Her legs still hanging over the ledge, gravity began to pull at her, and she scrambled to find a handhold. With her left hand, she found a small crack and dug her fingers in, crying out from the pain. With her other hand, she drove the tip of her staff into another nearby crack. Using all her strength, she pulled herself up. When she finally gained the relative safety of the stair, she allowed herself only a moment of rest before resuming her climb.

Higher up, in a place where two sets of stairs came close together, Catrin saw parts of the other stair that were new and hastily constructed. That was the stair Belegra and his men used.

Trying to decide between stealth and a clear path, Catrin finally decided on a safe climb; she would have to face Belegra one way or another, and she doubted surprise would give her any substantial advantage. Climbing between the two stairs was dangerous, but she hoped the rest of the climb would be easier. Movement and shouting from above gave her a start, and she flattened herself against the rock, hoping not to be seen.

Whoever it was went back inside, and Catrin completed the climb to the newly repaired stair. Following it up, she was constantly alert for signs of movement, and she thought she saw something moving through the trees below. Perhaps, she thought, it was Belegra's men. Knowing she might have only a short time before the soldiers returned, she climbed with haste, throwing caution aside.

When she reached the top of the stair, the wails were like a physical assault, but as soon as she stepped toward the entrance, it stopped. With the light behind her and relative darkness within, Catrin stood momentarily blinded.

"So, the Herald Witch has come to witness my triumph!" Archmaster Belegra said, his voice grating and raw.

Stepping into the chamber, Catrin barely noticed the exquisite carvings that adorned the entranceway or the ancient sculptures that lined the walls. It was the object in Archmaster Belegra's hands that drew her attention: a chunk of dragon ore the size of a melon that sparkled even in the dimness of the mountain hall.

A foul smell filled the air, and Catrin turned to a place where a doorway had recently been walled in and reinforced. Only a small hole let her see what was within. Pinkish and sickly, the dragon looked very unlike those she had seen in the vale, but there was little doubt as to his true nature. As soon as she looked at him, she knew his name: *Kyrien.* It came to her like a song filled with joy and life, despite what her eyes told her. His eyes locked with hers, and in that

144

moment, she knew what she had to do. With a deep breath, she drew power from the air and from her staff.

Quietly and humbly, another reason for her presence emerged from the shadows, his head down and his face concealed within the hood of his robe, Prios came. She knew him the instant he moved, and she turned back to face the one foe she had in the room. "You will enslave and corrupt no more, Belegra. Stand down now or I will attack."

Hysterical laughter threw him into a brief fit of coughing, but he regained his composure and faced Catrin with sudden clarity in his eyes, which narrowed as they beheld her. Disturbances in his energy field were so intense that it looked to Catrin as if his energy would collapse in on itself. "Burn," he said in a low and unfamiliar voice, as if he were a completely different person. His hands, gripping the dragon ore, sent ropes of fire and lightning sailing through the air toward Catrin, but she was not unprepared and created a shielding sphere around herself.

His attack struck her barrier with a violent impact that sent her reeling, nearly pushing her over the nearby ledge. Maintaining the protective sphere sapped her strength, and Catrin knew she needed to launch an attack of her own. Momentarily dropping her defenses, she hurled blue lightning at Archmaster Belegra, sending it with all the rage she possessed. Howling, she lashed out again and again, but he brushed her attacks aside as if they were little more than annoyances.

His laughter started as a deep rumble in his chest, but then he began to cackle, and in another moment of transformation, he spun and attacked. Balls of fire raced before bolts of fetid lightning, and a wave of nausea poured over Catrin as they approached. She hastily cast her defenses about her, but the onslaught threw her aside and pinned her to the chamber wall. Helplessly she watched as Prios joined the attack, his movements synchronized with Belegra's.

Inexorably, her sphere began to shrink under the pressure, and she could feel the heat on her face. Hot air burned her lungs as she sucked in desperate breaths, and still the attacks continued. Dizziness began to overtake her, and the world grew dark despite the flames that surrounded her.

* * *

The wailing drew Chase on, and he found himself in a rocky vale. When he saw grass stained with blood and a piece of the leather from Catrin's leggings, he was as frightened as he was relieved. There was too much blood, and he wondered how she could have walked away.

Turning to the mountain where the wails originated, Chase saw the stairways. He covered his eyes as he thought he saw a form moving up the rock face. Moments later, the wailing stopped, and Chase knew it must be Catrin. Taking off at a run, he climbed with abandon. Seeing flashes of light and hearing thunderous booms from above, he could only pray he got there in time.

* * *

Relent.

The command came just when the pain had reached its height, and Catrin was tempted to obey, tempted to just give up. It would be so much easier to let someone else be in control. She was so very tired. In the corner of her sight stood Prios, deep in the throes of compulsion, coerced to do that which was not his will. Kyrien, trapped in a tomb of stone, did not deserve such a horrid fate; she could not relent. They should suffer no more.

The pain began to fade, and her sphere slowly grew. Belegra looked spent, drenched with sweat and breathing hard, a wild look in his eyes. Prios looked worse, and Catrin knew Belegra would run him dry without another thought. Watching as a nimbus of power began to form around Belegra, who seemed to have found his strength, Catrin prepared a hasty attack. Prios lay, unmoving on the floor.

The nimbus grew brighter and more intense as Belegra drew an enormous amount of energy. The stone around his feet grew red hot, and he stepped back. Catrin launched her attack not on Belegra, but on the rock around him. Meanwhile, he cast a massive wave of raw energy at her, flames leaping out and forming the tortured faces of those

146

she had lost, and they howled at her as they came. At the last moment, she cast up a sphere to protect herself, but it was insufficient, and she was thrown, tumbling, to the back of the hall.

Belegra howled in glee as Catrin fell before his attack, but he also took two steps away from the super-heated stone. As he raised his arms for the killing blow, his aura glowing like the sun, Kyrien struck like a massive viper. His head and neck shattered the wood and plaster that filled the doorway to his prison. Before the wood and stone hit the floor, he snapped Belegra up in his jaws and bit down hard. It was over in an instant, and Catrin could hardly believe what she had just seen. Consumed from within by blue flames, Belegra began to burn.

With only his head and neck freed, Kyrien gave Belegra's body one last shake then cast it aside. An instant later, Chase ran into the cavern. Seeing Catrin on the ground, smoking, he charged in, looking for someone to fight. His eyes landed on Prios, who was trying to stand, and Chase descended on him, howling. Even Catrin's screams could not pierce his blinding rage; only Kyrien's fierce visage kept him from killing Prios. Kyrien moved his head between Chase and Prios and locked eyes with Chase.

The sword dropped from Chase's hand, and he turned away from the dragon. Then he ran to Catrin. She was trying to stand as he approached, and he helped her to her feet.

"Anything broken? Are you hurt?"

"I'm bruised and burned and scraped, but I think I'll make it. Prios?"

He moved from behind Kyrien slowly. His face was still concealed, and he approached with his head down.

"Who is this?" Chase asked.

"Prios was one of Belegra's cadre. He was enslaved and compelled to attack me, but now he is free," Catrin said, and the hooded face snapped up at her words. Reaching up, Catrin pulled the hood back and looked on the face of Prios for the first time. He was only slightly younger than she, and to her, he looked beautiful.

I am free?

"You are free."

147

"Why doesn't he say anything?" Chase asked, suspicious.

"He speaks in my mind," Catrin said. "He has helped me in the past, despite the risks, and I trust him. He comes with us."

"What about the . . . uh . . . dragon?"

"We need to find a way get him out of there."

"The walls are really thick, Cat. It would take days to chip him out even if we had the right tools, which we don't."

"We're getting him out," she said in her most commanding tone, but then she remembered the others. "Where are Strom and Osbourne and Brother Vaughn?"

"I sent them back to the ship after the Gholgi attacked. Osbourne hurt his knee, and Brother Vaughn broke a few ribs, I think. Strom went with them so they would not be helpless in a fight. I came looking for you."

"I knew you would," Catrin said with tears in her eyes as she hugged him. "Thank you. You've always protected me."

"Who knows what kind of trouble you'd get yourself into if I wasn't around? I'm just saving myself the hassle. So how are we going to get this dragon out?"

There is water nearby, and I have a bucket, and this might be of use to you.

Prios approached, holding Belegra's dragon ore, and he handed it to Catrin. Even before it touched her skin, she could feel its power, far greater than anything she'd ever experienced before, as if the greater size allowed it to contain exponentially more energy. Even after the massive amount Belegra had drawn from the stone, it still held an enormous charge. Yet there seemed to be flaws. Something was simply not as it should be, and she was hesitant to use the stone.

Desperate for a way to free Kyrien, her mind reeled with possibilities, but then she remembered what Prios had said: *There is water nearby.* "Fill everything you can with water and bring it back here," Catrin said.

"What?" Chase asked. "What good is water going to do? We need tools, Cat."

"The water will be all we need. Please help Prios," Catrin said as Prios was already moving to obey her command. In that moment she made a vow to talk to Prios, to help him understand that he had to do what she asked only if he believed it was the right thing to do. He was free.

Chase looked smug when he and Prios returned, each with a large container of water. "Are we going to scrub the stone away?"

"Stand back and be ready to throw the water at the rock on my command," Catrin said. Chase still looked unconvinced. Using the same technique she had used against Belegra, she heated the rock until it glowed like a hot ember. "Now!"

Chase and Prios moved in unison, and a wall of water rushed toward the rock. It struck with a hiss and a series of loud cracks, and several chunks of rock fell away. "We need more water," Catrin said, and Chase did not hesitate. Kyrien huddled at the back of his cell, but Catrin sensed he knew what she was doing, and he occasionally bugled in what sounded like an expectant call.

Chase and Prios returned just as the rock began to glow almost white. "Again," Catrin said. More chunks erupted this time as the structural integrity of the wall began to break down. With each successive time they threw water on the glowing rocks, more of the wall fell, but the process took time.

Kyrien lost patience and roared as he charged from the back his prison and threw himself against the wall with percussive force. Brittle stone fell before his desperate need, and the chamber walls exploded. Catrin, Chase, and Prios fled before the dragon as he charged to the entranceway, seeing the sunlit sky for the first time in his life. Before Catrin could even say good-bye, he gave a triumphant roar, leaped over the edge, and disappeared from view.

Running to the ledge, Catrin looked down to see Kyrien falling like a stone. He struggled to fully extend his wings, and even when he did, he still fell at tremendous speed. Suddenly, the air below was filled with activity. Other dragons, most larger than Kyrien, flocked around him. One of the largest, who Catrin thought she recognized as the one she had slept against, positioned himself directly beneath Kyrien, straining his wings to hold his own weight and that

149

of Kyrien. Perilously close to the treetops below, the dragons halted their fall and began to gain altitude.

Crying out to his brethren, Kyrien wobbled in the air as they left him to soar the winds on his own. Twice other dragons kept him from crashing to the ground, but he seemed to be gaining confidence as he got the feel for flight. Flexing his wings, he soared high into the sky. He gave one last cry before disappearing into the clouds.

Chapter 13

Procrastination robs the world of countless treasures.
--Massimo Arturo, scribe

* * *

For a moment, Catrin simply stood, motionless. So much had happened in such a short time that she found herself in a state of shock. Only when Chase moved to her side and took her by the arm did she return to her senses.

"Come over here and sit down," he said, and she let him lead her. On a huge chunk of what had once been part of Kyrien's prison, she sat. "How bad is your leg?" Chase asked, looking over her wound. "I don't understand. You took this wound yesterday, yet it looks like it happened weeks ago."

"I'm not sure," Catrin said, not wanting to admit what she had done, and very much wanting to keep the struggle with her subconscious a secret. No matter how ashamed she was of healing herself, despite the potential consequences, she was alive. Her heart broke a little when she silently vowed to bear no children, but she would not repeat the mistakes made by Enoch Giest. If she had no children, then there was no way Catrin could pass along any deadly traits. Still, tears slid down her face.

"Whatever the reason," Chase finally said, "it's a blessing. Are you in pain?"

"Only a little, but I'll be fine."

"Is Prios hurt?"

I am uninjured, but I need to rest.

His voice was timid in Catrin's mind, and he approached her slowly, his eyes downcast. When he reached the chunk of rock, he climbed up next to Catrin, curled into a ball, and slept.

Chase finished his inspection of Catrin's wounds. "Looks like you'll live. I think we should stay up here for the night. I'm going to try and find some wood for a fire and some food."

Prios did not move or even open his eyes, but his voice whispered in Catrin's mind: *Both can be found in the chambers at the back of the hall.*

"There is food and wood back there," Catrin said, pointing.

"How do you know that?" Chase asked.

"Prios told me."

"I thought he was asleep."

"Not quite yet."

Chase left to explore the back of the hall but not before casting a suspicious glance at Prios, who still appeared to be asleep. When Chase returned, his arms were laden with wood, and he placed it within the existing fire ring. With plenty of kindling, he soon had a small fire going. On his next trip, he returned with salted fish and some hard cheese.

"Not much left after this," Chase said as he and Catrin ate. "Not sure how Belegra expected to survive up here."

In a moment of panic, both Chase and Catrin realized that there might still be Zjhon soldiers about. They could be out hunting and could return at any time. Chase quickly stood, and Catrin drew a sharp intake of breath.

They are all dead. I, alone, survived.

"I thought you were sleeping," Catrin said.

I would, if you would stop flooding me with anxiety. When you worry, your thoughts boom in my head like thunder.

"I'm sorry," she said, embarrassed.

"You have to tell me what he's saying," Chase said, "or this is going to make me crazy."

"He says the rest of the Zjhon soldiers are dead. He's all that's left. I'll tell you the rest, Chase. I promise. But first I need rest."

"You two sleep. I'll keep watch."

* * *

Standing at the gunwales, Strom tried to relax, but his hands seemed to constantly clench into fists of their own volition. Osbourne and Brother Vaughn were recovering from their wounds and Strom was torn.

"You can't go back in there alone," Kenward said. "It's just too dangerous."

"Yet that is exactly what Catrin and Chase are doing. I'd be in no more danger than them. I can't just stay here and wait while they struggle to survive. I've already seen the dangers they face, and I don't know how they could survive it alone."

In a moment that brought Strom to tears, three of Kenward's crew came forward: Farsy, Bryn, and Nimsy. "We'll go with him," Farsy said. "Others volunteered as well, but we know we can't all go."

Kenward seemed torn, and he paced the deck while he considered. Nora stood nearby, watching him, and she tapped the toe of her boot on the deck. "I'm sorry," Kenward said, "I can't let any of you go. If you were lost, then chances are none of us would ever see our homes again. We simply can't afford to lose--by the gods!"

Everyone turned to see what had frightened Kenward, and Strom saw a terrifying sight. Like a wave of death, a black tide raced toward them. Like a single, huge organism, it moved faster than the swiftest horse. Strom braced himself and offered a hasty prayer, knowing they would need every bit of help they could get. No longer could he hope to find Catrin and Chase; now he could only hope to survive.

* * *

"Get up," Chase said. "He's gone."

"What? Who's gone?" Catrin asked, still trying to clear her mind of sleep. Outside, it was still nearly dark, only the blush of the false dawn gave any light.

"Prios."

With a wide yawn, Catrin sat up, her body stiff and sore. "He'll be back."

"How can you be sure it's not a trap? He could be going for help. I know he said the rest were dead, but I don't trust him."

"Prios and I are connected," Catrin said. "There is a bond between us that I cannot explain, but I know it's there. We can trust him. I assure you of that." As if to prove her

153

point, Prios returned to the hall in that moment, carrying a basket of freshly caught fish.

Breakfast.

"Thank you," Chase said after Catrin relayed Prios's words. "I'm sorry I didn't trust you."

Trust should be given only to those who have earned it. Maybe, someday, he and I will trust each other. Maybe today.

Catrin relayed his words, but Chase made no response; instead, he helped clean the fish while Catrin sliced the fresh roots Prios had found. Using Belegra's cook pot and a jar of fresh water from his stores, they made a bland but filling stew, and knowing they would need all the energy they could get, they ate all of what they had.

When they finished the meal, Prios took Catrin by the hand and silently led her to the back of the hall. Beyond the rooms used for storage and what had been sleeping quarters for the soldiers was the room Belegra had used. Inside were two rough stone slabs. One he'd used for a bed and the other as a table. On the table, next to the remains of a burned-out candle, was a stack of leather-bound books, and Catrin looked upon them with undisguised fear.

The books are not evil. They are just books. Perhaps you can do some good with them.

Despite his words, Catrin reached out for the books with trepidation, haunted by the fear that Belegra had left a trap for her. When she lifted the books from the table, though, nothing happened, and she felt foolish. Taking those and a few other items that could be useful, she loaded them into her pack. Chase and Prios rummaged through the stores and filled packs for themselves.

As they reached the entrance of the hall, Catrin looked out over the mountains, down the river valleys, and to the sea. There, the *Slippery Eel* waited. "Let's go home," she said.

* * *

"Prepare to fend 'em off," Kenward said as the tide of dark shapes gathered near his ship, hiding beneath the waves, waiting to strike. This was not an act of curiosity; Kenward could feel the hostility. Unwilling to leave Catrin and Chase behind, he kept the *Slippery Eel* moving, but the dark shapes followed them wherever they sailed. With great speed and endurance, they moved faster and farther than the wind could drive the *Eel.* "We can't outrun them--whatever they are."

"Not sure we can fight 'em either," Nora said. "If they are Gholgi, as Brother Vaughn has guessed, then they have tough, armorlike skin that we are unlikely to penetrate with spears. If they try to board us, we must repel them as we would any other foe, but if they attack the underside of the ship--"

"We're helpless," Kenward finished the thought for her. "Put us under full sail. Let's just see how long these things can keep swimming."

* * *

Finding the way back to their boat proved to be more difficult than Catrin had imagined. Surrounded by dense forest, it was easy to lose their way, and each time Chase had to climb above the canopy to gauge their course, they lost precious time. As daylight began to fail, chilling fear nearly paralyzed Catrin, who knew the Gholgi would come. If only she knew when.

Climbing and cutting their way through the underbrush while trying to remain alert for danger was exhausting, and Catrin swayed on her feet, taken by a spell of dizziness. The world seemed to shift and move, and only the tree trunk she found herself clinging to kept her from falling.

Chase cursed and stopped. "I know you're tired, Cat, but we can't keep stopping," he said. "If we don't make it back to the ship before dark, we could be in big trouble."

"I know. I'm sorry," Catrin said, ashamed of her own weakness.

"You've been through a lot. I suppose it's to be expected, but you're going to have to push yourself. Rest for now. I'm going to climb up and make sure we're going the right way."

Catrin lost track of how many times they had stopped and how many times Chase had changed their direction after one of his climbs. The jungle looked the same no matter how far they went, and she started to fear they would never get out.

"We're getting closer. I promise you," Chase said as he climbed back down, but Catrin lacked the energy to respond. Prios moved without complaint. When Catrin rested, he rested, and when she walked, he walked with her. Like a second shadow, he always seemed to be right behind her, and she took comfort from his presence. He was living evidence that she had done something worthwhile, and that knowledge helped to keep her moving. Somewhere, up in the clouds, Catrin imagined Kyrien soaring on the wind, and the image made her smile. That made two good things, and she moved ahead with newfound energy.

It was Chase who called the next break, and Catrin dropped to the ground, suddenly weary once again. The sun was beginning to sink, and their journey took on a new sense of urgency. Though Chase said they were nearing the boat, Catrin wondered if he was saying that just to keep her moving. At the moment, she no longer cared which it was; all she wanted was to be free of the jungle. The longer she stayed under the canopy of green, the more she felt she would never leave.

As they cut through a thicket of bramble, though, the landscape changed. Ahead, huge granite boulders, only their tops free of lichen and moss, rose from the jungle floor and blocked the way ahead. Chase climbed up first; struggling to get a solid grip on the slippery surface. He clawed through the soft moss and dug his fingers into hidden cracks. When he reached the top, he secured a rope to a nearby tree and tossed the other end down to Catrin. Even with the rope, the climb was treacherous, and Catrin cried out when she lost her footing. With only the rope holding her, she crashed into side of the rock, slamming her wounded leg into a sharp corner. When she finally reached the top, her leg was soaked in blood; her scabs had been ripped open.

Prios made the climb without difficulty while Chase bandaged Catrin's leg. She was tempted to heal herself again but feared the consequences. Already the barrier between her conscious and subconscious minds was breaking down, and she did not want to risk damaging it further. Despite her vows, she feared other, unforeseen ramifications. Still, every painful step tempted her.

Beyond the stones lay a narrow valley that sloped gracefully downward.

"Now we just need to keep moving lower. Eventually we should find water, and from there we just follow the shore until we find the boat."

Bolstered by Chase's confidence, Catrin moved as fast as she could, and they started to make what seemed like real progress. The land continued to slope downward, and when the wind shifted, the sound of running water drifted to them. Ahead, the small valley they followed opened into a much larger valley. Beyond one last hill, they found a sheer drop. A few tenacious trees grew from the side of the mountain, but they were widely spaced.

"I'm going to look for the best way down," Chase said. "Wait here."

Catrin and Prios found a shady spot and leaned against the spongy moss.

"I think I see where we left the boat," Chase said when he returned. "There looks to be a way down, but it won't be easy."

"Let's not waste any time," Catrin said as she stood. "I just want this to be over."

Chase led them along a meandering path, where they followed a ledge that was, at times, only a hand's width across. Using his knife to create handholds in the soft limestone, Chase did what he could to make the climb easier. There came times, though, when they had no choice but to jump between large rocks and boulders. Chase led the way, and some of the rocks moved when he landed. Catrin could only hope they would stay in place long enough for her and Prios to cross. Each landing brought new levels of pain. Blood seeped through Catrin's bandages, and at times dizziness nearly overcame her. Her vision became cloudy and blurred. Chase allowed her to rest, but the breaks were kept short. Even when they did stop, Catrin found it impossible to relax in such precarious positions.

When they finally reached the shore, her will was nearly spent. Soaked with sweat, her hair hung down into her eyes, causing them to sting and burn. Her legs trembled with every step, and her breathing was labored.

Be strong.

Having Prios behind her, enduring the same trials yet never complaining, helped Catrin to remain focused. She could not fail him now, not when they had come so far.

"There it is!" Chase shouted, triumphant. Catrin made it to the boat before she collapsed to the ground. Prios helped Chase gather wood for the signal fire. Unable to find much dry kindling, Chase shaved bits of bark into a pile. Prios struck the flint, and each spark was like a ray of hope. When one finally caught and the air filled with smoke, Catrin began to believe they might actually make it.

As the fire established itself, flames leaped high into the sky, but Chase said it still was not enough. He and Prios gathered as many pine branches as they could find, creating a pile near the fire. When they had what they considered to be enough, they threw it all on top the fire at once. For a moment, it looked as if they had extinguished the fire, but then great billows of smoke began to pour around the pine needles. In a blinding flash, the fire erupted with its full strength. Popping and hissing, it sent flames and burning embers high into the twilight skies.

"And now," Chase said, "we wait."

* * *

"Damage report!" Kenward shouted with the slightest hint of panic in his voice, his knuckles white from clutching the wheel.

"The hull's not been breached, but they beat joints loose in places. We've got a thousand small leaks," Bryn replied.

"You're making too much speed for the shape we're in," Nora said. "The *Eel* will come apart if we keep this up."

With the wind at his back, Kenward could not resist the speed. He needed to get away from the boiling Gholgi to give his crew time to make repairs. Though none of the beasts had shown themselves, Kenward was now convinced it was the Gholgi they faced. These creatures were clever and strong and, if nothing else, determined.

"Maintain current speed. Make repairs as best as you can. Keep in mind that we'll most likely get attacked again."

"Yes, sir," Bryn said before spinning on his heel and running belowdecks.

"It's your ship," Nora said. "I'm going to supervise the repairs. Send someone for me if you need any advice to ignore."

Drawing a deep breath, Kenward hoped he was right. All of their lives were at stake, and he had never felt more vulnerable. In all of his close encounters, he had always been confident he would somehow survive, but now he had a sick feeling in his stomach.

"Smoke, sir! The signal fire's been lit!"

"Boil me," Kenward said, knowing he needed to make repairs before going back into shallow waters; that was where the Gholgi wanted him. "What am I supposed to do now?"

"I just saw a bright flash, sir, as if something exploded," the lookout yelled, and an instant later, what sounded like a thunderclap reached them.

"Set a course for the signal fire!" Kenward yelled, his mind made up. As his gut continued to churn, he wondered if he was taking his final risk.

* * *

The attack came swiftly and nearly silently. No smell announced the presence of the Gholgi since the attack came from the water. Charging to shore, nearly a dozen Gholgi attacked. Chase jumped to his feet and ran to meet them, howling. The first Gholgi raised its mighty clawed hand to strike Chase down, and Catrin reacted quicker than she ever had before. In the span of a breath, she drew on the power around her and unleashed it in a single action. A bolt of electric light slammed into the Gholgi, scattering them and leaving some stunned, but others were quick to mount another attack.

159

After Catrin's instinctive release of power, she noticed it had very little backlash. Feeling only slightly drained, she used the new technique to fire off bolts of energy at every approaching Gholgi. Each strike stunned its target, but it was not enough to stop the attack, and more Gholgi were emerging from the water. One terrified glance at the water revealed hundreds of dark shapes moving toward the shallows.

Concentrating on the two Gholgi that were bearing down on Chase, Catrin pulled Belegra's chunk of dragon ore from her pocket. Drawing on it, her staff, and the air, she prepared to deliver a more powerful blow, but before she released her attack, Prios's voice thundered in her mind: *You are not strong enough alone. Use me.*

Like a flash flood, he gave himself to her completely and utterly, and she was overwhelmed by the very essence of him. It took only an instant, but it seemed much longer to Catrin. Praying her momentary hesitation had not cost Chase his life, she attacked. Ropes of fire and lightning raced across the shore and struck thunderous impacts. The shoreline was suddenly littered with smoking Gholgi forms; others had been tossed back into the water.

Limping, Chase retreated. All was still for a moment, and over Chase's shoulder, Catrin saw the *Slippery Eel* as she rounded the bend. In the next instant, though, her hopes were dashed. Undaunted, the Gholgi resumed their attack, and now they came in even larger numbers.

"Stay behind me!" Catrin shouted and no one argued. With Prios still open to her, Catrin allowed both of them to draw from her staff and the oddly disjointed energy of Belegra's dragon ore. As soon as she opened the energy to him, Prios pulled deeply, and she could sense his shock and wonder.

It's so beautiful.

Almost drawn in by his fascination, Catrin had to pull herself back to the fight. Gholgi were advancing toward her, and to her horror, the *Slippery Eel* also seemed to be under attack. With a cry of anguish, she attacked. Again the Gholgi fell before her fury, and again it was not enough. It seemed an endless supply of Gholgi waited for their own chance to

160

attack. When she looked out to the *Slippery Eel*, her last glimmer of hope began to fade.

* * *

Kenward watched as his ship was overwhelmed. Gholgi clung to the *Slippery Eel*, pulling her lower in the water. Some tried to board the ship, but most seemed content to simply pull the ship under with their sheer weight. One of those bold enough to make the deck had his mother cornered, and he rushed to her aid. The beast turned as he came, screaming, and Kenward thrust his spear into its reptilian eye. Issuing a shrill scream, the Gholgi dropped back over the railing.

"Go for their eyes!" Kenward shouted, but he knew it would not be enough; there were simply too many.

* * *

Swaying on her feet, Catrin prepared to deliver another blast of power. Prios was nearly drained, and she could ask no more of him. Using her energy alone, she cast out a desperate attack. In the momentary pause it created, she watched as the *Slippery Eel* was slowly and inexorably pulled under water. Gholgi clung to the ship like a writhing mass of ants. The attack on land began again, just as the *Slippery Eel*'s prow dipped below the water.

Above the roar of the attack, a keening wail could be heard that made every Gholgi take pause. Looking up, Catrin saw a circling cloud of dragons. Calling out in unison, the mighty serpents folded their wings and dived. Many struck the water, full speed, and others pulled up to skim over the shore. In the next instant, the air was filled with activity and the screams of the Gholgi.

Catrin watched in awe as Kyrien swept down in front of her and cast the Gholgi aside. Using his head and tail, he sent them flying through the air. His brethren continued to strike the water, looking like giant seabirds.

"Now's our chance," Chase shouted above the din. Prios and Catrin raced to his aid as he began sliding the small boat to the water.

Kyrien stayed near Catrin and snapped up any Gholgi that came too close. Once they were in the water, though, the situation became even more dire. Dragons continued to crash into the river, only to launch back into the skies a moment later. Tossed by growing waves, Catrin and the others barely held on. When she looked around, Kyrien was nowhere to be found.

Though progress was slow, the *Slippery Eel* grew ever closer. The ship was now riding higher in the water, as most of the Gholgi were now fighting for their lives. Catrin, Chase, and Prios rowed as hard as they could and approached the *Slippery Eel.* Apparently not wanting to waste time retrieving the boat, the crew dropped a boarding net over the side. Catrin leaped to the net first; the others followed. But her leg no longer wanted to hold her weight, and she had difficulty climbing. When Chase reached the deck, he leaned over the gunwale and extended his hand to her. "Grab on, Cat. I'll pull you up!"

Exhausted, she reached out to him, but before their hands met, a reptilian claw reached from the water and grabbed her legs. Desperate, Chase extended himself further, kept on the ship only by Prios, who grabbed him by the ankles. His hand connected with Catrin's, and she clung to it. With all her strength, she tried to hold on, but slowly she began to slip.

"No!" Chase screamed. "Don't you dare let go!"

There was nothing more she could do; she had no strength left, and she felt her fingertips sliding over his, as the Gholgi's grip grew ever tighter. Just as she thought she would succumb, the Gholgi released her and screamed, its lower half engulfed in Kyrien's jaws. After tossing the Gholgi away, Kyrien nudged Catrin from behind, and she let Chase pull her onto the deck. The last thing she saw before she passed out was Kyrien, wheeling in the sky, circling over the ship.

Chapter 14

Our weather is controlled by the ocean currents. Should they ever falter, all will lament.
--Sister Meigan, Cathuran monk

* * *

Coming awake with a start, Catrin sat up in her hammock. Her head spinning, she wiped the sweat-soaked hair away from her face. The door opened, and daylight streamed in.

"It's good to see you awake," Osbourne said as he closed the door. "I brought you some broth."

"Thank you. How long did I sleep?"

"Not that long. Since last night. You look horrible."

"Thanks," Catrin said before sipping the broth.

"Brother Vaughn wanted me to report back on your condition. You rest."

The broth was weak, almost tasteless, but it warmed Catrin's belly. After a yawn and stretch, she climbed from the hammock. Her legs were unsteady, and she leaned on the door for a moment before opening it. Cool sea air greeted her, and she breathed in deeply, taking strength from it. The decks were near empty; by the sound of things, most were belowdecks making repairs. Brother Vaughn and Osbourne emerged from the hold and walked toward Catrin as soon as they saw her.

"Back to bed with you," Brother Vaughn said, holding his ribs and sounding like a scolding father. Osbourne walked with a severe limp.

"The ship needs repairs, and everyone is needed," Catrin said.

"You'll be no use to us if you drop from exhaustion, not to mention the loss of blood. Your wounds are healing exceedingly well, but you still need to rest."

"I will, but first I need to know what dangers we still face."

"Things have improved a great deal," Brother Vaughn said. "The dragons have driven off the Gholgi, and the crew

163

has been able to make many of the needed repairs. There are men on shore now gathering materials to make additional repairs."

"The dragons are still here?" Catrin asked.

"Only your dragon remains," Brother Vaughn said. "He's kept a vigilant watch, and there have been no more attacks."

"Kyrien? Where is he?" Catrin asked, and Brother Vaughn pointed.

High above, resting on an outcropping of rock, Kyrien sunned himself. Somehow sensing Catrin's gaze, he extended his serpentine neck and looked back at her. Then he gave a triumphant call. Moments later he leaped from the rocks and soared above the *Slippery Eel*.

"You see?" Brother Vaughn said. "We are well protected. Now back in you go."

Captivated by the sight of Kyrien soaring majestically on the thermals, Catrin was held in thrall, but she allowed Brother Vaughn to escort her back to her cabin. Once inside, she realized he was correct about her condition. The short walk left her winded, and she collapsed back into the hammock, her dreams filled with wings and green-flecked, golden eyes.

* * *

Master Beron walked in silence, his mind consumed with the dilemma he faced. Master Edling wanted him to convince the others to declare everyone north of the Wall a traitor, but Master Beron disagreed. Only the threat of poison in his food or a knife in the ribs kept him from siding with the others.

Through the halls of the Masterhouse, he walked, taking corridors he rarely used just to delay his audience with Master Edling. When his legs began to ache and he had still come up with no solutions, he gave up hope. As he walked into Master Edling's apartments, he was a beaten man. "I'm sorry, sir," he said. "I cannot convince the others. They still care for their countrymen, and they fear the wrath of the Herald."

"I *told* you I would attend to the Herald myself!"

"I believe you, but they don't believe me. They cannot understand that you have the power to protect us from her."

"Come, then," Master Edling said, his robes gliding across the floor as he led Master Beron from his apartments. "I'll show how I will defeat the Herald. Then you can convince the others. If you don't do it, I will. I'm certain it would be better for them if you made them believe. My methods might be slightly less gentle."

Master Beron cringed. Master Jarvis had always been a good friend to him. He was kind and honest. The same could not be said for Master Edling, but still Beron struggled against his own fears. Should he flee? Should he, too, go north of the Wall? Would they even accept him there? His thoughts were interrupted when Master Edling made an unfamiliar turn. "Isn't this a servant passage?"

"Keep quiet, or I'll silence you myself."

Master Beron closed his mouth and allowed Master Edling to lead. After three more turns, which Beron committed to memory, Master Edling stopped. He turned his back to Beron and, in some unseen way, triggered a doorway to open. "Get in there."

Beron walked into the darkness, not knowing what to expect. Master Edling closed the door before lighting his lamp. Beyond two short halls, they came to a room filled with treasures of all varieties. Master Edling walked straight to an oddly shaped, metallic rock, which rested on a supple piece of red cloth.

"A gift from the gods," Master Edling said, his eyes full of fervor. "Dropped from the sky, it was delivered to us hundreds of years ago. The gods have blessed us. We will prevail over the Herald. I'll show you the scriptures."

Master Beron looked at the strange stone, wondering if a weapon from the gods would be so formless, but as he looked at it, he saw magical symmetry and graceful lines all over it. What had first looked like big holes, under a careful eye, were each a work of art. It looked as if the winds of a billion years had scoured the rock's surface into patterns. Then he read the scripture.

In the hands of the righteous, the sky stone will capture the power of the mighty one.

"I'll take her power and use it as my own. I'll bring true power back to the Masterhood," Master Edling said.

* * *

"We've made the best repairs possible with the materials available to us, sir," Bryn said. "There's not much more we can do. We've stopped all the leaks, and we have additional pitch ready should we need to patch any new leaks."

"Your crew has done well," Nora said with a firm nod.

"Thank you, Mother," Kenward said. "A better crew I could not ask for."

"On that we agree," she said.

Bryn flushed, embarrassed by the compliment. Catrin stood at the gunwales, her strength returning. Given her leisure while she recovered, she spent most of her time watching Kyrien and his kin. Though Kyrien kept constant vigil, other dragons occasionally joined him, and their synchronized acrobatics drew more than just Catrin's eyes.

"Such fearsome beauty," Nora said as she joined Catrin.

"I can't make myself look away."

"You've an attachment with Kyrien; that much is clear. He seems a noble and loyal beast to protect us in such a way. I would never have guessed such a thing would happen."

"They are more intelligent than I would have thought possible," Catrin said. "Kyrien and another spoke in my mind; they spoke not in words, but in images and emotion. They asked me to save Kyrien from Belegra, and I suppose they are repaying the debt."

"Whatever the reason," Brother Vaughn said, "they have saved us all. I've always loved flying creatures, but these dragons are beyond my wildest expectations. None are as large as the skeleton found in Faulk, but they are undeniably beautiful. Their ability to communicate makes them even more remarkable."

For a while they simply watched as Kyrien and two other dragons danced in the skies. Much of the crew stopped to watch as others joined the dance. Like a flock of birds, the dragons moved in unison, as if of a single mind, changing directions so dramatically that it was a wonder none collided.

"We're ready to raise our anchors and set sail," Kenward said. "We've only to fill the hold with fish before we are ready to leave this place. I assume we are to travel back to the Godfist?"

"Yes," Catrin said. "I'm ready to go home."

"I suppose the safest route will be to go back the way we came. There may be a shorter route to the Godfist, but we've no way of knowing."

Belegra had a map.

Turning at the sound of Prios's voice in her mind, Catrin looked for him. It took a moment before she found him reclining in the shadows. Remembering Belegra's books, Catrin turned back to Kenward. "I think we have a map."

"What?" he asked, clearly excited. Few things seemed to excite sailors more than maps and charts.

"Before we left the mountain hall," Catrin said, "we took some books from Belegra's quarters. I had completely forgotten, but I think we should look there first." After retrieving her pack, she rummaged through and found the leather-bound tomes. Holding the first in her hand, she was loath to open it, but she remembered Prios's words: *The books are not evil.* Running her fingers over the unadorned leather binding, she made herself open it.

The pages were of finer quality than any Catrin had ever seen before, and the text had been meticulously scribed. Much of what she saw seemed to be equations and formulas, and after leafing through the pages, she set it aside. When she opened the second volume, she immediately found what she was looking for. Kenward, Nora, and the others stood by, waiting with undisguised anticipation. Folded in half was a finely woven canvas with a colorful map painted on it. The crease down the center had damaged parts of the map, but it was otherwise whole. Kenward drew a sharp intake of breath when she handed it to him.

"By the gods!" he said. "It's all here. The Firstland, the Greatland, the Godfist--all of it. And look here, there are at least three chains of islands I've never seen or heard of. What a treasure!"

"Taking this route," Nora said, "we can make it back in half the time."

Catrin looked at the map, trying to figure out why the thought of taking a different route made her stomach hurt. The map gave no indications of any danger save a large expanse of open water, but something told her emphatically not to go that way, and she was torn. "Can you think of any dangers that we would face taking the direct route?"

"There are always dangers," Nora said, and she pointed to a place on the map. "Most of these waters are unfamiliar to me, but there are some parts I have traveled. The biggest danger I think we would face are storms, and we could run into those anywhere."

Still, Catrin could not shake the feeling, and she decided to give her instincts credence. "Something is telling me not to go that way. I cannot explain it, and can find no reason to support it, yet I feel compelled to heed it."

"Sometimes we must listen to our instincts," Kenward said, "especially when they contradict the most likely course. Given your magic, I would be inclined to follow your gut. In my younger days, I would have taken the shortest course no matter what you said, but now I have seen too much, and I find myself given to caution."

"It's certainly taken long enough to beat some caution into you, fool boy," Nora said, but her eyes shone with pride.

"Are you certain about this?" Chase asked as he forced himself into the cramped cabin, trying to get a better look at the map. "I don't want to spend another year at sea if we don't have to."

"I can't tell you why, Chase, but I feel very strongly about this. I've no desire to prolong the journey home, but the thought of going back any way but the way we came makes me ill."

"It's decided, then," Kenward said with a sigh. "I'll have to save exploring those waters for another journey."

Under Kyrien's watchful eye, they fished until the *Slippery Eel* sat heavy in the water. As Kenward set a course for the Keys of Terhilian, Catrin stood at the stern watching Kyrien. As the Firstland faded in the distance, two other dragons joined Kyrien. They escorted the ship to deep water, but as the sun began to sink below the horizon, the other two dragons refused to go any farther. Circling, they called out to Kyrien, and he seemed torn. After several long and tense moments, the other dragons turned on their wingtips and soared back to the Firstland. Catrin watched, also torn. Part of her wanted Kyrien to come with her, to be a part of her life, but she wondered what kind of life he could have without other dragons. In the end, she knew she needed to do what was best for Kyrien. Opening herself to a trickle of power, she did her best to communicate with him using only her mind: *Go. Be free. Live well!*

His only response was a mournful call; then, after diving down and soaring low over the deck, he flew after his brethren, back to his home. Catrin watched with tears in her eyes, hoping he would live a happy life. Though she had known him only a short time, she left the Firstland with what felt like a gaping hole in her heart. Prios joined her and seemed to share her sadness.

I will miss him too. I was responsible for delivering him to Belegra, which is something I may never be able to forgive myself for, yet somehow he found it in his heart to do just that. I always thought he hated me. He could have let Chase kill me, or he could have killed me himself, but he did not. I cannot say I understand it, but I will forever be in his debt.

"Perhaps, someday, you will get a chance to repay that debt," Catrin said.

I don't see how I ever could, but I suppose it's possible. No one can say what the future will hold.

* * *

In the following weeks, Catrin spent much of her time with Brother Vaughn. Together they learned everything they could from Belegra's books. One volume was about the physical laws of her world; it was this tome that was filled with equations--most of which only made Catrin's head hurt, and she doubted she would ever find any of it useful. Brother Vaughn had little more success, and they set that book aside.

The second seemed of little use at first since it contained descriptions of mythical creatures, from harpies to bearbulls, most of which neither Catrin nor Brother Vaughn believed existed. When Brother Vaughn flipped to the section that described dryads, though, Catrin became intrigued, especially since much of what it said rang of truth. "I thought of those other creatures as mere fairy tales, but I know dryads exist. Could these other creatures really have once existed?"

"I suppose it's possible," Brother Vaughn said. "Let's see what other creatures are described." Turning the pages carefully, he passed a section describing giant birds called phirlons and another on glowing sea serpents known as godhairs. It was when he reached the section on dragons that he drew a sharp breath. He read aloud: "Of dragons there are three types: *verdent, feral,* and *regent. Verdents* are most common and are by far the largest dragon species. Despite their size and power, they are docile and easily tamed. All *verdent* dragons have mottled bluish-gray coloring.

"*Feral* dragons, as black as night, are as ferocious as their name would imply. Generally, *ferals* are solitary creatures that only congregate during mating season, but there have been incidents recorded where groups of *ferals* have attacked *verdents* who intruded on their territory.

"*Regent* dragons are the most rare and intriguing species. *Regents* seem to live more like ants than dragons. That is to say that they live in colonies and have specialized roles. Each colony has but one female--the queen. There are many types of *regent* males: warrior, protector, hunter, and nurturer are but a few."

"So Kyrien is a regent dragon?" Catrin asked.

"I would say he fits the description, and the skeleton found in Faulk would have to have been a verdent."

Seeing a vision of skies filled with all three types of dragons, Catrin felt a chill run down her spine. The thought was thrilling and terrifying.

"*Regent* dragons have other remarkable qualities," Brother Vaughn continued. "The ability to change the color of their skin to blend in with their surroundings is among the most formidable trait. Regents are so skilled in camouflage that they can become nearly invisible in almost any environment. It is their innate ability to transform noonstone into dragon ore, though, that makes these creatures the most highly sought after."

Pulling Belegra's dragon ore from her pocket, Catrin held it up. It caught the light and cast it about in disorganized fashion, which detracted from its beauty. "So that was why Belegra wanted Kyrien," she said. "For this."

"It would appear to be so."

Nothing could be worth the torture Belegra inflicted upon Kyrien. She was tempted to cast the stone into the sea, but Catrin came to see that even though the way the stone was created was evil, the stone itself was not. When she began to view it as a gift from Kyrien, a piece of him that she could take with her, it became a cherished treasure.

The book gave few more details, and they set it aside. The third volume gave Catrin chills, for it told of ways to enslave the mind of another. Chilled by the gruesome and cruel techniques described in painful detail, Catrin decided that this book truly was evil. "This is knowledge that no one should have. I think we should burn it."

Brother Vaughn seemed appalled by the idea of burning a book at first, but as he looked through the rest of the book, he came to agree. There was no joy in the act, but Catrin felt a little safer knowing it was gone. With any luck, those skills would be lost forever.

Catrin's thoughts turned to all that had been lost, and tears gathered in her eyes. When one fell to the floor, Brother Vaughn looked up. "Will you tell me what's bothering you?" he asked.

"I just feel so alone," she said. "It's not that you and everyone on the ship are . . . It's just . . ."

"I miss them too," Brother Vaughn said, and Catrin let her emotion flow. "May I share something with you?"

"Please do," Catrin said with a sniffle.

"What is there between us? Right now. What's separating you and me?"

"Nothing, I guess," Catrin said.

"Nothing? Really."

In the silence that followed, Catrin tried to understand his meaning, but then something occurred to her. "Air?"

"Air. Indeed," Brother Vaughn said. "Now I want you to step away from everything for a moment, including the air."

Catrin smiled, knowing it was impossible. "I suppose I could submerge myself in water."

"Not for long. But the point is that you and I are parts of the same system. We are parts of the world, and we cannot separate ourselves from it. Everything I do influences you, and everything you do influences everyone and everything else. Do you understand?"

"I think so," Catrin said.

"Since we are part of this enormous system, we are always connected and can never truly be alone. And even when we seem to depart from this world, our energy remains. In this sense, we are one and we are eternal."

His words gave Catrin solace, and she turned her thoughts back to anything that could help her in the future. Again she looked at the dragon ore she held. So precious and so very rare, she was afraid she would drop it and shatter it into tiny pieces. Oddly shaped, it felt clumsy in her hands. The stones in her staff had been masterfully cut, their symmetry somehow balancing them. Then she remembered Imeteri's Fish; it had been such a simple carving, yet it, too, had symmetry and balance. "Do you think the shape of the dragon ore could enhance its effects?" she asked.

"The thought never occurred to me," Brother Vaughn said, "but I suppose it's possible. Do you have reason to believe it could?"

"The stones Mother Gwendolin gave me have been carefully cut, where Imeteri's Fish was just a simple carving. The one thing they have in common is that one side seems to balance the other. When I hold Belegra's stone, it feels unstable, out of balance."

"Perhaps you should have a gem-cutter cut it for you? Or you could carve it yourself. You did say that Imeteri's Fish was only a rough carving. Surely you could do just as well," Brother Vaughn said.

Catrin turned the translucent stone in her hands, and as she looked at it, a simple but elegant shape became apparent to her--the shape the stone wanted to become. It was as if all she had to do was peel away the husk that shrouded the stone's true form. "Could I be so bold as to try to carve it myself? I've no skill for art or carving. I might destroy it."

"I suppose you must follow your heart."

* * *

Cradled by her hammock, Catrin closed her eyes. As had become a bit of a ritual, Prios chose this time to spend with her. Though walls separated them, it was as if he were sitting beside her.

"Is it not difficult for you to talk to me without touching me?" she asked aloud, despite the fact that she had only to think of saying it to him for him to hear. "You could come in here while we talk if you'd like."

There is a bond between us that I do not understand. I believe I could speak with you over almost any distance without the slightest strain. It is something I share with no one else. Perhaps it is your abilities, but I wonder if it isn't something else . . .

Catrin let his unspoken question go unanswered, afraid of things she was not yet prepared to face. Grateful that he could not read her thoughts unless they were directed to him, she changed the subject. "Do you think I should try to carve the dragon ore? I'm afraid I'll only destroy it."

I know nothing of the properties of dragon ore, but I, too, sense its flaws despite its purity. When I look at nature, I see varied shapes and forms of life, yet those forms are not chaotic or random, as the shape of Belegra's dragon ore seems to be. My instincts tell me that giving it orderly shape and form will give it new life. I cannot be certain, and there is the risk that you will destroy it, so I am hesitant to give council.

"It would be so much easier if someone would just tell me what I am supposed to do."

I've lived my life doing what others have told me to do. While not being responsible for my own destiny may have been easier, I certainly would not say it was better.

173

"You make a good point," Catrin conceded. "I suppose I'll just have to stop my whining and get on with it." She could almost hear Prios chuckle.

* * *

As the sun rose over the sea, the lookout called out: "Land!" His call drew everyone to the deck. Having seen nothing but waves for months, it was a thrill to see land, even if they would only pass it by. When they neared the Terhilian Lovers, the sun cast a ruddy glow, and there, perched upon the man's outstretched arm, waited Kyrien. Glimmering like a jewel, he spread his wings and extended his tail. Dropping his head down, he wove back and forth hypnotically. No one spoke, and Catrin was held in thrall, not wanting to move or speak for fear he would fly away, but he just watched them as they slid past. Not long before he would have been lost from sight, he slipped from his perch, spread his wings only part of the way, and slammed into the water.

Watching for him to emerge, Catrin waited at the gunwales for most of the day, but he did not show himself. She was left to wonder if his presence was but a final farewell.

"He's a remarkable beast, your Kyrien," Nora said as she walked to Catrin's side.

"I had hoped to see him again, but I think he's gone."

"With such a rare and mystical creature, I don't suppose you'll ever know what to expect."

* * *

In the light of her cabin, Catrin prepared herself. Before her was the dragon ore and the sharpest knife she could find. To the side sat a leather bag she would use to collect the chips and shards, each one precious. Taking a deep breath, she picked up the knife before she lost her nerve. Using only light pressure, she pulled the knife against the stone. Not even a scratch was made in the glossy surface. Trying again, she used greater force but achieved no greater effect.

174

Brother Vaughn watched with anticipation. "Apply your will," he said.

Opening herself to a trickle of energy, she tried to keep the torrent from pulling her away. Despite greater understanding, her power remained difficult to moderate, and a bead of sweat formed on her brow. Directing her energy along the fine edge of the knife, she pulled it toward her, and blade parted stone. A tiny shard separated from the dragon ore and sat, perched, atop the gleaming knife.

"Well done," Brother Vaughn said. "Now do it again."

* * *

"When we get back," Osbourne said, "I'm gonna eat for a week. Ham, bacon, sausage--anything but fish."

"Bread and apple butter," Strom said.

"A big, juicy steak with potatoes," Chase added.

"Slices of pepper sausage with chunks of smoked cheese," Kenward said from behind them, and they all turned. "Aye, a seafarer I may be, but I've a love for land food."

"Do you think we'll ever make it back home?" Osbourne asked.

"We'll make it," Kenward said. "And when we do, the first meal is on me."

"I'm going to hold you to that," Strom said.

"You've all earned it. I've spent most of my life at sea, and I can think of no passengers I'd rather have on my ship. Hopefully you'll find some reason to take to the seas again someday."

"So there's no chance you'll stay on the Godfist?" Strom asked.

"Not for long," Kenward said. "I tried it once, but life on land didn't suit me. All those invisible lines that divide one man's space from another's were beyond my understanding. The sea is the sea. No one can claim it or take it away from me."

In a way, Osbourne could see his point, but it did nothing to dampen his longing for home. To feel the grass between his toes or to run through the forest would be

175

glorious indeed. Things that had seemed mundane, even boring, in his old life now had new meaning, new significance. If ever they make it home, he thought, his life would be forever changed, and he would no longer take for granted the things he now knew he loved the most.

After finishing their meal in silence, they dispersed, each having tasks waiting. It seemed on a ship, the work was never done.

* * *

"If we run full sail," Kenward said, "we could make to the shallows just before the full moon."

"We need to fish while still on this side of the shallows," Nora said. "Or have you forgotten the sharks? Your ship is in no condition to face any foe, let alone make full speed. It would be wisest to take it slowly and fish while we wait out the cycle of the moon."

Pacing the deck, Kenward struggled. Why must his instincts always push him to do the exact opposite of what his mother suggested? He valued her council, no matter what she thought, but he had learned to follow his gut. "We can't sail the shallows with a full hold, and we'll have to fish on the other side either way. Raise full sail," he said. Nora made an annoyed sound in her throat and walked away.

"She doesn't look happy," Chase said as he approached.

Kenward just shrugged. "I have that effect on her."

* * *

Wiping the sweat from her eyes, Catrin squinted, trying to figure out the best way to make the final cut. Before her was the physical manifestation of the image she had seen in her mind. Despite her rudimentary carving skills, it was, in its own way, beautiful. Turning the tip of her blade carefully under a delicate section, she trimmed away a tiny sliver, though she nearly cut herself when someone shouted: "Shallows ahead!"

After carefully placing the sliver in her now nearly full bag, Catrin went to the gunwales, secretly hoping to find Kyrien waiting for her.

"Get the gear ready. We fish," Kenward said, and the crew scrambled. Despite their efforts, the fish simply weren't biting, and they caught only a few small sharks. As the light began to fade, the frustration was palpable. "We need to catch enough fish to feed us for a while. I didn't want to fill the hold, but I didn't want to starve either. If we don't catch something soon, we are going to have to wait another moon before we cross the shallows."

"Aye," Nora said. "Nothing to be done for it but to keep trying."

"Fins to port, sir!" called the lookout.

Glossy fins parted the water, tossing a wake on each side as they came. Then, as if they understood the fear it would instill, they slipped beneath the dark water. Catrin tried to prepare herself for an impact, but not knowing exactly when it would come made it nearly impossible. When the sharks did hit the ship, it felt as if all of them hit at once, and the *Slippery Eel* rolled to one side before slowly righting herself.

"Pull in the trawl tubs!" Kenward ordered. "As soon as they are in, we raise full sail and make for the shallows. Prepare yourselves!"

In a frenzy of activity, the crew readied the ship to come about, but the men retrieving the trawl tubs cursed. They had caught something, and whatever it was, it was big.

"*Now* the fish decide to bite," Strom said as he helped the men struggling to turn the windlass.

"Sir, some of our repairs have been knocked loose. We're taking on water," Bryn reported.

"Lock the windlass," Kenward said then, with a single stroke of his belt knife across the tensioned rope, cut the trawl away. "Full sail. Now!"

The *Slippery Eel* thrummed as the sharks slammed against the hull again, and the crew needed little urging to make speed. Catrin clung to the railing, a sick feeling in her stomach. The sharks seemed determined to sink them, and she knew that, in the water, they would make an easy meal.

177

Though the moon was nearly full, a thick covering of clouds blanketed the skies, and the shallows were barely visible. Sailing full speed into those waters seemed in itself suicide, and that was assuming the sharks didn't get them first.

"There's someone in the shallows, sir! Light ahead!"

Chapter 15

To depend solely on a single food source is to risk starvation.
--Ruder Dunn, farmer

* * *

Near complete darkness hindered the crew's efforts to find a clear path when entering the shallows. Though the firelight was still distant, it cast dancing reflections across the water, making it even more difficult to find obstacles. In a bold spectacle, the sharks pursued the ship into the shallows. At times it seemed they would surely become trapped in the sand, yet they remained a threat.

"Bring out the spears!" Kenward ordered. "There's no place for them to hide in the shallows, and I want them to feel our sting!"

Catrin watched as crewmen leveled long spears at the sharks. Some simply stabbed at those that drew too close, others threw their spears with all their strength into the sharks that circled the ship. Most had little effect or simply missed their mark, but one landed a mortal blow. The badly injured shark thrashed wildly, churning the water, and its brethren turned on it, quickly tearing it apart. The grisly display made Catrin's stomach churn as she imagined what it would feel like to be pulled apart. Deeply disturbed, she kept her eyes toward the firelight.

The closer they came, the larger the fire grew, as if feeding off their very energy. Occasionally, a dark silhouette blocked out parts of the fire, but little more could be seen. When finally the sharks were left behind, Kenward slowed the ship. "It would be risky to go any farther in these conditions," he said. "We could do it if that fire wasn't ruining our night vision. I want to know who started it."

"You're starting to show the wisdom of a seasoned captain," Nora said.

"If you call being scared out of my shorts wisdom, then I guess it's so."

"Fool boy."

179

"Drop the boats," Kenward said. "Arm yourselves and be ready for a fight. I've no doubt they know we're here, and they may be laying in wait."

Despite the fact that whoever it was probably already knew they were coming, the crew did their best to remain silent. After the boats had been lowered, Catrin stood next to Chase, waiting her turn to climb down. "You stay here," he said. "We'll go find out what's going on."

"Not a chance," Catrin said, and she grabbed the railing and jumped over. Scrambling down the boarding net, she gave no one else the opportunity to dissuade her. Waiting on the ship would have been pure torture; better to see for herself.

Farsy climbed into the boat with her, handed her an oar, and dipped his own. Soon they glided through the relatively calm waters. The fire could be seen through the withered remains of saltbark trees, many of which appeared to have been smothered in volcanic ash. An oily film coated the water and at times was so thick that it clung to their oars. As they moved past a small island, their view of the fire was finally unobstructed, though there seemed to be no one about.

"Do you see anyone?" Farsy asked in a whisper.

"No," Catrin said. The fire was built on a wooden platform that extended between the roots of a saltbark tree and a nearby rock outcropping. Looking back to the other boats waiting in the distance, she saw Chase slip into the dark water.

* * *

"Looks like a trap," Chase said. "Hold back." He and Bryn used their oars to slow the boat, keeping it in relative darkness. "Wait here." Flexing the muscles of his arms and shoulders, Chase silently lowered himself into the water. With his belt knife between his teeth, he slipped beneath the surface.

Swimming as far as he could on a single breath, Chase moved to the other side of the fire, and there he slowly broke the surface. Not far away, someone else watched from the water. Giving them no time to escape him, Chase moved closer. With one swift motion, he brought his knife up to the man's throat. "One move and I give my knife a good yank."

Behind him the water stirred, and Chase had no time to react before the tip of a crude spear was driven under his chin, slamming his mouth shut.

"One move and you'll be a head on a stick."

* * *

Trying to locate Chase again, having lost sight of him when he went underwater, Catrin looked about, cursing the darkness and the light. A commotion on the far side of the platform got her attention, and she leaned out far, trying to get a better look.

"By the gods! Is it you?" came Chase's voice over the water. "Benjin! Fasha!"

Still overextended, Catrin's knees buckled, and she nearly fell face-first into the water, but Farsy grabbed her and pulled her back into the boat. Their boat swayed, nearly capsizing, but Catrin looked up in time to see Benjin climb from the water.

Standing on the platform, the flames casting a rosy glow over him; he looked nothing like the man Catrin remembered. Long, mostly gray hair was plastered to his face and fell to his shoulders. His beard, which he had always kept trimmed, was now long and straggly. Thinner, but still well muscled, he wore only a loincloth.

A moment later, Fasha and Chase joined him. She wore little more than Benjin, and her skin shone like gold. Catrin could form no words and began to sob. A wave of relief crashed over her, and she tumbled in the surf. Only Farsy's strong hands kept her from falling over, and she clung to him, overwhelmed by emotion.

"I'm here, li'l miss!" Benjin said, his voice rough and gravelly. Catrin could take no more. Standing, she jumped into the water and swam as fast as she could to meet Benjin, who immediately swam to meet her. When at last they touched, Catrin latched on to him and would not let go. Still sobbing, she clung to him all the way back to the *Slippery Eel*.

181

"I thought you were dead," she said haltingly. "We searched--"

"I know you did, li'l miss. I know. The currents carried us away, and though we saw you, you could not see us. You never made it close enough to hear us, but we know you tried."

As the water slipped by, Catrin looked up the see a dryad peeking around her saltbark tree. With a silent thank you, Catrin closed her eyes and cried.

* * *

Shaved, washed, and clothed, Benjin looked more like the man Catrin remembered, but the gray dominating his hair and beard made him look much older. As he raised a mug of water, his hand trembled, and she tried to hide her concern.

"A few planks of my deck held together," Fasha said. "Benjin and I used it as a raft and paddled our way back to the shallows. We nearly lost the raft when the cloud of fire came. We both ducked underwater and held our breath for as long as we could. When we came back up, the raft was far away."

"Fasha is a strong swimmer," Benjin said, pride in his eyes. "She caught up to it and brought it back to me."

"You could've caught it yourself," Fasha said, "if you hadn't already begun to take a chill. Thought I was going to lose him for a while there, but the saltbark leaf seemed to help a great deal--that and being dry and warm."

"Wood was hard to find," Benjin said, "and neither of us wanted to be without a fire. When I was strong enough, we swam to the Zjhon ship and, each day, we brought back more wood. The Zjhon had fairly well stripped the ship of anything else of use, but we were happy to burn what was left."

"I wanted to build a boat and sail back into trade waters, but Benjin insisted you would come back. Thank the gods he was right. Otherwise, I might've had to feed him to the sharks."

Catrin told the tale of their adventures. Benjin and Fasha listened, obviously having a difficult time believing all they heard. As if he knew when his name was being spoken, Prios joined them, keeping his eyes downcast.

"Do not fear us," Benjin said. "You helped save Catrin, and for that I'll always be grateful."

Prios bowed his head to Benjin and Fasha then slipped into the shadows, seemingly reluctant to be the focus of attention. When Catrin began to tell more of Kyrien, a hush fell over the room, and Benjin looked thoughtful. "You're attached to this dragon in some way?" he asked.

"I won't claim to understand it," Catrin said, "but yes. I think so. He was waiting for us when we reached the Keys of Terhilian, and part of me hopes to see him again, but I don't know if I ever will. He's so regal and beautiful, I find it difficult to describe. Belegra was willing to torture and destroy him . . . for this." Holding out her hand, she revealed the dragon ore carving.

Even in the dim lamplight, Catrin's panther gleamed, its simplicity making it all the more striking. Smooth lines and subtle curves showed the mighty cat, alert and ready to pounce. So aggressive was its stance that it was uncomfortable to view the carving from the front, yet there was playfulness about it.

"Where did you get that?" Benjin asked, reaching his hand out slowly, seemingly almost afraid to touch it.

"Belegra used Kyrien to create dragon ore. I brought his chunk of ore back with me, but it seemed unbalanced, as if it needed to be in a different form. So I carved it."

"How did you come up with the cat shape?" Osbourne asked.

"It's a panther, I think. I just looked into the stone before I started carving, and I could see the shape of the panther already inside it, waiting."

Waiting for you to set it free.

Catrin gave a start and looked up to meet eyes with Prios.

You set the panther free. Just as you did for me and for Kyrien. You freed the panther from a prison of stone, but you have forgotten something, something special, something important.

183

"Is something wrong, li'l miss?"

"I'm fine," Catrin said. "Sorry. Prios can speak in my mind, and he was reminding me that I've overlooked something." Looking into the eyes of the carving, Catrin opened herself to it, seeking its name.

Koe.

More a thought than a voice in her mind, the name came to her and she spoke it aloud. It felt powerful and right, and though the panther looked no different than it had before, Catrin found she saw Koe in a new way. The name felt right.

It's a good name, Prios said in her mind.

"Seems quite fitting," Benjin said at almost the same time, and others nodded in agreement.

"I saved all the chunks and slivers of stone that I cut away, and I plan to experiment with them. My gut tells me there is a great deal I can learn from them."

"You must use caution," Benjin said. "You know the power of dragon ore and how devastating a mistake could be."

"I know," Catrin said as she carefully slid Koe back into her pocket.

"Can Prios speak in others' minds?" Fasha asked suddenly. "I mean, other than yours, Catrin?"

I could speak to Belegra and the others in the cadre. I never tried with anyone else except you. It is more difficult over distance. I find it easiest if I can touch the person I wish to speak to.

Catrin relayed his words, and Fasha seemed disappointed, but Benjin looked thoughtful.

"If someone can hear Prios," he said, "then that would mean they almost certainly have access to Istra's power."

Yes, Prios answered in Catrin's mind, and she relayed his answer.

"Prios," Benjin said. "Would you mind trying to talk to those of us on this ship? If we know someone has access to the power, then maybe Catrin can help them develop their abilities."

"I'm not so sure how much help I'll be," Catrin said.

I want to do this. You can free these people too. I want to help you free them all.

184

His words were an inspiration, but they also brought tremendous responsibility, the weight of which was nearly crushing. It made her feel as if she alone were responsible for the fate of the world. The feeling passed, and she told the rest what Prios said. His words brought tears to Fasha's eyes, and Benjin shook his hand. Prios seemed unsure of how to respond, but then he reached out and laid his hand on Benjin's shoulder. Benjin's eyes showed disappointment when Prios simply shook his head.

Chase and Osbourne were the next to be disappointed, but then Prios laid his hand on Strom's shoulder.

"I heard him! He said, 'Be free'!" Strom cried out and Prios nodded his head. Catrin and the others were stunned, and no one said a word. Prios continued around the room, and when he laid his hand on Fasha, she gasped. In the next moment, she underwent a transformation. First her face flushed, then she smiled, then she cried. Prios simply nodded when Kenward, too, heard his words.

Brother Vaughn and Grubb were the only others among those left on the ship who could hear Prios. Grubb seemed more confused than excited. In contrast, the rest seemed to have nothing but questions, and Catrin sighed, knowing answers were far too rare.

* * *

As the hammock cradled Catrin, the motions of the ship lulled her, and she let her mind wander. So much of her world had changed, and she couldn't imagine what would come next. With the help of Prios, she had attempted to teach the others how to access Istra's power, but they had no success. The others simply seemed incapable of connecting themselves with the flow. Maybe someday she would find a way to teach others, but for the moment, she made herself think about other things.

Images of her father and uncle and her home flooded her mind. Tears coursed down tracks that Catrin thought might carve valleys in her flesh if she cried any more, but still the tears came.

You will see your home again. And you will set them all free.

Prios's voice was like a whisper in her mind, and Catrin wondered if she had only dreamed it, but sleep claimed her in the next breath. His voice whispered in her dreams, caressing her, and she wrapped herself in his energy like a warm embrace.

Sleep well.

* * *

In the morning light, the lookouts scoured the waters for a safe course. Retracing their route back through the massive fallen columns, they moved into slightly deeper water, and for a while Catrin felt almost safe. With Benjin by her side, the world seemed a brighter place. Sadness still clung to her for the loss of so many others, but at least he had been returned to her, as if the gods had truly shown mercy. Fasha never seemed to be far away, and Catrin wondered at the change in both of them. The looks they exchanged often spoke of more than friendship.

Even in calm waters, there was much work to be done, and most of their time was spent assisting the crew. Weakened repairs were mended, and the *Slippery Eel* was once again watertight. When the end of the shallows finally came into view, Catrin felt a stirring in her stomach. She was another step closer to home, but no one could know what awaited them in deep water.

"Get the fishing gear ready," Kenward ordered, and the crew began making preparations, all the while watching the seas for any signs of sharks. After the trawls had been dropped, everyone waited in tense anticipation. Knowing they must fish or starve, the threat of sharks had them all on edge. Kenward took no chances, though.

"Pull in the trawls!" he commanded. "If we caught anything, there'll be blood in the water. I want to be well away from here before we drop the tubs again."

Though the fish were biting, what they caught was small, and Kenward's precautions made the process of filling the hold painfully slow. Big sharks were sighted on several occasions, but Kenward did his best to use the wind and currents to his advantage, and they filled the hold without

186

any attacks. Exhausted, the crew finally allowed themselves to relax.

Catrin stood at the stern and watched the water slip away, silently hoping to see Kyrien flying on the winds. Prios stood by her side but said nothing, comforting her with his presence alone.

* * *

By the light of a small lamp, Chase looked at his companions and smiled. He and Strom and Osbourne had been through a great deal together, and now Prios was quickly becoming a part of their group. Chase found that he had sorely misjudged Prios. His quiet and reserved demeanor was unnerving. The fact that he had no tongue made it almost difficult to look upon him for the images it brought to mind, but Chase was beginning to see beyond those things. Slowly, Prios revealed himself as a vibrant personality with both a mischievous streak and a sense of humor.

Though there was always work to be done on a ship, Chase liked to make certain that they all spent some time together, and their late-night talks often lasted until the sunrise. Most times Catrin would join them, but on this night she had complained of a headache and gone to her hammock earlier than usual.

Strom began telling tales, and Prios seemed enthralled by his dramatic reenactments of events. After hearing stories of how Chase had trained at being stealthy, Prios made eye contact with Chase. Using his amazing ability of expressing himself with only his facial expressions and body language, he sized Chase up, smiled, and issued an unspoken challenge. Though Chase could not hear Prios speak in his mind, he had no trouble deciphering the challenge: If you are such a mighty sneak, then prove it!

"What would be the hardest thing to steal on this ship?" Strom asked with a knowing grin.

"Catrin's staff?" Osbourne asked.

Prios turned his nose up, and Strom snorted. "Too easy."

187

"She never takes Koe out of her pocket. I bet she sleeps with him under her pillow."

Prios gave a firm nod.

"Koe it is," Strom said.

Chase smiled, put his hands behind his head, and yawned. "Is that all?"

A sly look crossed Prios's face, and he waved for Strom to lean closer. Reaching out, he laid his hand on Strom's shoulder.

"Ha!" Strom barked. "He says to make it a real challenge, I will stand guard at the prow and Osbo will stand guard at the stern. If either of us sees you, then you've failed."

"And if I succeed?"

Prios shrugged, seeming to think it was unlikely, and that just made Chase even more determined.

"If you succeed," Strom said, "we'll all bow down and show due respect for the master sneak."

"Good enough for me," Chase said.

* * *

Osbourne strained his eyes and ears, trying his best to catch Chase in the act. Though a part of him wanted Chase to succeed, it would be a true victory only if they did their best to stop him. At the slightest sound, Osbourne whipped around and ran to the gunwales. Had he heard a splash? Watching the dark water slide by, he saw nothing beyond the usual wake left by the *Eel*. Convinced he'd been hearing things, he returned to his post.

No more sounds, save the snapping of sails, the creak of rigging, and the sound of the water rushing by, broke the silence. Even the crew was silent, as if they knew what was transpiring, and Osbourne found the stillness unnerving. When Strom walked around the corner, he nearly leaped from his skin.

"Did you see anything?"

"No," Osbourne said. "I thought I heard something, but I didn't see anything."

Strom just shook his head, "I didn't either, but Prios came to get me, and Chase is all smiles. How do you think he got by us?"

"I don't know," Osbourne said. "I think he may have tricked me."

"Let's go find out."

As they entered Chase's cabin, Osbourne was surprised to see Chase as dry as tinder. "I was certain you'd gone over the side."

"That's what I wanted you to think," Chase said with a triumphant grin.

"So let's see it," Strom said, his arms crossed over his chest.

Chase just grinned and reached for his pocket, but then the color drained from his face, and his victorious bravado suddenly changed to anxious desperation. For a moment, he searched his pockets, and then he searched the cabin. "She's going to kill me."

"You never actually stole it, did you?" Strom asked, seeming almost hopeful.

"I swear to you: I took it, and now it's gone."

Tense silence hung over the group, and Osbourne thought Chase might actually cry. When Prios's shoulders began to shake, the others turned to him, thinking he was overcome with remorse, but he surprised them all when he made the first sound any of them had ever heard from him. Though the gift of speech had been taken from him, he proved that Belegra had not taken the life from him when he laughed. So pure and joyous was his laughter, that the others simply waited in silence to find out what could possibly have tickled him so.

With a look of apology, he ended Chase's torment as he produced Koe from a concealed pocket in his shirt.

"How did you--? When did--? Oh, for the love of everything good and right in this world, forget it. I don't want to know," Chase said, and without saying any more, he stormed into the night.

Osbourne looked at Strom, and for the first time in a long time, they laughed.

189

"That really wasn't very nice," Catrin said when Prios told her about how he had tricked Chase. A sly smile crept across his face, yet a hint of blush shaded his cheeks. "And I would appreciate it if you would challenge him to steal someone else's things next time." Again, Prios simply smiled in response. Every day they spent together seemed to bring them closer. With increasing frequency, he showed that, in many cases, he could communicate without the need to speak in her mind. It seemed he had a talent for expressing himself without speech or words. Others, too, had made note of this talent, and Catrin was grateful for it, as it seemed to make his life aboard the ship much easier. Knowing he could communicate in other ways just made the times when he did speak even more special.

Though I look forward to seeing you reunited with your family and your homeland, I must admit that I am afraid.

"Afraid? What are you afraid of?"

What if your people do not accept me? What if your family does not like me? I'm not certain my story will give them reason to trust me, and I fear I will only make things worse for you.

With his shoulders hunched and his eyes cast down, Catrin could feel his pain and anxiety. Though she tried to put herself in his position, to understand how he must be feeling, she found it impossible. The circumstances of his life were just too far from anything she had ever experienced, and though she could sympathize, she knew she would never completely understand. "Once they come to see your true nature, they will come to feel as I do."

And how, exactly, do you feel about me?

Though he did not truly speak, it was as if Catrin could hear the tremble in his voice. Something in his emotion was betrayed to her, and she sensed his fear and anxiety. In that moment, she realized the courage it had taken for him to ask. "I think . . ." she hesitated, and he raised his eyes to meet hers. In them, she saw not only fear, but hope as well. "I think I love you."

* * *

When land was finally sighted again, Catrin could barely contain her excitement. All of them had known the *Slippery Eel* was too small to make the journey to the Falcon Isles safely, but they had unanimously chosen expedience over caution. Storms had chased them and rogue waves appeared without warning, but somehow they had survived. The Falcon Isles were the last stop Catrin planned to make before she returned to the Godfist, and she did not intend to stay long. Nora insisted they take a week to make proper repairs, but Catrin hoped the job could be done in less time. Each day seemed longer than the last, and she wasn't certain how much longer she could stand the anticipation.

As the smaller islands slid by, Catrin moved to Nora's side. Fasha and Benjin stood not far away, and they turned when Catrin addressed Nora. "Will you leave from the Falcon Isles to go back to the *Trader's Wind?*"

"A big part of me wishes to do just that, but I know I would only spend my days worrying over your fate. I've come too far to leave you just now. I must see this to the finish. I wish to see you reunited with your family, and only when you are safe will I return to my ship," Nora said with a firm nod.

"Thank you," Catrin said. "I owe you and your family a great debt. I only hope I can find a way to repay you someday."

"Nonsense," Nora said. "We've only done what was right. You owe us nothing. Given the chance, I'd do it all again."

"Trade vessel ahead," the lookout called, and the crew gathered at the gunwales, anxious to see another human face. It was thrilling to see someone besides her shipmates, and excitement ran through her as the ship slid by. The crew of the trade ship eyed them with suspicion, but a few were brave enough to offer a wave. There was the chance that hostile ships would also be in the area, and most kept their eyes to the seas, but there was still an air of celebration aboard the ship. Grubb prepared a special meal using spices

191

and stores normally kept under strict ration, and many a tale was told. Catrin smiled and laughed more than she had for a very long time, and when some of the crewmembers began to sing, she danced.

* * *

Straining under the weight of the planks she carried, Catrin asked Benjin to stop so they could rest. The walk from the lumber mill to the docks was not long, but the way was crowded and it took effort to weave their way through. When a man passed by whom Catrin thought she recognized, she assumed she must be mistaken.

"Things have changed," Benjin said, reading her face. "That was Kenmar Wills. You know him because he used to live in Harborton. It would seem there are many people here from the Godfist. This entire town has grown up in the time we've been gone. I can only imagine what we'll find when we return to the Godfist."

Catrin tried not to let his words dampen her excitement, but beneath her desire to get home was a petrifying fear that things had changed too much, that her home no longer existed. With a grunt, she lifted her end of the planks, and they began walking back to the *Eel*.

"That's the last of it," Benjin said when they finally reached the deck.

"Take the rest of the day off," Kenward said. "We've got the materials we need now."

"I need to go look for someone," Catrin said after retrieving her staff.

Benjin frowned. "Nat Dersinger?"

"Yes."

"If you must," Benjin said with a sigh. "I don't want you going alone, though. Take Chase with you."

Though she wanted to go alone, Catrin didn't argue. She'd considered asking Prios to come along, but what she truly needed was time to talk to Nat--alone. Chase seemed to agree with Benjin and followed her down the gangplank. "It'll be good to have my feet on solid ground for a while," he said, and despite his casual tone, Catrin knew he would come whether she wished it or not.

Though solid, the land itself created feelings of uncertainty, as there were still signs of devastation everywhere. It seemed unfathomable that an eruption so very far away could cause so much destruction. A distinct line stretched from coast to coast, showing how high the water had gotten. It was a wonder anyone survived. The docks and the buildings that stood were apparently new construction using materials recovered after the water receded.

Most of the people they passed were busy with their own tasks and paid no attention to Catrin and Chase. A few cast suspicious glances; others hawked their wares. Catrin stopped to look at some sausages, knowing how Benjin loved them. She bought three varieties, and after she'd paid, she asked the man if he knew of Nat Dersinger. The man's face turned from friendly to sour, and he just pointed to a place at the end of the docks, where civilization ended and the forest began. Catrin thanked him, but he seemed eager to have her away from him, and she and Chase began walking toward the end of the docks.

When she saw birds take flight from behind a nearby building, Catrin wondered if word of her coming were already on its way to the Godfist. If it were, there was nothing she could do about it, and she just kept walking.

"We're not going to be able to find anyone out there," Chase said, but then he stopped short when a tall man stepped into their path. A skirt of reeds covered his loins, but the rest of his body was covered in red paint, with white and black markings painted strategically to make him look better muscled than he actually was. Atop his head was a crown of vines, and the black paint around his eyes gave him an angry appearance. He leaned on a simple wooden staff, but only when he spoke did Catrin recognize him.

"Greetings, Catrin."

Chapter 16

Evil often hides beneath a veil of righteousness.
--Fetter Bains, agnostic

* * *

"Come," Nat said, and he led them to a narrow but well-worn trail that wove through the rotting mass and into the forest. "It's not far."

"Why are you dressed like that?" Chase asked.

"I have joined the Gunata, a tribe native to the islands. I married the daughter of a chieftain, and I have become a leader within the tribe."

"You're married?" Catrin asked, and Nat smiled. Despite the paint he wore, it was the warmest smile she'd ever seen from him. There was a light in his eyes, and the fear fled from her; all that remained was the desire to meet the one who made Nat so cheerful. "That's wonderful. I'm so happy for you!" Charging forward, she hugged him, getting his paint all over her clothing.

"Come. I must bring you to the elders. They've been waiting for you."

"Waiting? How did you know we were coming," Chase asked, suspicious.

"I had a vision," Nat said without hesitation. Chase rolled his eyes but said no more. Beyond a turn, they came to a place where the trail emptied into a lush meadow. The land rolled gently and was blanketed in thick grasses. In the middle was a large fire surrounded by the silhouettes of people, most of which stopped and turned to watch them approach.

Speaking in a tongue Catrin did not understand, Nat announced them. None of the Gunata spoke or approached; they simply watched as Catrin and Chase followed Nat to a massive log. Here he sat and gestured for everyone else to be seated. Catrin sat next to Nat and Chase beside her. From the crowd of Gunata, one woman approached. Dressed in a wrap of woven palm adorned with flowers of every description, she came straight to Catrin. Going to one knee, she kissed Catrin's hand. "Thank you," she said in a thick accent, but the look in her eyes effectively conveyed her message.

"Catrin, Chase, this is my wife, Neenya," Nat said. Neenya wore a warm smile, but her eyes were timid. Catrin returned her smile. Neenya sat on the other side of Nat, and now the entire group was seated in a circle around the fire. "When I arrived here, the Gunata seemed to be waiting for me, just as they have waited for you. I tried to communicate with them, but they only pointed to the mountain. Neenya took me there. The way was difficult, but what I found there was worth it. Atop the mountain is a sacred place, a place where the visions are much stronger and clearer. I must take you there. That is what they are waiting for."

"You and your visions," Chase said, clearly disgusted. "We're finally ready to go home, and you want to drag Catrin into the jungle because of a daydream."

"The visions are far from daydreams," Nat said in a level voice. The Gunata seemed unsettled by the tone of Chase's words. "I don't know how to convince you, but I will try. Things are seldom specific in my visions, but as I said, they are stronger atop the mount. In a vision, I saw Catrin riding a wave."

"That's it?" Chase asked.

"Let him finish," Catrin said.

"Catrin rode atop a white cat--a panther, I believe," Nat said.

Chase's eyes went wide and he choked, which set him into a fit of coughing. Catrin simply reached into her pocket and pulled out Koe. When the Gunata saw the shining cat, they all began to talk at once. Nat just nodded. "Will you come?" he asked, looking Catrin in the eye.

"I will."

* * *

"I don't like it," Benjin said.

"I agree," Chase added.

"I'm going," Catrin said. "You can choose to believe whatever you wish, but I believe Nat's visions deserve

195

credence. After all, he's been right before. Kenward said he'd wait for us, and Prios can contact me if there is trouble, so let's just go and get it done. Then we can go home."

Benjin and Chase seemed to realize that arguing would get them nowhere. After grabbing their packs, they followed Catrin down the gangplank. Waiting below, dressed for hiking, Nat seemed annoyed that Benjin chose to come along, but he said nothing; instead he just led them back onto the trail. As they walked past where the Gunata were gathered, Neenya joined them and took the lead. She, too, was dressed in leathers.

Nat dropped back to walk beside Catrin. "There was something else puzzling about my vision," he said in a low voice meant for only Catrin's ears. "I see the stones you have mounted in the staff, and I suppose that explains the dragon with gleaming eyes, but the dragon in my vision flew."

"Then it was another dragon you saw. His name is Kyrien."

Nat stopped and stared at Catrin a moment but said nothing as Chase and Benjin stood waiting. It was a while before he spoke again. "You've seen a real dragon?"

"Yes. More than one."

Shaking his head and muttering under his breath, Nat walked in what seemed a daze. "I had hoped you would prove my visions false, but you have not. There have been other visions since, each more terrifying than the last. There are troubled times ahead for our world, Catrin. We must prepare."

"What did you see?" she asked.

"I cannot even describe the horrors I've seen, but I can tell you this: There will be a time of great prosperity that will lull most into complacency, but you must be vigilant. You must remind them of the danger that lurks just beyond the horizon. You must learn to live beneath the soil, and you must learn to grow food there, or you and yours will perish."

"What dangers do you foresee? What foe do we face?"

"It's impossible for me to say. I've seen death flow from the skies and the seas. I've seen the land itself coil up and strike you. In my dreams, though, you have stood before the coming fury. You, alone, have the power to save us all; you

196

have but to find it, and find it you must, for you do not yet possess the strength you'll need."

"Strength she'll need for what?" Chase asked, and Nat made an annoyed sound.

"Nat's visions bring dire warnings of a peril we have yet to face," Catrin said. "For that, I will need strength."

Chase seemed to want to say something more, but he bit his lip and remained silent. The forest grew thick around the trail until the trail itself disappeared. Following Neenya, they meandered through lush greenery and vicious needle-vines. Neenya did her best to choose a clear path, but still they had to remain always watchful for danger. Nat explained that Neenya's sharp hiss was a warning when danger was near, and Catrin jumped every time she heard it. Sometimes she failed to even see what danger Neenya warned of, but other times she saw snakes, dangerous plants, and once, a bright red scorpion.

"The blood scorpion is said to have a sting like fire," Benjin said as he avoided the small but deadly creature.

Neenya seldom stopped, but when she did, she generally collected edible fruits, berries, nuts, and roots. On one occasion, though, she stopped in a thicket of tall, stalklike plants with green stems as thick as a man's fist. Using her long knife, Neenya cut down one of the stalks, carefully cutting along one of the many brown rings that divided the stalks into sections. After handing each member of the party a section, she showed them how to cut the top open and drink from the strange plant. The milky juice was sticky and sweet with a tangy aftertaste, but it left Catrin feeling refreshed.

As darkness began to fall, Neenya immediately chose a place to make camp and set about building a fire. The place she chose to camp looked as if it had been used recently; Neenya built her fire on the remains of another.

"It is not safe in the jungle at night," Nat said. "Only fire will keep the predators at a distance, and even then you must be cautious. There are snakes here that can swallow a person whole."

"Was this your camp?"

197

"Yes. Neenya and I have camped here before. There are several campsites along the way that we may be able to find. Others have already been reclaimed by the jungle."

Catrin pulled a fallen log closer to the fire, and after checking it thoroughly for scorpions, she sat.

While everyone was busy setting up camp, Nat pulled Catrin to the side. "The visions I had were of challenges that await, but I know there are more immediate dangers you need to be aware of. I'm as certain as the sun."

"And you think I will learn something from seeing this place?"

"I can only say what I feel," Nat said. "All my instincts say you must go there."

Catrin said no more, and when Benjin approached, Nat seemed to suddenly realize he had some task waiting for him.

"What did he have to say?" Benjin asked.

"He thinks it's important that I go to the mountain," Catrin said. "I think he believes I will have a vision."

"What do you think?"

"I'm not sure. I should be excited about a place that might give me some insight, but I have a sour feeling in my stomach. Either way, I have to do this for Nat. I hope you can understand that."

"I suppose I do, li'l miss," Benjin said, and he patted Catrin on the shoulder as he rose to look for food. "The world always looks brighter on a full stomach."

* * *

With one arm holding a cloth over her face, Catrin climbed, trying to keep the sand out of her eyes, nose, and mouth, but it was impossible. The wind played tricks, growing calm only to suddenly return full force, driving sand and dirt before it.

"We should wait until the wind dies down," Benjin yelled through the cloth he held over his face. Catrin barely heard him as the wind screamed and growled around them.

"It will not get better any time soon," Nat said. "And then it will rain."

Careful not to lean too heavily into the wind, Catrin tried to be ready for when it died down without warning. Already she had stumbled twice and nearly fallen, only Benjin's firm grip on her jacket had kept her upright. Choosing her steps with greater care, she tried not to look down, for every step took them higher.

When they finally reached the chamber atop the mountain, Nat led Catrin in. Within, the wind still howled at her, but it no longer touched her, and Catrin instantly felt safer. Much of the floor was covered in a layer of dirt, but what was exposed was a marvel. Intricate patterns and circular drawings coexisted in orderly chaos, and rods of colorful metal were inset in the floor, bisecting it at regular angles. In the ceiling of the chamber were three precisely sized and spaced holes that let in sunlight. To her right stood a large opening that looked out over the world below. Amazed by how far she could see, Catrin was overwhelmed by the sense of height the view gave her, and her guts constricted.

"Come here and look out to the seas," Nat said.

"I can't," Catrin said, suddenly terrified.

"It'll be fine, li'l miss. I'll be right here holding on to ya."

Slowly, deliberately, Catrin moved toward the opening. Then she stuck her head outside until she could no longer see the chamber walls in her periphery, her face exposed to raging currents. For a moment she simply stared out across the landscape, but then her vision began to swim. Only the feeling of Benjin's grip kept her from screaming. Slowly he began to pull her back, but something was happening. "No," she said. "Just hold me."

Benjin did as she asked, and she watched as the landscape morphed.

A crowd gathered outside the Masterhouse. With their arms in the air, they chanted. Above, on a raised dais, stood her father, his hands tied behind his back.

"Treason," said a thundering voice, and Catrin shuddered as its deep vibrations assaulted her being. "The penalty is death!" His words hammered Catrin's chest like a physical blow. Howling, she ran forward as the headsman raised his axe. The crowd parted before her, but a single figure rose up to dominate her sight. The glowing face of

Istra stood between Catrin and her father, and she screamed, howling in frustration.

Gasping for breath, Catrin fell back into Benjin's arms, but only a moment did she allow herself to recover. A tickling around her nostrils and a warm sensation brought her hand to her nose, and it came away covered in blood.

"We've got to get her down from here," Benjin said with a scathing glance at Nat.

"We have to hurry," Catrin said. "Have to get home."

* * *

"Is she hurt," a voice called, and Catrin stirred.

"She just needs rest," Benjin said, his deep voice close to her ear.

Only then did Catrin realize she was being carried, and she pulled her head away from Benjin's neck. "How did you get me down?"

"Chase and I took turns carrying you."

Unable to imagine how difficult it must have been to carry her down the mountain, Catrin just closed her eyes and let Benjin carry her to her cabin.

"We have to get back to the Godfist, or they're going to kill my father," she managed to say before sleep claimed her again, and she saw the shock in Benjin's eyes, though she never heard his response.

* * *

"How close is the *Eel* to being fully repaired?" Benjin asked.

"There are one or two places where we may need to reinforce a cracked beam or the like," Kenward said, "but she's seaworthy."

"Is there any way we can make extra speed for this trip? We have good reason to believe that Wendel is in mortal danger."

"There's not much we can do but run light," Kenward said. "Problem with that is you can get awfully hungry before the fish start biting."

200

"Is it a chance you'd be willing to take?" Benjin asked, locking eyes with Kenward. Both knew the stakes.

"I'd be willing to take that chance, and perhaps one more," Kenward said with a sly wink. "I had some new sails made and some extra rigging hung. Mother thinks I've lost my senses, but I know the *Eel* can take the speed, and more speed means less time spent hungry."

"That's your problem, fool boy," Nora said. "Always thinking with your stomach."

"Aye," Kenward said. "Keeps me well fed. We've no more time to waste, I suppose. I'll just make sure the crew is done loading, and then we'll be under sail."

* * *

Standing at the prow, Catrin held onto the railing as the *Slippery Eel* knifed through the water, her extra sails filled with wind and driving her forward with tremendous force. Even so, no amount of sail could make the journey from the Falcon Isles to the Godfist short, and Catrin was made to wait. Most of her time was spent pacing the decks like an angry cat, her hand caressing the carving in her pocket. At those times she thought she might be more comfortable in the form of a panther than anything else, and she wondered about something Barabas had once said. She wondered if she had ever truly lived as a panther, or a butterfly, or even a whale. It seemed too strange to be true, yet she felt an affinity to each of those creatures, and she was left to wonder.

The others tried to keep her company, but they, too, were anxious, and their anxiety poured over Catrin like a wave. Eventually she found herself alone, driven to near madness by the waiting. Unwilling to do nothing, she began to experiment with ways to make ship move faster. At first, she tried pushing more air into the sails, but her efforts were both ineffective and extremely draining, thus she abandoned that approach.

In a moment of sudden clarity, Catrin wondered of she'd ever lived as a bird. The thought gave her an idea. After a lot of thought and experimentation--moving her hand up and down in the wind and feeling the way the air currents changed--Catrin decided to try using a narrow band of energy, like a wing, to slice the air. Her first attempts had no noticeable effect, but as she formed her wing of energy into different shapes, holding it at varying angles, she suddenly felt tremendous drag applied to the ship. It was not the desired effect, but it was a significant effect with relatively little effort. Reversing the curve of her energy wing produced an equally significant increase in the ship's speed; it was as if she were lifting the ship, causing it to ride higher in the water.

Before she went any further, she searched for Kenward, who was arguing with Bryn over the ship's suddenly erratic performance.

". . . can't find anything wrong, sir," Bryn was saying as she approached.

"Then look again," Kenward snapped.

"Bryn, wait," Catrin said, and though he turned his head, he kept moving.

Kenward met Catrin's eyes and called Bryn back. "What's this about?"

"I wanted to see if I could make the ship go faster," Catrin said, and Kenward's eyes bulged. Of all the things he'd seen her do with the power, the thought of her propelling *his* ship seemed to disturb him greatly. "At first I only managed to slow us down, but I reversed my technique and the ship seemed to speed up."

"By the gods," Bryn said. "*That's* what that was?"

"I've never felt anything like it before," Kenward said, and Nora, who had been inspecting the ship for problems, now stood at his side. "It was as if we'd emptied the hold and lightened the ship. Can you do it again?"

"We have no idea how this will affect the ship," Nora said. "It would a dangerous thing to try, and knowing you, that's all the incentive you'll need to try it, but you've been warned." After wagging her finger in Kenward's face, she walked away.

"Do you think it's safe for me to try?" Catrin asked, now unsure of herself.

"I'll put the men in the hold on guard, and they can tell us if there are any problems developing. I'm anxious to reach the Godfist on your father's behalf and yours. Nothing would make me happier than a way to shorten this particular voyage."

"Then I'll try," Catrin said. "I'll use only a small wing at first."

"A wing?" Kenward asked, but then he shook his head. "Forget I asked. I'm not certain I want to know yet. Maybe you can tell me afterward."

The conversation had drawn attention, and most of the crew stopped what they were doing long enough to at least steal a glance at Catrin. She stood at the prow, her arms cast wide, her staff in one hand and Koe in the other. It took her a moment to find the correct angle and curvature again, but when she did, she felt the ship surge ahead.

"You're doing it!" Kenward shouted, his face a mixture of horror and fascination, which turned more and more to excitement. "Damage report!"

"The hull is showing no signs of stress, sir," Bryn said. "If anything, I'd say there seems to be less stress."

"Catrin, you may use a larger wing," Kenward said with a firm nod.

Bending her will to the task, Catrin opened herself to more power, and she expanded the size of her wing. As she applied her will, she could almost see her diaphanous formation of energy take shape. The ship rose higher in the water, and the crew stood in shock as the ship moved faster than ever before, but there was a sudden lurch when Catrin lost her concentration.

I'm sorry I surprised you.

Prios's voice in her mind and the energy he lent her gave Catrin the power to test larger wing formations and even multiple wings on each side. When she used two large wings, level with the deck, and a pair of wings from the top of every mast, everything changed. The ship moved at unbelievable speed.

"May the gods have mercy!" Nora said. "We're flying!"

Chapter 17

The greatest gifts are those not expected.
--Missa Banks, healer and mother

* * *

The wind blowing in her face, Catrin let the salt air refresh her and keep her alert. With Prios to bolster her, she kept the ship sailing on the winds. Others had tried to help-- those who had heard Prios in their minds--but Catrin was unable to connect with them. Their energy was inaccessible to her, and she decided it would be best if it remained that way.

Only during storms and times when Kenward thought there might be fish did she and Prios rest. Although, some of Kenward's recent requests for time to fish seemed contrived, and Catrin suspected Benjin convinced him to lie for the sake of getting her to rest. In truth, she scolded herself for abusing Prios. How she used her own energy was her choice, but she had no right to choose for Prios. Seeking him out, she sat beside him and apologized.

You have not coerced me. What I've done, I've done of my own free will. I am free, and no one will ever enslave me again. For now, I must rest, and so should you.

Though she left feeling silly, it made Catrin feel better to know that she was not misusing her relationship with Prios. His dedication to her cause bolstered her will, and she went to her hammock smiling. Soon she would be home.

* * *

"She's coming," Master Jarvis said as he tucked away the message.

"Yes," Humbry said. "I heard. Wendel has not always been my favorite person, but he always seemed to have good sense. It would be good to see him reunited with his daughter. You had Catrin as a student. Didn't you?"

"I did. She was an average student. If I remember correctly, she was easily bored, but she was a good girl overall. I don't think she would hurt any of us. Well, except for maybe Edling."

Humbry chuckled. "Has Beron been at you to side with Edling again?"

"He never stops."

"I thought he might follow me here," Humbry said. "I don't care what they say, Jarvis. I think we should try to make peace with Wendel and his followers."

"They disobeyed a council edict," Master Jarvis said. "Though it was an edict I was tempted to go against myself. I just don't see how we can convince Beron or Baker Hollis."

"I'll do what I can," Humbry said. "A day doesn't go by that one of them doesn't show up at the farm and talk until my ears hurt. Maybe, this time, I'll do all the talking."

* * *

"No one's ever going to believe this," Kenward said as the *Slippery Eel* skimmed across the water.

"Perhaps it's a tale best not told," Nora said.

"The best ones always are."

"On *that* we agree," Nora said.

"I worry about them, though," Kenward said. "They've been at this for weeks, and Catrin is becoming more and more reluctant to take time for rest. It will do no good to reach the Godfist in time if she has no energy left. The physical exhaustion alone would be enough to put most men abed."

"Women are tougher than men," Fasha said.

"Prios doesn't seem to be faring poorly," Kenward countered, but Fasha just rolled her eyes and walked away. "Hopefully he'll not have to endure much longer. It's impossible to say how much time we've saved, but I think we should be getting close."

"I agree," Nora said.

Walking to where Catrin and Prios stood, in what looked like a deep meditative state, Kenward cleared his throat and spoke softly, hoping not to startle Catrin. The thought of his ship suddenly dropping from the air made his stomach hurt. "Can I talk to you while you work?"

"Yes," Catrin responded, her eyes still closed. "It's more difficult when I divide my attention, but I can do it for a short time."

"We should be nearing the Godfist," Kenward said, and he would have sworn the ship surged ahead with his words. "Normally we would only dock at the cove or along the southern coast, but I can't say what things are like on the Godfist these days, and I want your opinion."

"It would take too long for us to travel around the desert, but I also agree that we should probably avoid the harbor."

"Besides going to the harbor," Benjin said as he approached, "landing on the northern tip of the Godfist, where the Zjhon built their lift system, may be the shortest and safest route."

"I agree," Catrin said.

"It's settled, then," Kenward said.

* * *

With their destination set, Catrin felt a renewed sense of urgency. The duration of their voyage and the additional burden of propelling the ship had dulled her panic, despite knowing her father was in no less danger. There was simply no more she could do, and she made herself accept it.

Beside her, Prios made no complaint, but she could sense his exhaustion as poignantly as her own. Cold weather made their task even more difficult. Still, Catrin could not relent--not yet. Every moment brought her closer to the Godfist, closer to her father and her home, and she doubted she could sleep even if she tried.

"Sails to port, sir!"

The lookout's call sent a thrill through Catrin as she realized they must be getting very close. The vessel on the horizon had the look of a fishing boat, and it seemed unlikely that they would be more than a day from shore.

"Catrin," Kenward said. "I don't think we should let anyone see us sailing like this; it might cause a panic. We should make the rest of the trip under sail alone."

Though she agreed with his sentiment, Catrin was loath to release the energy that flowed through her, and when she did, her exhaustion became acute. Still, she refused to leave the deck, despite the icy winds that drove in heavy cloud cover. She didn't want to miss the first sighting of the Godfist, and she remained at the prow, straining her tired eyes. Prios showed that he had better sense and went to his cabin to rest.

* * *

"You can't be thinking of going?" Jensen asked. Wendel unrolled the message and read it once again.

Wendel,
The people have suffered enough. Let us put an end to this struggle. Come to the Masterhouse immediately so that we might settle this matter peacefully.

This letter will serve as notice to all guards. Wendel Volker is to be assisted on his journey to the Masterhouse, and he is to be treated with respect.

I will await you.
Master Edling

"It's obviously a trap," Jensen said.

"We must at least make an attempt at peace," Wendel said. "I owe that much to Catrin."

Jensen looked angry and frustrated. "You'll go alone? Into the hands of those who've already tried to have you killed?"

"I know who we're dealing with," Wendel said. "Edling is not all powerful. There are others who remain that have good sense. I'm sure if I could talk to Jarvis or Humbry, I could convince them to truly make peace."

"This entire meeting is on their terms. I don't like it. We should request neutral ground."

"I don't like it either, but I'm saving my energy to fight for peace instead of territory."

"I suppose you have a point, but I still don't like it," Jensen said.

* * *

"Land!" Catrin called out, proud to have been the first to see her homeland in the distance, and the sight of it was agonizingly sweet. She longed to raise the ship up and fly, but she honored Kenward's wishes. Chase and Prios came to stand by her, just as she caught a whiff of cold but stale air.

"We're almost there," Chase said, but there was something else in his voice and stance. Looking to the sky, he sniffed. "Do you smell that?"

"I smell something foul," Catrin said. "It smells like the shallows did before the mountain exploded."

Chase stayed a moment longer then went in search of those he wanted to thank for all they had done for him, which left Catrin and Prios alone.

"We're nearing my home," Catrin said, "but I doubt I'll be welcomed. There are more dangers ahead, and I'll not ask you to take any more risks. You've done enough. You deserve to live the rest of your life happy and free."

I go where you go. No matter what dangers we face.

"Thank you," she said, unable to find words that would express what she truly felt.

Clouds gathered and darkened the late afternoon, and the foul smell grew stronger, as if the clouds themselves were rank. Cold wind descended and drove the *Slippery Eel* through choppy surf. Catrin went to her cabin in search of warmer clothing. In her pack she found the jacket that Rolph Tillerman had given her, and she pulled it on for the sake of sentiment as much as warmth.

Benjin entered the cabin. "Chase, Strom, and Osbourne are waiting in the galley. I think we all need to sit down and plan out our next moves. We're not out of danger yet."

"Let's go."

The heat of the galley was a welcome change from the frigid air on deck. Catrin sat next to Chase and made eye contact with Strom and Osbourne, but no one spoke a word as they were faced with fears they could no longer deny.

Catrin wondered if her father and uncle were alive, or if Strom and Osbourne had family left to go home to. Fear knotted her stomach, and she began to sweat.

Benjin must have sensed the mood as he entered the galley. "Whether good or bad, the time has come to get the answers to the questions we've had. Though I hope we can all be reunited with our loved ones, we must prepare for the possibility that we may have suffered losses as well." No one else spoke. A pall of sadness hung in the air. "Do not mourn what might not be lost. Be strong for a short time more, and then we'll know. Get your packs ready. Kenward has given me coin and some supplies in case we have need."

As if summoned, Kenward entered. "Sorry I'm late. We're not far from what looks to be the new northern harbor. There're plenty of lights. We can come in, quietly, at the very last dock and probably not be seen, but it's doubtful. Most likely they'll know you're coming. We can go farther east, but not under darkness. The reefs are simply too dangerous to approach after dark."

"What do you think?" Catrin asked everyone gathered.

"This is our homeland," Chase said. "I say we land tonight at the new harbor."

"We need to be careful," Benjin said.

"I agree with Chase," Strom said. "I say we land now."

"Me too," Osbourne said, and everyone turned to Catrin, waiting for her vote.

"We land now," she said.

"Gather your things," Kenward said with an enthusiastic smile. "You will be home soon."

* * *

Only a few lights remained as the *Slippery Eel* glided into the harbor. Catrin had already bade farewell to Kenward, Fasha, Nora, Brother Vaughn, and the rest of the crew, and already she missed them. Three fishermen watched the *Eel* with fear and suspicion as she glided into a slip. The crew scrambled to secure the ship and drop the gangplank.

Tears filled Catrin's eyes as she waved a final farewell; then she walked down the plank. Not liking the way the narrow walkways along the docks moved as she walked, she held her breath until, once again, she placed her feet on the firm soil of the Godfist. Ahead, the three fishermen stood at a long table cleaning fish by torchlight. Even in the darkness, seabirds gathered around to fight over the scraps. The men stopped and watched as Benjin, Catrin, Chase, Strom, Osbourne, and Prios walked by. All three had the look of the Greatland about them, and none chose to speak.

"Good evening," Catrin said as she passed. The men just stared back, seemingly frozen in fear. "How do we get up there?" she asked, pointing to the lights that still illuminated the lift. One of the men pointed to a wide path that led to the lift, and she supposed she would just have to find out when she got there. Her heart raced at the sight of shadowy forms moving at the base of the lift and voices that floated from the shadows.

When they reached the torchlight, the area was clear, and a man was extinguishing the remaining torches. The other people were packed into one of the large wooden boxes that were attached to massive lift ropes. Like oversized crates, the lift boxes could transport people and goods to the tops of the steep cliffs.

"Wait," Benjin said as the man approached the last torch. "We need to get to the top."

"Not tonight you won't," the man said. "This's the last trip up for the day, and we're full up. You'll have to come back in the morning."

"Who goes there?" a voice called from inside the box, and the door flew open. Catrin recognized Cattleman Gerard before he managed to squeeze out of the crowded box. "Benjin? Is that really you?"

"Greetings, Gerard, it's good to see a familiar face," Benjin said. "Where's Wendel?"

"He's gone south of the Wall for the peace treaty. Won't be back for days."

"How about Jensen?"

"He's in Lowerton."

"Where?" Chase asked.

"Ah, yes. Sorry," Gerard said. "I forgot. Lowerton is the new settlement, south of here but north of the Wall." He turned back to the people in the box. "Hey! You all get out of there. These people need to get up top right now. Hurry up!"

A debate raged briefly within the box; then Catrin heard someone say her name. A moment later, people poured out. Watching Catrin and her companions as they boarded the now empty crate, no one said a word. Cattleman Gerard entered the giant crate, which could easily hold forty people, and closed the door behind himself. Catrin watched through the cracks as one of the men yanked on a long rope that hung down from above. Slowly, the crate began to rise into the air, swaying gently at first, but sudden movements often sent it swinging into the timber framework, which groaned in response. Catrin and the others held on tightly to loops of rope that hung on the walls at regular intervals.

A platform came into view, and the crate stopped above it, making them step down as they disembarked, but Catrin didn't care; she was another step closer to her father. The others could go to Lowerton and search for their families, but not her. She was heading south. "What is the Wall you mentioned?" she asked.

"Edling's Wall is what they call it," Gerard said, and already Catrin didn't like it. "They built it after we fled the cold caves. They hit us while we were vulnerable and drove us as far north as they could, and since then, they've held us here. They've been building the Wall to divide north from south ever since. But now there are talks of peace. Your father's gone to the Masterhouse to end the fighting."

Determined, Catrin grabbed a nearby torch and began marching south. The others scrambled to catch up.

"Have you seen my mother or Miss Mariss?" she heard Strom ask, and she slowed a bit so she could hear the answer.

"They're in Lowerton, 'long with Jensen and Osbourne's parents. They've had no end of worry over you, and it'll be an honor to escort you to them."

Catrin nodded, her heart lightened to know no one else stood to lose a parent. Quickening her step, she challenged the rest to keep up.

211

Chase reached her side and cast her a sidelong glance. "You're going to the Masterhouse."

"I can't risk losing him," Catrin said. "I have to go."

"I'm going with you," Chase said as he grabbed her by the arm, making her stop.

"I coming too," Strom said. Benjin crossed his arms over his chest, and Osbourne did the same.

"I can't protect all of you. I can only protect myself. I must go alone."

"No," Benjin said. His stance and that of the others told Catrin that none of them would back down, and she relented. Somehow, she would have to keep them all safe.

Gerard led them along a well-trodden roadway, and after a series of sweeping bends, they gained the shelter of the valley. Ahead waited a bizarre town. "Welcome to Upperton," Gerard said.

Along the dirt roadway stood cylindrical, wooden buildings, and Catrin gasped. The others turned as she stopped, her hands covering her mouth. There stood what remained of the mighty greatoaks, and Catrin was filled with gratitude that they would live on as shelter from those in need. It seemed a fitting tribute. "Why did you use the greatoaks?"

"It was cold," Gerard said. "We needed housing. Your dad suggested we use the fallen greatoaks. It was a lot of work getting them here, but we used the ships we had to tow them to the lift. Took all our ingenuity to get them up here, but a couple of Greatlanders came up with a way to do it. Heck, they dragged a bunch of 'em to Lowerton as well."

Men and women gathered in the streets despite the cold, and Catrin guessed news of their coming had preceded them. No one spoke as she and her companions walked into town. Just as Catrin could make out faces of the townspeople, a cold wind gusted, bringing with it the foul smell. Everyone watched in horrified amazement as snow began to fall, for it was no ordinary snow. As if dipped in blood, each walnut-sized flake was a deep crimson.

The people of Upperton moved back into their homes, driven by fear. Surely this was a bad omen, and Catrin felt a wave of futility wash over her. What could be worse than having the darkest possible portent coincide with her return to the Godfist? The storm intensified, casting a filter of red over the entire landscape. Soon snow began to accumulate, making it look as if the land were bleeding.

The sound of wings caught Catrin's ear, and she turned to see three birds flying south. Everywhere she went, it seemed, someone was watching and waiting.

"We can't make the journey to Lowerton in this," Gerard said, "whatever it is."

"I doubt we'll be welcomed into anyone's home now," Strom said.

"I don't know how you do the things you do, Catrin," Gerard said, "but I don't believe this has anything to do with you. I was there when you were born. You're no threat to me or any other right-minded person. You can stay with me tonight, and we'll set out for Lowerton with the sunrise. By then the snow should've stopped."

The insides of the greatoak buildings were remarkable. Much of the furniture was carved directly from the walls, and the furniture that was freestanding was obviously made from the same wood. With the exception of the stone hearth and chimney, the mighty trees provided all the needed materials.

"There's not much food these days," Gerard said as he brought out a wooden platter covered with nuts and dried berries. "Next year'll be better. When the terraces are complete, we'll have all the food we need. The Greatlanders have it all figured out. Until then, we just have to squeeze by."

"I thank you for sharing what you have," Benjin said. "It was a long journey, and it's good to be home and with friends."

"That's prob'ly where ya should stay," Gerard said.

"Catrin believes her father is in danger."

"That he is," Gerard said, "and he went there knowin' it. He went 'cause he believes there's a chance to end the fighting. If you go south of the Wall, you might just ruin our best chance for peace."

Catrin sat, staring at the fire, conflicted. How could she be certain her vision would come true? How could she put

213

everyone else at risk on the basis of something she did not understand? In her gut she knew. She had to go south; every instinct agreed. "I'm sorry, Gerard. I mean no disrespect, but I must go. I know my father is in trouble, and if he's in trouble, I doubt peace will follow."

"Sometimes, we must follow our feelings," Gerard said, thoughtful. "If you're goin', the best place to get over the Wall would be the eastern guardhouse; there're no breaks in the wall near there, but the wall is not very high. We keep a close watch on the guards, and the two fellows stationed there are terrified of you: Carter Bessin and Chad Macub. Their only job is to make sure no one comes over the wall, and they seem to be getting a bit complacent."

The names slammed into Catrin, and sudden memory overwhelmed her. Once again, in her mind, she entered the clearing where Peten, Carter, and Chad were attacking Osbourne. In her mind she saw Peten charging down on her then the world flying away.

"I'd wager they are scared," Strom said. "I would be too."

Catrin came back to herself, and in a moment that seemed to prove she would someday heal, she laughed. "We're going to scare the wind out of 'em."

"First," Benjin said, "we have to get there. I suggest we get some sleep. It's going to be an early start."

* * *

Knee-deep, crimson snow blanketed the landscape, giving everything a surreal appearance, which made Catrin feel as if she were walking in a dream. She pulled her hood closer as the wind blew, and drifting snow clung to everything. Beyond a large rock overhang, though, the wind died, blocked by natural rock formations.

Not far ahead roared a swollen, red waterfall, and Catrin recognized the plateau from afar, suddenly realizing that she was now approaching it from the same direction as the Zjhon army had, so long ago. Most of them had died here.

Looking around, Catrin noticed large mounds on the valley floor, and she no longer had to wonder where those

214

she killed were laid. A great sadness welled up in her as they passed the gaping wound in the plateau, though it was already partly overgrown by bushes and trees that poked out of the snow.

Beyond, Catrin saw the terraces for the first time. Like giant snakes, one on top of another, following the contours of the land, the low, stone walls made for a mind-bending view. As soon as she saw them, their design made perfect sense; by creating narrow but level platforms down the slopes, they gained much valuable land for planting.

The roadway ahead was obstructed as a crowd of men worked with hammers and picks to finish the construction of a terrace. Two men argued in the middle of the road, and they seemed oblivious to the group as they approached. Then one of them looked up and saw them. "Whoa! You folks stay as far to the right as possible. Look out for falling rock." He shook his head and started to turn back to the other man, but when his eyes passed over Catrin, he stopped and watched her walk by. "Hey! Wait!"

Catrin was tempted to simply keep walking; she had no time for interruptions, but something in his voice made her stop.

"Where'd ya get that coat?" he asked. "I had one just like that. It even had the same tear on the shoulder."

"Rolph Tillerman gave it to me," Catrin said. "Are you Martik?"

"Yes!" he said, his eyes going wide, and he grabbed Catrin by the arms. "You saw my father? How was he? And my mother? And Jessub?"

"Yes," Catrin said. "I spent time with all of them. They're fine, though they miss you dearly. Wait. I have something for you." Catrin reached into the coat pocket and pulled out the drawing Jessub had given her. It showed Martik with Catrin hovering over him, protecting him.

Martik received it with wonder, and when he opened it, he was stunned. He stood for a moment with the look of a man whose thoughts were far away.

"I promise I'll tell you more when I return," Catrin said, "but I really must be--"

A loud cracking sound filled the valley, followed by shouting. As Catrin turned to look, she saw a large section of rock dislodge itself and roll forward until it crashed to the ground.

"Need help over here!" someone shouted, and everyone scrambled to help. Catrin watched as people lifted rocks away from where a man was trapped, but her eyes were drawn away, lured by a far more ghastly sight. Revealed by the fallen rock were flowing lines and graceful curves lit by an inner glow. Catrin recognized it immediately from the image that was burned into her mind. It was a Statue of Terhilian.

Chapter 18

There is permanence in every action and inaction; each is a choice and cannot be undone.

--Enoch Giest

* * *

"We were just working at the base there," a man said. "Then the whole rock face got unstable and collapsed on us."

A crowd gathered after all the men were pulled from the rubble. Women and young people, who had been nearby preparing lunch for the workers, now tended the wounded. All other eyes were drawn to the glowing curves of Istra's dress.

Catrin moved to stand before it, and she turned to face the crowd, pulling her hood down as she did. "Many of you know me; others may only know of me," she said. "I'm Catrin Volker, and this land is my home. I mean no one any harm. I only want us all to be safe. Right now we are not. What you see is part of a Statue of Terhilian, and it's an immediate threat."

"What can we do?" someone shouted from the crowd.

"I believe I know a way to neutralize the statue," Catrin said. "It will be dangerous to everyone nearby. Please take the children back to Lowerton. I wouldn't want them to be endangered or frightened." Women gathered the children, and soon only adults remained. Catrin wondered a moment that she, Chase, and the others were now adults, but that thought was driven out by what lay ahead. "I'm going to attempt to drain the negative core, but I need more rock cleared away. Here. We need to expose the base."

Despite the danger of another rockslide, men worked feverishly to clear the stone away from the statue, and Catrin waited, drowning in frustration. She couldn't leave the statue behind. She could get killed south of the Wall; then there would be no one left to destroy the statue. It was too dangerous to use her powers to remove the rock since she might set off the statue in the process. With tears in her eyes,

217

she knew she had to choose the needs of her people over her desperate desire to save her father; she had to wait.

When a large, squared corner became exposed, Catrin rushed in to run her senses over it. Her staff in one hand and Koe in the other, she opened herself to the flow, and energy surged through her. With effort, she moderated the flow and kept her balance. Like the others, this statue had positive and negative cores kept apart by a thin layer of insulating material. Remembering how the positive charge had overwhelmed her with its energy, Catrin quailed. Barabas had attacked the negative charge, and she decided to do the same.

Using her staff to establish physical contact with the statue, her fingers resting in the grooves created the last time she attempted to destroy one of these statues, she reached out to the negative core. Slowly her flow of energy penetrated the crystal-like stone that made up the statue and, as it drew close, there was an enormous pop and a flash of light. In the next instant, Catrin was drawn to the statue like nails to a lodestone. Irresistible force pulled her closer until her flesh pressed painfully against stone, and she thought she might be crushed.

The negative core ravaged her with its insatiable appetite for energy, and she felt herself slowly being drained of life. Drawing from her staff and Koe alike, she did what she could to satisfy the core, but still it demanded more. It all happened so fast, Catrin could hardly catch up. Prios reached her side and latched on to her, trying to pull her away. Then, in what must have been an effort to help, he sent his own energy surging through her. Just as it had done with her, the negative core greedily pulled him closer.

With Prios now pressing against her, also trapped, Catrin felt certain she would die. Slowly, though, something was happening to the negative core. The outer edges were beginning to break down, and the deterioration began to take place more rapidly. Drawing a ragged breath, Catrin used every energy source around her, and some in the crowd were shocked to find themselves suddenly hurtling toward the statue. With the last of her will, Catrin flooded the negative core with a positive charge, and the chain reaction reached a white-hot zenith before it vanished without a sound.

Those drawn from the crowd caught themselves before they collided with Catrin and Prios, and everything grew very silent. Catrin did her best to remain standing, but Prios fell backward, still gripping her, and she fell. Prios grunted as she landed on him, and she rolled away. For a moment she rested. Her body had been drained, and it quivered with weakness. Standing was impossible, and speech was difficult, but she managed to grunt Benjin's name.

"I'm here, li'l miss. I'm here."

"Carry me. South."

* * *

Between a pair of oversized guards, Wendel sat, waiting for his fate to be decided. As soon as the red snow had begun to fall, fear spread. Edling had pounced on the opportunity, and Wendel went from peacemaker to traitor in a matter of moments. They said Catrin was back on the Godfist, but he didn't believe them. It was all just a ploy to be rid of him. Jensen had been right.

"In an act of cowardice and indifferent malice," Master Edling said, addressing the other members of the council, "Wendel Volker and his daughter, Catrin, have inflicted our home with a blood scourge. We had hoped the memory of its creation had been lost to time, but the Herald has found a way. You see it all around you. What further proof could you require?"

Master Edling sat, looking smug. Wendel looked at the other council members, but none of them would meet his eyes, and he knew he'd already lost.

* * *

A blurred, red and brown landscape slid by, and Catrin tried to get her eyes to focus. After some squinting and eye rubbing, she saw that she was on a sled, Prios beside her. Four large men pulled the sled, and Catrin sat up too quickly, causing her vision to swim and her head to ache. Then she

219

saw Benjin and Chase, who both called for a halt when they saw she was awake.

"How're you feeling?" Benjin asked.

"Better," she said, but she feared the truth was obvious: her body was drained and needed rest.

"We're nearly to Lowerton."

Propping herself up with the blankets and pillows loaded on the sled, Catrin watched as Lowerton came into view. Again word had preceded them, and the roadway was lined with people, only this time there was no fear. Here were the people who knew her best, and they waited in silent tribute, each holding a candle. Catrin wiped her tears as the first few faces slid by. Some she knew, others she didn't, but she finally felt she was home. Around the gentle bend awaited a sight Catrin could not have expected. There, standing taller and wider than any other building she'd seen and constructed out of six huge shafts of greatoak, stood a building with a weathered and chipped sign hanging above its double doors. Even through her tears, Catrin could read it: *The Watering Hole.*

From the double doors charged two women, their hair flying in the wind as they hoisted their dresses and ran. "Miss Mariss, Miss Bryson," Catrin said as she tried to stand, but her legs refused to support her. Seeing Strom rush to his mother's arms made Catrin's heart ache; it was a sweet ache, but it made her yearn for her own reunion. A moment later, Osbourne's parents arrived at a run. His mother lifted him from the ground and refused to let go. "Stay," Catrin said to Strom as his eyes met hers. "You and Osbourne belong here. I couldn't take you from your parents now. Please. Stay. Live happy lives."

Both Strom and Osbourne seemed torn, but they came to see her truth, and they waved a long good-bye as the sled began moving once again. "Come back to us," Strom shouted.

Farther along, a man stood in the middle of the roadway, his hands on his hips. Chase shouted as soon as he saw his father. He ran ahead and embraced Jensen.

Catrin watched with joy and envy. "Hello, Uncle Jensen!"

"There's my girl," he said as he crouched down by the now stopped sled. "I've missed you."

"I've missed you too, but I have to find my father. He's in danger."

Jensen put his arm around Chase, who now knelt by his side. "I'm sorry, Cat. I didn't want him to go. He thought he'd be safe, but I've been so worried. Can you be certain he's in danger?"

"I'm as certain in this as I've ever been in anything. I have to save him."

"That's good enough for me," Jensen said. "I'll gather those trained to fight, and we'll go get your dad."

"No," Catrin said. "I need to take Edling by surprise. Benjin, Prios, and I will make our way there by stealth. You, Chase, and everyone else stay here. If we don't return, it'll be up to you to keep these people safe."

Jensen took Chase by the arm and led him away, but Chase stopped and turned. "I can't stay here. Not now. Not after everything we've been through. I'd never forgive myself."

Catrin wanted to protest, but the look of pride on Uncle Jensen's face kept her from saying anything more. She hoped she could keep him safe.

* * *

Cruel light poured into the cell, and Wendel shielded his eyes with his hand. Silhouetted in the doorway, his guards waited, and he knew better than to keep them waiting long. Already his bruises and injuries made it difficult for him to walk.

Into the council room they led him, and he was brought to the seat of the accused, a place he'd never thought he would find himself, especially not accused of the highest crime. It seemed a horrible dream. None of this could be real. If only he could wake.

"On the charge of treason, how do you find Wendel Volker?" asked Constable Fredin.

"Guilty," Master Edling said.

"Innocent," Master Jarvis said, despite the glares he received.

"Innocent," Humbry Milson said.

Master Edling looked as if he would explode, but then a guard burst into the room, breathing hard.

He came to Master Edling and went one knee. "An urgent message, sir."

Master Edling's eyes went wide with feigned surprise and fear. He passed the message to the other members of the council and waited.

"I request a new vote," Humbry said, his voice trembling.

"No!" Wendel cried out.

"On the charge of treason, how do you find Wendel Volker?"

"Guilty," Master Edling said.

"Guilty," Humbry said.

"Innocent," Master Jarvis said. One more guilty vote would condemn Wendel to death, and he waited without wanting to hear. He wanted so much to wake.

"Guilty," Baker Hollis said.

On the floor lay the discarded message.

The Herald is coming for you.

* * *

Crouched in the snow behind a mighty elm, Catrin waited. Downhill stood a rudimentary guardhouse, and smoke poured from the small hole in the roof that served as a chimney. Occasional conversation drifted on the wind, and Catrin felt some remorse. Despite their differences, Carter and Chad were her countrymen, and she truly meant them no harm. Scaring them was simply the easiest way she could think of to get to her father. Nothing would stand in her way.

From the far side of the guardhouse, where Benjin, Chase, and Prios crouched, Benjin gave the signal. With a deep breath, Catrin prepared herself. Still feeling drained, she relied heavily of her staff and Koe as she drew a trickle of

222

energy. "I know you're in there," she said, her voice amplified just enough to give it a chilling effect.

Shuffling could be heard from within. "Who's out there," Carter asked, his high-pitched voice laced with fear.

"You knew I would come for you," Catrin said. "Both of you."

"You best just be gone," Chad said, "or we'll come out there after you."

"A threat?" Catrin asked as she drew more power and stepped out from behind the tree. Wisps of blue lightning rolled across her fingers, and she moved her hands in elaborate patterns, trails of light streaming from her fingertips. Speaking words she remembered from books in High Script, she did her best to sound like a wizard of legend, incanting some horrific spell.

"I'm not afraid of you!" Chad challenged, but his aura reeked of fear, and Catrin gave the signal.

"Then you will die!" she shouted, throwing her hands back. Both Chad's and Carter's eyes flew wide as her energy began to reach out for them like fingers of death. Horrified, they watched and never saw Benjin, Chase, and Prios coming. In an instant, it was over. Both Carter and Chad were tied, gagged, and left to sit by their fire.

Benjin even tossed a bit more wood on the fire. "Someone should find them before they freeze t'death." Before he left, though, he removed the short sword and scabbard from Chad's belt. Chase took Carter's sword then helped Catrin over the Wall. Benjin helped ease her down the other side. Even that slight exertion taxed her body and her will. Each step was a challenge, and she weaved as they hiked through the trees.

"We need to rest," Chase said.

"I'm fine," Catrin said. "We need to keep moving."

"Passed out or dead, you'll be of no use to anyone, Cat," Chase said. "Take a short nap at the very least. Please."

He's right.

Catrin cast Prios a scathing glance, but then she let herself admit that they were right. No matter how much she wanted to move forward, she was in no condition to travel, let alone fight. Prios was in nearly the same condition, and she could sense his own inner struggle. "Carry us," Catrin begged.

Benjin nodded in submission.

Chase shook his head. "Better than nothing, I suppose." Chase lifted Catrin easily, and she settled herself so her weight was balanced across his shoulders. It was far from comfortable, but sleep claimed her before Chase had taken three steps.

* * *

As her head leaned back, resting against the snow, Catrin's eyes flew open. Not far away, she heard a distinct and undeniable sound: a feed bucket being slammed against barn walls. In an instant her senses collided. Sound, smell, and even the shadows told her the same thing: she was home. She was not just on the Godfist; this was her farm, her home, and the light streaming from around the barn doors told of a new occupant. Suppressed rage, kept sealed away for so long, suddenly burst forth with its fullest fury. Her breath coming in ragged gasps, she sat up. Benjin, Chase, and Prios crouched nearby, listening and watching.

Crawling at first, Catrin pulled herself forward; then she stood. Slowly and unsteadily, she walked to where they were hiding.

"I'm going in there," she said as she swayed on her feet.

"Get down," Benjin whispered through his teeth. "He's just about done pickin' hooves. We wait until he puts the horse in a stall. Then we go in."

Catrin waited, but she remained standing, certain that if she sat down, she'd not rise again. Through the crack between the doors, she could see only the man's legs as he walked the horse into a stall. Benjin leaped up and Chase matched his stride. Quickly but quietly, they rushed to the barn doors. While the man was still in the stall, they slipped inside. Catrin walked a meandering course behind them, dizzy but more determined than ever. Prios guided her to the barn door, and she slipped inside.

"Just come out real slow," Benjin said, wielding only his belt knife. The man slowly stuck his head out of the stall, and his eyes grew wide when he saw Benjin. When his eyes reached Catrin, he took a step back. She recognized him.

"Easy, Gunder," Benjin said as he sheathed his knife.

"They said you were coming," Gunder said as he trembled. "I didn't believe them."

"We're your friends," Benjin said.

"Yes," Gunder said, still looking terrified. "Yes, we *are* friends. I . . . caught your mare for you. And . . . and . . . you saved my pig that time it got caught in the fence! You remember, don't you?"

"Yes, Gunder, I remember. We're friends."

"Oh, thank you," Gunder said. "Thank you for understanding."

"Why are you here?" Catrin asked, her fury unabated.

"The Masters keep horses here," Gunder said, his eyes cast low. "I'm to care for 'em."

Catrin's anger could find no target. This man was her friend. Once again she made herself stuff the rage down inside, deep in her gut where she could contain it.

"What's the news on the treaties?" Benjin asked.

Gunder looked from Benjin to Catrin. "I'm so sorry," he said. "There'll be no treaty. The blood scourge, as they're calling it, has everyone scared out of their wits. It gives the Masters power since only they know the will of the gods."

"What about Wendel?"

"Charged with treason," Gunder said in a low voice. "I'm so sorry. He's to be executed tomorrow. I thought he had a chance. The council argued for days, but when they heard you were comin', fear won again."

His words were like a punch in the stomach, and Catrin reeled. Could it be that she was bringing about her vision by her very attempts to stop it?

"Where?" Benjin growled.

"The Masterhouse."

"Boil Edling in grease," Benjin said. "We'll never even get close. They know we're coming."

"They do," Gunder said, "but they won't be expectin' you to look like a wine barrel."

In the darkness, Catrin tried to anticipate the next bump; already she was covered in bruises. It seemed like days since they left the cold caves, bound for the Masterhouse. Gunder would make his delivery of wine, cheese, and meat as scheduled, and Catrin could only hope his wagon would not be thoroughly searched. The hole, through which she had her only access to fresh air, seemed terribly small from inside the barrel, but she could see through it. When she wasn't gulping for air, she watched the landscape slide by.

The sound of hooves and wagon wheels on wood echoed around her, and Catrin watched as they crossed over one of the many small streams that ran through the lowlands. As the wagon turned, Catrin got a clear view of the countryside. Seeing the Masterhouse in the distance knotted her guts, though she was struck by how much smaller it was than she remembered it. Somehow, her travels across such vast distances had forever changed her perception of the world. Life had been so much easier when her world had extended only as far as the top of the lake. Now everything was different.

As Gunder drove the wagon into the line at the guardhouse, Catrin began to tremble and sweat. Time moved slowly, and she thought she might never get out of the barrel. The wood slats seemed to move ever closer, constricting her like a giant snake. Her face pressed against the wood, she sucked air through the hole and tried to calm herself.

"Delivery for the banquet," she heard Gunder say.

Closing her eyes, she held her breath. Only when the wagon began rolling did she draw another breath. Gunder angled toward the kitchen service entrance, and Catrin watched as a flurry of servants prepared for a gathering, even as crowds of people were already arriving. The Masters would treat her father's execution as a banquet, a reason for celebration! Barely able to contain her anger, Catrin ran her fingers over Koe, the feel of him giving her comfort.

Outside the barrel, hidden in the straw, her staff awaited, and she missed the feel of it in her hands. Afraid someone might recognize it, she had covered the heel and much of the shaft with mud. It was a poor disguise, but it was the best that she could do.

When the wagon stopped, Catrin waited, her inner tension mounting. Servants unloaded the cheese and other supplies, and she knew they would come for the wine soon. A gentle knock was her cue, and she carefully pushed the lid open and to the side before crawling out. Benjin emerged from his barrel a moment later, his face a mask of pain, but he made no sound. Bruised and cramped, Catrin understood his pain, and she stood as quickly as she could. Chase and Prios soon joined them.

Moving with increasing haste, she pulled her staff from the straw. Benjin and Chase were ready with their borrowed swords.

"That's all I can do," Gunder said. "They'll know you're here soon--one way or 'nother. You'd best do whatever ya can now. I need to be away from here before I'm found out. I'll see you north o' the Wall." Without another word, Gunder walked away, looking as if nothing were amiss.

Catrin envied his ability to mask emotion. She jumped at the sound of servants returning, but then there was big uproar from the great covered terrace that stood as the Masterhouse's main entrance. There, a crowd gathered. This was not an expectant crowd, ready for feast and revelry. There was sadness in the air, and something far more horrible in Catrin's perception: acceptance. These people did not want to see her father put to death, but none would stand up to stop it, perhaps believing themselves powerless.

Before the servants could return, Catrin pulled her hood up and walked hunched over, as if in need of the staff to support her. Benjin kept his eyes low, and they did their best to blend in with the crowd. Chase and Prios stayed separate but nearby. When finally Catrin got a glimpse of those on the terrace, she saw a pair of meaty guards holding her father, who hung between them, a haunted look in his eyes. He looked so much older than Catrin remembered, and her rage returned. He could not defend himself, and these cowards would take him from her.

Fate left her no more time to contemplate, for she saw a servant rush up to Master Edling. After the servant whispered in his ear, Master Edling ran his eyes over the crowd, searching for her. Despite nagging fears, Catrin knew she had no more time to waste. This was her last chance for salvation. As she cast back her hood, she threw her arms wide. Holding her staff high, she opened herself to the flow. In her weakened state, the flood of energy nearly washed her away, but she bit her lip and made herself endure. Benjin raised his head and drew his sword, a look of pessimistic determination on his face, as if he fought a battle he knew he would lose.

Angry, red plasma crawled over Catrin's hands and arms, and the crowd parted, rolling away like rippling water from around a tossed stone. Before her, Catrin saw her father, his guards, the Masters, and the members of the council. For a moment the sight of Baker Hollis, the man who had killed her mother and aunt, distracted her. He had stolen from her the most precious things, and now he stood in accusation of her father. A growl escaped her throat as she approached.

Master Edling watched and smiled. "Come, Miss Volker. Join your father!"

For an instant, Catrin hesitated. She sensed no fear from Master Edling, and her instincts shouted in warning. Fear poured from every other soul present but not Edling; he was like a stone. Step after step, Catrin drew closer to him and to her father.

When Wendel heard her name, he raised his tired eyes and screamed. "No! Get away from here, Cat. I don't want you to see this!"

Catrin longed to embrace him, but she turned her gaze to Edling as if she could bore holes in him with her eyes.

"Go ahead. Run away," Master Edling said, standing behind a lectern of stone. "Spend the rest of your life trying to picture it in your mind, all the while knowing you left him to die."

"Lies!" Wendel shouted, and one of the guards cuffed him on the back of the head. Catrin lashed out at the guard; a rope of lightning and fire sent him flying backward, and he landed in a smoking heap. Again Edling smiled, and Catrin gathered all her fury and rage. Determined to incinerate him, she launched her attack. Quicker than she would have thought him capable of, Master Edling ducked down, picked something up, and thrust it in front of him. The object was like nothing Catrin had ever seen. The size of a melon but with a pocked surface, it looked metallic, and it drew Catrin's energy just as the statue's negative core had done.

With a thunderous crack, her energy exploded over the stone yet was utterly absorbed, and the stone demanded more. Her energy rushed out of her body like a draining flood, and she knew there would soon be none left; she would die.

Use my energy.

At her side, Prios waited, but Catrin knew it would not be enough. He would only become a slave to the stone, and Catrin could not allow that. "Attack the building," she said through gritted teeth. "Don't get close to Edling's stone."

Rolling forward, Prios surprised everyone as he leaped into the air. Spinning as he flew, he unleashed a rapid series of short energy bursts. Looking like balls of pure fire, they slammed into the tops of the columns that supported the terrace roof with concussive force. Chunks of the roof began to fall even as the flagstone shook.

"Kill the prisoner!" Master Edling shouted above the din.

"No!" Catrin wailed, driven to her knees by sadness and weariness.

I'm coming.

More like an expression of emotion than exact words, Catrin felt the message.

In a moment that would forever remain clear in her memory, one of the guards surrounding her father drew his sword. Reaching back, he gritted his teeth as he prepared to thrust, but then he was suddenly cast into shadow, twisters of dust and dirt rolling through the air. With a triumphant cry, Kyrien grabbed Wendel in one claw and used the other to send Master Edling tumbling over backward. Like rolling thunder, each flap of his wings sent people sprawling. Grabbing a shocked Benjin in his free claw, Kyrien turned on his wingtip and soared back into the sky.

"No!" Wendel screamed as he disappeared into the clouds. "Catrin!"

Chapter 19

Though the years may change us, we see each other as we were.
--Ort Sisteva, wanderer

* * *

With the connection between her and Edling's stone broken, Catrin reeled. Prios reached her before she hit the ground, and he lent her energy; her head swam with it. All around, people panicked. Many sought to flee, others seemed frozen by fear. The guards pulled Master Edling back to his feet, and he wiped the blood away from his nose. Before Catrin could compose herself enough to stand, he stooped to retrieve his stone. Prios lashed out, again using only short bursts of energy. Edling deflected each one with his stone, but he was losing ground.

Do not connect yourself to him. Disconnect from the energy before it reaches him.

It had never occurred to Catrin before, but even in her muddled state, it made sense. Struggling to stand on her own, she let Prios bolster her strength, and they attacked in unison. Edling could not block every attack, and he was sent spinning. At the same moment, a brief buzzing filled Catrin's hearing, as if a bumblebee had flown past her ear; then there was another. Looking up, she saw arrows raining from the sky; archers lined the trembling roof.

Before she could draw enough energy to protect herself, the sky went dark as Kyrien intercepted the hail of arrows; some bounced harmlessly across the flagstone, but Kyrien cried out as he soared away. Using his wing, he took a parting swipe at the archers, knocking three from the roof and sending the others sprawling. With another cry, he wheeled and swooped, plucking Chase and Prios from the crowd, like pulling grapes from the vine. His thoughts flooded Catrin's mind as he gained the clouds: *Your flock is safe, my queen.*

On the terrace, only Master Edling and two of his guards remained, all others had fled. Demanding all her body had left to give, Catrin charged Master Edling, howling as she came. He held up his stone and she laughed. Then, using short bursts of energy, she attacked the flagstone, sending a shower of fist-sized rocks and debris into his face. Both guards went down, and neither tried to rise. Only their breathing gave any indication of life. Master Edling teetered and looked as if he would fall, blood trickling down the side of his face.

Catrin took advantage of the opening. Rapid bursts flew toward Edling and he screamed. Energy slammed into him and sent him spinning. As Catrin stopped her attack, Master Edling stood facing her on wobbling knees. With finality, she issued one last attack, sending a ball of lightning and fire soaring into Master Edling's chest. Tumbling over backward, he landed in a sprawl of arms and legs. Catrin knew she could easily finish him, but she'd had enough of killing.

For a moment she stood, swaying on her feet and breathing deeply. Then, from the corner of her vision, she spotted movement. There, someone crouched behind a collapsed bench, but he could no longer hide from Catrin, and he must have known it, for he stood.

"*You,*" Catrin said, a haze of blood clouding her vision.

"Please," Baker Hollis said. "Let me explain."

"*Explain?* You want me to let you *explain?* Did you let my mother or my aunt explain? Did you?" she demanded, and he cowered before her wrath, but she was denied retribution. A blast of wind cast Baker Hollis's hair away from his face, and Catrin drank in his fear. She wanted him to suffer for what he'd done, but quick as a snake, Kyrien snapped her up in his jaws, somehow keeping her secure without impaling her on his daggerlike, back-turned teeth. In the next moment, she was soaring through the skies, and the beauty of it was almost enough for her to forgive Kyrien. He'd deprived her of revenge, but he had saved all that was truly precious to her, and she let her anger slip away.

Her father was safe.

* * *

In a clearing north of the Wall, Kyrien landed and gently lowered Catrin to the ground. Benjin and her father

232

approached with concern on their faces. Only when Catrin stood did either of them visibly relax. Kyrien craned his neck and brought his eyes level with Catrin's. She saw his pain, felt it as her own. Slowly he extended his wing, and Catrin ran her hands along the smooth skin that covered his wing structures. At the second joint, she found a broken shaft protruding from his flesh, blood seeping slowly from the wound.

No one spoke; all were seemingly mesmerized by Kyrien, who watched Catrin as she worked, making low noises in his throat. Using both hands to get a grip on the slippery and splintered shaft, she pulled. With a wiggle and a jerk, the shaft and point came free, and Catrin stepped away from Kyrien's wing. In the next breath, he turned and flapped his mighty wings and, using his powerful legs, thrust himself into the air.

"Wait!" Catrin shouted. "We should clean your wound!" Kyrien trumpeted in response and sent her a vision of him swimming in the seas, letting the salt water cleanse him. As she turned, though, nothing mattered more than reaching her father, and she collapsed into his arms, sobbing.

"Oh my dear Cat. You've come home to me. I'm so sorry. I let you down."

"No you didn't," Catrin said. After wiping her nose, she wrapped her arms around him and held on tight. "You're here. That's all that matters."

* * *

Inside the new Watering Hole, a fire burned in the hearth, and the aroma of food drifted from the kitchens. Catrin thought it was perhaps the happiest moment of her life. Sitting in the same room with her father, her uncle, Chase, Strom and his mother, Osbourne flanked by his parents, and Prios by her side, she could hardly believe it. Laughter filled the hall as exaggerated tales were told, and Catrin raised her mug. "I want to thank you all for being here. Without the people in this room, I would certainly be lost."

233

Those gathered cheered and raised their mugs. Miss Mariss emerged from the kitchen with a roast over potatoes and onions. For the first time that any of them had ever seen, Miss Mariss sat down to eat with her guests. "We're all family here," she said, smiling. "You all can help yourselves." A moment later, the door opened. Kenward entered, followed by Nora and Fasha, all grinning like fools. "Here comes the rest of the family now."

"You're not giving away our greatest secret, are you?" Nora asked as she walked up behind Catrin and kissed her on the top of her head. "It's good to see you didn't get yourself into too much trouble. I had a hard time keeping Kenward from running off to save you." Kenward actually blushed.

"So what's this well-kept secret?" Catrin asked.

"Ah, the fish is off the hook now, Sis," Nora said with a wink at Miss Mariss.

"'Sis'?" Chase asked. "You two are sisters?"

"That is to say we were fathered by the same man," Miss Mariss said, "but sisters we are. I inherited the good sense to stay on land."

"And I got the good looks," Nora said. Kenward laughed, and she smacked him in the back of the head. "Fool boy."

The door opened again, and Brother Vaughn entered. "Many pardons for my tardiness. I saw the most fascinating variation of finch on my walk, and I simply had to find its nest."

"Please sit," Miss Mariss said, not completely out of her role as hostess, and she handed him a plate. As they ate, a silence fell over the hall, conducive to quiet introspection.

"There is something I don't understand," Osbourne's father, Johen, said. "What is this 'blood scourge'? Does anyone know? Will it really poison the crops?"

"I have a theory," Brother Vaughn said. "In the great shallows, far from here, we passed an enormous mountain. It exploded from within and sent a cloud of fire and ash high into the sky. This was also the source of the giant wave that assaulted your harbor, the Falcon Isles, and other places in

234

the world. The red snow had the same smell I remember from the shallows, just before the mountain exploded."

"But how could something so far away cause red snow here?"

"Just as the oceans carried the great wave," Brother Vaughn said. "The winds must have carried some of the fouled air here. I don't think there'll be any long-term effects, save perhaps fear."

Johen looked doubtful, but Catrin felt a great relief. The red snow was a frightening anomaly, and it made her feel better to have a more practical explanation.

Looking at her father, she marveled at his strength. His hair had gone gray, and he walked with a limp, but his eyes still held the same steely strength. Even when he smiled at her, his face at its softest, there was strength of conviction.

Benjin looked older too--all of them did--but his relationship with Fasha seemed to be bringing out a much younger personality. Catrin watched them as they laughed; there was excitement in their eyes as they discussed plans for the future. Catrin lacked their enthusiasm; ahead she saw a long and difficult road, and she wasn't certain she would ever be truly happy again.

Peace had not been made, and she doubted her attack on Master Edling would endear her to those who already considered her the enemy. Despite having forgiven Kyrien for pulling her away, she had a burning in her stomach, and she knew it could only be quelled by resolving her anger toward Baker Hollis. He had said he could explain, but there was no explanation that could be sufficient; no circumstances could have warranted such a cowardly act. If he'd had his way, Catrin, too, would be dead. Trying to recall the image of her mother and aunt became frustrating, as all she could form was a vague and gauzy image. Memory was fading, and she could no longer picture their faces in her mind.

"I have men looking for Baker Hollis," her father had said, but it came as a shock when a man arrived with an urgent message. "Catrin, Jensen, Benjin, Chase," Wendel said, his voice a harsh baritone that sounded only barely in control. "Come with me." All conversation stopped, and anxiety poured from everyone in the room. Catrin urged Benjin forward, wanting to escape the confined emotion. Her father led them to one of the buildings not built from a greatoak, made instead of pine with a thatch roof. Reddish water dripped onto the dirt floor as the snow inexorably melted. On a crate, with his hands tied, sat Baker Hollis. A well-muscled guard stood behind him, alert and seemingly ready for any threat.

"Untie him," Wendel growled. Baker Hollis rubbed his wrists and began to cry. Everyone who was crowded into the small room had reason to want him dead. By the look of him, trembling and crying, he seemed poignantly aware.

Chase stood with his hands balled into fists, and Catrin had never seen Uncle Jensen so enraged. The pain that radiated from them was nauseating, and Catrin nearly fled, but she had to know. If she did not witness this, no matter how painful, she would never forgive herself.

"Why?" her father demanded.

"I'm so sorry," Baker Hollis said. "I didn't know it would kill them. They made me do it."

"Who?"

"The Greatlanders," Baker Hollis said.

"How did they *make* you?"

"They took my little Trinda. What those monsters did to her, I'll never know, but she's never been the same. I should have killed her, freed her from the horrors, and let them kill me, but I couldn't do it. It wouldn't have saved Willa and Elsa, even if I had. The Greatlanders would've found another way. Please forgive me."

Wendel stood, hovering over Baker Hollis, seemingly on the verge of exploding, but then he seemed to deflate. "The people responsible still hide in the Greatland?" he asked in a voice just above a whisper.

Catrin thought it the most frightening voice she'd ever heard. "The person responsible is dead," she said, only then releasing her anger. She had been ready to rip Baker Hollis to pieces, but now she could find no target for her fury. She remembered the look that haunted Trinda's eyes; she remembered the pain she had plainly seen for so many years. How could she blame Baker Hollis for wanting to protect his

236

daughter? "Arbuckle Kyte ordered their deaths, and mine, but now he's dead. It's over. There's nothing more we can do."

Uncle Jensen wheeled in frustration and kicked the door, which fell before his fury.

Chase bent down and looked Baker Hollis in the eye. "If you ever endanger my family again, I'll hunt down you, your daughter, and everyone you ever loved. If you get threatened into hurting us again, I suggest you come to me first."

Baker Hollis nodded, sweat dripping from his nose.

Chase followed his father into the night, also venting his rage on what remained of the door.

Benjin left Catrin and Wendel alone with Baker Hollis. Catrin sat in silence, trying to reconcile her feelings; her father seemed frozen in time. "I'm sorry about Trinda," Catrin finally said, and Baker Hollis looked up in surprise. Confusion radiated from him, as if he suspected a trap. "I'm sorry about her pain and yours. I'll never get my mother or my aunt back, and you'll never be able to fix what happened to Trinda. For those things, I am truly sorry. I don't like you, and I'm still angry, but I won't kill you." Her words fell like rolling thunder, and there was finality in them.

"Release him," Wendel said, and he turned to leave. Catrin followed him and rushed to catch up when she saw his shoulders begin to shake. For a moment he allowed himself to cry, to once again mourn the loss of his true love, but then he drew a deep breath. "You're stronger than I," he said without looking up. "I couldn't be more proud of you, Catrin. You've grown to be the woman I always knew you could be."

"I draw my strength from you."

"I would've killed him if it weren't for you," Wendel said, still staring at the ground. "I wanted so badly to hurt him, to make him feel my pain." Wendel raised his eyes to Catrin's. What she saw there was not weakness; it was vulnerability presented as a gift to one he knew would not hurt him.

"I love you, Daddy," she said, and he held her tightly as they cried.

"I love you too, my little Cat."

Warmer weather banished the blood scourge, and the memory began to fade. No longer did people instantly react in fear, and Catrin felt she was making progress at winning back her own people, but it still felt good to be out in the wilderness with only Chase and Prios, searching for the underground lake.

"I'm tellin' ya," Chase said, "it's this way. I recognize that outcropping of trees." Already he'd been convinced three times, and all three times they were disappointed. Catrin found it hard to believe that someplace where they had spent so much time would be so difficult to find, but those memories, too, had begun to fade. Prios just shrugged and followed Chase. He'd become more open lately, using the chalk and slate Uncle Jensen had given him to communicate with those who could not hear him in their minds. In some cases, he used the slate simply because hearing his voice was something not everyone was prepared for, and some people did not seem to understand his gestures and body language. The slate and chalk appeared to remove a barrier of fear that seemed to keep many from becoming close to him. Now he seemed to enjoy using it for fun, as if it had become a game for him.

Chase stopped and turned when Prios tapped him on the shoulder. Prios held up his slate. *Hungry,* it read, and Chase laughed. Prios had written the word hours ago, and at regular intervals tapped him on the shoulder, showing him the same word. From his pack, Chase produced three of the pepper sausages he knew Prios wanted. Since the first time he'd tried one, he'd wanted little else. Prios smiled and accepted the sausage. Chase shook his head and put the other two back. He tossed Catrin an apple, and he nibbled on some cheese, saving the sausages for the next time Prios held up his slate.

Satisfied, they continued their search, and Catrin started looking higher, trying to find the peaks she remembered to orient herself by them. It was not something she was skilled at, but the direction she guessed was the same as the path

Chase chose next, and she moved with renewed confidence. "Look!" she said as they moved past a pile of large rocks overgrown with bushes.

Up above rested the rotting remains of the screen Chase had once made to hide the light of their fire. Seeing the place brought back feelings of fear and anxiety, but there were also good memories. Catrin climbed without regret and felt the same sense of awe when she entered the man-made passage. Piles of walnuts still lay where they had been left. Much of the food was gone, and the shelves were overturned, most likely raided by scavengers.

Chase found a salted perch that was nearly whole. "I wonder if it's still good," he mused, holding it up as if he were about to eat it. Prios wrinkled his nose and shook his head; then he smiled and pointed at Chase's pack. Chase laughed and produced another pepper sausage.

Catrin looked beyond the remains of their camp and used her imagination. She pictured all the openings cleared and repaired and boats floating across the hidden lake.

"Now that we've found it again," Chase said, "what will you do?"

"I'll prepare for the future," Catrin said. "I believe what Nat said, and even if he is wrong, what do we stand to lose? If we don't prepare, we stand to lose everything."

"You know I'll help in any way I can," Chase said, and Prios moved to her side.

He smiled and nodded. *I will help.*

"The first thing we need to do," Catrin said, "is make sure we can find this place again. Then we'll go back and talk to my dad and Uncle Jensen. We'll figure something out."

* * *

As they walked back into Lowerton, Catrin saw a young boy running down the middle of the roadway, and she was struck by recognition.

"Elma!" he shouted as he ran, and Catrin laughed.

Prios squeezed her hand. *Elma?*

"It's a long story," she said.

239

"I tol' you I was gonna be a great adventurer some day, didn't I?" Jessub Tillerman said. "I sailed all the way to the Falcon Isles and then on t' the Godfist. Just like my dad!"

"Did your gramma and grampa come with you?" Catrin asked. Jessub was bigger and older than when she'd seen him last, and he seemed offended by her question.

"Yeah," he said. "A whole shipload o' people came from the Greatland. Most came t' see you, but I came t' see my dad!"

"Your father is a fine man," she said.

Jessub seemed to forget all about being insulted. "D'ya really have a dragon? What's 'is name? Where is he? Can I see him? Did he really pick ya up in his teeth? How come you didn't die?"

Catrin tried to answer his questions, but each answer spawned a dozen new questions, and she was exhausted by the time she reached the Watering Hole. Her father and a room full of people, some she recognized, some she didn't, waited within. Seeing Milo and Gustad made her smile, and she ran to embrace them.

Rolph and Collette Tillerman moved through the crowd to greet her. "When Martik said his skills were needed here, I knew we had t' come," Rolph said.

"I'm so glad t' see ya," Collette said, and she hugged Catrin.

A moment later, Brother Vaughn approached with a beautiful woman on his arm; they both smiled. "Catrin, this is Mirta Greenroot. You've never met her, but she received a gift from you. It was to Mirta that I sent the pyre-orchids you harvested."

"Thank you, Lady Catrin," Mirta said. Her genuine smile and the twinkle in her eyes endeared her to Catrin instantly. "So much sickness has been stopped because of your gift. I dried it and ground it to powder. Whenever sickness began to spread, I was able to save people and prevent further spreading. I sent powder to healers across the Greatland. Your efforts saved hundreds if not thousands. Now I bring pyre-orchid to your people, as a gift."

Tears filled Catrin's eyes, overjoyed to know that she may have actually saved more lives than she had taken away.

240

It did not banish her remorse, but it did make her feel much better about herself. "Thank you, Mirta. It would seem you and Benjin deserve more credit than I. He insisted we harvest the flowers, and you made certain they did not go to waste. You have a generous heart. I thank you for coming so far to deliver your gift."

"I think I'd like to stay here," Mirta said, suddenly shy, and she looked up at Brother Vaughn.

"Be welcome, Mirta," Catrin said, and Brother Vaughn smiled. Wendel approached. "We found the cavern," she said to him.

"I knew you would," Wendel said. "Before you returned, I wasn't well enough to search for it myself, and no one could find it armed with only my description. With a lot of work, it could be a good, safe place. Many of these people have come here to help you. All you need to do is ask."

"You're right," Catrin said, overwhelmed by the responsibility and expectation. So much had happened in so short a time, she had difficulty gathering her thoughts. Remembering how Mother Gwendolin had used the viewing ceremony as a way to find clarity, Catrin wondered if she couldn't create her own ceremony.

She stood up on a chair to address the crowd. "I want to thank you all for coming . . . and for everything you've done along the way. A new day has come, and we must prepare for what lies ahead. I feel I have a purpose I must fulfill, but I must first grasp the true nature of that purpose. When I return, I will enlist the aid of all who are willing."

Chapter 20

The sum of our lives can be judged only by what we leave behind--our legacy.
--Fedicus Illiani, historian

* * *

Hiking along the wide trail that had been created to get the greatoaks to Lowerton, Catrin prepared herself for meditation. Pulling her layers of clothing tighter, she tried to clear her mind as much as she could, but she was easily distracted. Knowing Chase was following her didn't help. He'd made no mistakes, and she had no reason to believe he was really there except a strong feeling, but that was enough for her. The feeling of his presence was so strong, she kept expecting him to walk out of the trees.

When the trail opened into the meadow, Catrin was transformed, transported back to the first time she'd entered the hallowed grove. She saw the trees as they were then, and she could still feel their energy and that of the stone. Perhaps she had not utterly destroyed the grove after all; perhaps some energy remained, dormant . . . waiting.

As she approached the stumps and grisly remains, she winced, but the energy drew her on. A few mighty trunks still lay where they had fallen, as if waiting for some use to present itself. When she reached the center of the black stone, she realized it did not look as terrible as when she had seen it last. Wind and rain had cleaned away the powdery grit, and now the black stone, though pocked, had begun to regain some of its luster.

Sitting with a crater between her crossed legs, she dug the tip of her staff into the stone. Holding her staff in one hand and Koe in the other, she closed her eyes and relaxed. In her mind, she traveled to the grove of the past and located the visual representation of her center amid the mighty greatoaks. Suffused by the energy around her, Catrin could feel the trees. She could see them and touch them. To her, they were still real, still alive. As she leaned forward, she had the strange sensation of moving downward, as if her staff were sinking into the stone. She kept her eyes closed, not wanting to leave her state of consciousness.

Dryads peeked around each of the trees in her mind, and they sang to her. There were no words, only melodies, but they were rich and delicate, like the tinkling of a fine bell over the sound of pounding surf, backed by the whisper of the wind through leaves. Birds sang their varied songs, somehow in harmony with the dryads, as if nature itself were playing her a chorus.

A feeling of security enveloped her, and she was washed with the relief of tension she hadn't even known she'd been holding on to. No one could touch her here; no one could harm her. She was safe. It was not something she could tell herself; her body had to believe it before she could truly relax. The physical world vanished from her senses, supplanted by the world of energy and possibilities. For a time, Catrin simply bathed herself in its warmth. No concerns pulled at her focus, no worries drained her energy. Here, she was perfect.

Slowly she began to process her thoughts. As always, some were painful, others whimsical. She dealt with her feelings and emotions and was left with only questions of practicality. How would she convince people they needed to learn to live underground? History and Nat's visions agreed. There had already been times when man had to retreat within the land, and Catrin knew she must succeed.

Though she thought she had cleared her mind and dealt with all her worries, an ugly, gnawing fear rose to the surface: *Prios*. Already she had feelings for him, and she suspected he felt much the same, but she had promised herself. After using her powers to heal herself, she'd sworn she would never have children. How could she take away from Prios the ability to pass on his line? How could she ever explain to him? Would he understand?

Suddenly, her calm and relaxing place became a maelstrom of anxiety. Then something, which felt like being tucked in by one you love, washed over her and brought calm. Everything would be as it should. She now knew what she must do.

243

With a course charted, she felt the anxiety drain away as if it had never been. The decision put her in a receptive frame of mind, and images began to spring forth, seemingly from the nothingness.

She saw a great hall and an underground complex capable of supporting thousands. Instead of a spooky and forbidding place, she began to see it as a thriving microcosm, a miniature ecosystem tucked inside the safety of a mountain. No longer was the hidden lake little more than a curiosity to her; it was a place where they could stock fish. She pictured underground farms fed water and fertilizer from the lake. The vision of her new home gave her great pride, though she had yet to do the work. She would; she knew she would. Seeing it here, in this world of energy, was as good as it being, and it brought tears to her eyes.

Resolved, she felt herself relax even further, and it felt as if, once again, her staff sank lower into the stone. Deep, rhythmic breathing propelled her from one moment to the next, and finally her mind was quiet, free of conflict. The song of nature took on new layers of beauty as it rose to a thrilling crescendo, and Catrin let herself ride the enchanting melody.

The feeling she was being watched made her look about, and not far away, she saw the mental wall that separated her conscious and subconscious minds. Light streamed through the hole, which was now significantly larger, and for a moment Catrin became alarmed. Then from behind a mighty greatoak stepped what looked like a goddess in the flesh. She came, and Catrin gazed upon her own subconscious with awe.

"You are ready now."

"Who are you?" Catrin asked, terrified because she already knew the answer.

"I am you. I am Catrin. Perhaps, to avoid confusion, you would like to call me Elma?" her alternate self asked with a knowing smile.

Catrin's fear was overcome, finding humor and ease in its place. "All right, Elma. I have been afraid of you because I don't want to go insane or hurt anyone. And . . . there is something else . . ."

244

"I know," Elma said. "I cannot tell you what mysteries lie ahead, for I do not know, but I can assure you that I will do no harm. History does not always repeat its mistakes. If you do not trust life, then your line is condemned either way. Whether you choose to have children whose own children might die terrible deaths or if you decide the risk of passing on a deadly trait is too great, the result will be the same. Only if you give life an opportunity will there be a chance."

Elma's cold but practical logic penetrated Catrin's mind, and she came to see truth in it.

"You are ready now."

"Ready for what?"

"Shirlafawna gave you a gift. It was left in my keeping, and now I present it to you. You are ready."

"I remember Shirlafawna's gift," Catrin said, confused. "After I talked with her, I could see the other dryads."

Elma laughed. "That gift you gave yourself. You took a great risk when you chose to believe. Seeing the dryads was a reward you made for yourself."

Catrin sat in wonder, waiting with unbridled anticipation, as Elma approached. In her hands she held a globe of orange light that pulsed from within. Holding it to Catrin's forehead, Elma pressed with her delicate fingers, and the globe began to slide forward. Warmth and understanding flowed through Catrin. The globe entered her and became a part of her, albeit a part she was yet to comprehend. Her staff thrummed under her fingers, and a wave of power washed over her. Invigorated and charged, Catrin felt as if she'd been made anew.

"We must prepare now," Elma said, and Catrin did not have to ask for what. Visions filled her mind, images of death and destruction for all mankind. "We cannot allow this to happen."

Catrin nodded, and as she did, Elma walked between the greatoaks and gradually faded until she could be seen no more. Slowly, Catrin's awareness of her physical body returned, and she opened her eyes only to find near complete darkness. Only the blush of the false dawn gave any hint of shape or form, but then the sun peeked above the mountains. Fingers of light caressed the land, and Catrin felt the warmth on her face. Around her the world sang of a new day, a new chance for life. When she focused closer, finally seeing the staff before her and a serpentine tail wrapped around her, she gasped.

Kyrien met her eyes as she craned her neck to see. His eyes sparkled with inner light and excitement, and he nudged her back to the staff. There, she found a treasure beyond any reckoning or expectation. Shirlafawna's gift was in the form of life. From the staff sprouted fresh, green growth, and under each voluminous leaf, was a tiny, golden acorn. Twenty-four in all, there were enough to replant the entire grove. Catrin's heart sang. The fates had been kind to her, allowing her the chance to undo one of her greatest mistakes.

In that moment she thought of Barabas. His last action had been to prevent her death. He had sacrificed his life so she could live, so she could behold the beauty of a new day. She remembered all her fallen friends, all those who had helped her despite the dangers and had paid the ultimate price. She remembered what they all had done, and she loved them for it.

Epilogue

At the center of the new grove, Nat stood, stupefied. Never had he imagined such a thing. In the center of the stone, Catrin's staff--the staff his family had guarded for generations--stood, embedded in the rock itself, and it bloomed. It produced no more acorns, only flowering buds of purple and blue, but it lived and grew! Shrouded by branches, leaves, and flowers, the shaft was barely visible. Nat had to get down on his knees and peer under the growth to see the shaft, and the steely gaze of the dragon met him, its gemmed eyes pulsing with an inner glow. Protruding from the heel, the wooden shaft looked more lustrous than ever, though it seemed no larger than he remembered it.

Evenly spaced, the new greatoaks grew, lean and straight. It would take thousands of years for the mighty leviathans to gain their predecessors' majesty, but the process had begun, and now it was a task only time could achieve. To know that some future generation would come here and see greatoaks that had sprung from the staff his father had given into his care all those years ago gave Nat an immense feeling of accomplishment along with gratitude to Catrin.

Neenya stood in awe of everything she witnessed on the Godfist. Nat had wanted to protect her from the rest of the world, to allow her to live her simpler life among the Gunata, but civilization encroached on the lands held by native peoples, and no longer were the Gunata innocent or ignorant. It was Neenya who convinced him to come back to the Godfist because she feared for his life. Now they were here, and he wondered what he could do. How next would unexpected events overturn his world?

* * *

"She's ready," Fasha said.

Benjin wasn't certain if she was referring to the *Dragon's Wing* or Gwen. At five years old, his daughter was a roaring terror wrapped in innocence. One look from her big, blue eyes melted his heart. He was helpless. Running his hands over the polished wood, he looked for imperfections, trying

247

to decide if they needed another coat of sealer and a few more weeks of polishing before making their sea trials.

"She's ready," Fasha insisted.

Still, Benjin made one final inspection of the *Dragon's Wing*. Carved from a single greatoak, it was like no other ship on all of Godsland. While Fasha and Catrin had been pregnant, Benjin and Prios had worked, carving the masthead, which extended back along the sides of the ship. Modeled after Kyrien, the ship looked as if it were flying, even as it sat in dry dock.

For a moment, Benjin stopped to revel in his new life. Letting go of Catrin had been difficult, but he knew Prios would take good care of her. It was on their wedding day that Benjin's life forever changed. With tears in her eyes, Fasha had asked him to marry her. *She* asked *him*. He still couldn't believe it. For weeks, he'd been trying to find the words to ask her, all the while helping organize Prios and Catrin's wedding. He'd been afraid of somehow making Catrin's day less special and never found the right moment to ask. Fasha had chosen the moment, and he loved her for it.

Catrin's wedding day was filled with tears of joy, and the ceremony touched everyone who attended. Later, when Benjin was asked to speak, he could no longer contain his news, and though he was terrified, he announced his engagement to Fasha. The celebration that followed was one he would never forget.

The familiar sound of bare feet running across the deck alerted Benjin to a coming storm.

"Are we ready, Daddy? Can we go now? Momma says I'm going to love the sea. Can we go now, Daddy? Can we? *Please?*" The last question was punctuated by one of Gwen's most practiced and effective looks.

"Yes. We can go now." Benjin gave the order, and horses were brought in. Hooked to thick lines that ran through a massive pulley, the horses pulled.

Unlike ships built from many small pieces, the *Dragon* was a whole. She didn't creak or moan as she slipped along the guide planks. She entered the water with what sounded like a sigh of relief. In the water, she looked much different than Benjin had imagined. Her wingtips, though close and tight to the ship, soared just above the water line, making the ship look vulnerable where Benjin knew it was strong.

Using Brother Vaughn as his voice, Prios often joked that the carving they did made the wood stronger. As if they were peeling away the bits that were hiding its true form. Looking at it now, Benjin couldn't believe he'd been a part of creating it.

"Fasha, my wife," Benjin said as he wrapped her in his arms, "I love you, and I think you should be captain of this ship."

"I'll need a cook," she said, and they both laughed.

Gwen charged by at full speed. "Can we *leave* now?" she asked without slowing.

Together, Benjin and Fasha raised the sails and let the wind drive the *Dragon's Wing* for the first time. Without a sound, save for the flap of canvas, she sliced through the water.

"Wait!" a voice carried across the water. "Hey! Wait for me!"

A loud splash followed, and Benjin turned to look. Then he just shook his head and laughed. He'd forgotten that he promised Jessub he could come on the maiden voyage. Every few days, the boy would show up and check on their progress, and he must have known they were getting close. Now he swam toward them. Fasha slowed the ship as they waited for Jessub.

Benjin dropped the boarding net over the side, never having expected to use it so soon. "Up you go," he said as he pulled a soaked and exhausted Jessub aboard.

"You were gonna leave without me," Jessub accused.

"It's my fault," Fasha said as she threw Jessub a towel. "I convinced him to sail today. I should have told him to wait for you."

"Yes, ma'am," he said, and Benjin barely contained his laughter. For all his energy and bravado, Jessub feared Fasha's wrath more than anything, which, Benjin supposed, only showed that the boy had good sense.

"Come on, Jessub!" Gwen demanded as she led him to the prow. "Look! I'm flying," she said as she stuck her arms out to the sides. A moment later, she was bathed in shadow. Kyrien soared low over the prow, just above Gwen and Jessub.

"Wow," Jessub said, his jaw hanging slack.

"We're flying!" Gwen said.

Benjin watched in amazement, hoping the likeness would not offend Kyrien. Unlike the tales of dragon riders, Catrin had no control over Kyrien. He was a free creature, and he went only where he chose. It was a fact that Benjin knew bothered Catrin and terrified others, but there seemed no way to change the dragon. In truth, Benjin liked him just as he was.

As if to show his approval, Kyrien rested his chin on the carved image of his head and flew with his eyes closed, letting the motion of the ship guide him. Benjin watched in amazement. A moment later Kyrien trumpeted and tipped his wings. Soaring high into the sky, he disappeared from sight.

In deep water, Fasha raised more sail, and the *Dragon's Wing* flew across the water--free.

* * *

The Watering Hole bustled with activity, and Miss Mariss carried platters laden with food between the many crowded tables. Warm weather had blessed them with record crops, and finally their livestock were plentiful again. Children were born, and the towns of Lowerton and Upperton grew faster than anyone could have imagined. Martik's marvels of engineering made farming possible in otherwise impossible places, and it seemed starvation was no longer a threat.

One of the guests yelled for Miss Mariss and she turned. Prios stood near the doorway, his slate in hand. "Sinjin?" it said.

"That boy best not be in my kitchens again. He'll eat us all back into starvation," Miss Mariss said before she stormed into the kitchen. From behind a cutting block, a small hand reached up and grabbed three pieces of bacon. "You'd best get outta my kitchen, boy!"

With a guilty smile, he darted from the kitchen. Miss Mariss chased him out with a broom, but she was not fast enough to catch him. Prios stood shaking his head as Sinjin darted out the doors and ran down the streets, eating his bacon without slowing.

* * *

"Do you really think we're going to discover anything?" Strom asked Osbourne as they hauled more sand through the halls.

"Who knows?" Osbourne said. "Milo says if we look hard enough, we're bound to find something."

"All I know is we've been through at least fifty bags of sand already, and I'm getting tired of carrying them."

"Me too."

As they returned to the mighty hall where Catrin conducted her experiments, Milo pulled a crucible from the furnace and began to pour it into the mold. Strom watched as Catrin waited for the exact right moment to insert the sliver of dragon ore. She looked older, as if the weight of her responsibilities had aged her more quickly than the rest. Still there was strength about her . . . and determination. She never gave up on one of her ideas; at most one might be set aside for further contemplation.

Strom wondered what it was that made her so sure things were going to go badly in the future. Things were going so well, he thought perhaps they should all take some time to enjoy themselves. Instead he was hauling sand to the furnace. Osbourne gasped beside him and Strom watched. Each time she had tried, Catrin had produced a brilliant light that lasted only a few breaths, but this time, as the molten glass captured the charged sliver in its embrace, a warm, steady glow radiated from it. Even as it cooled, the light continued to shine. No one spoke for a long time until the glass was cool enough to touch.

Catrin picked it up in her hand and smiled. "Sometimes the smallest things can make the biggest difference."

About the Author

Born in Salem, New Jersey, Brian spent much of his childhood on the family farm, where his family raised and trained Standardbred racehorses. Brian lives with his wife, Tracey, in the foothills of the Blue Ridge Mountains. After years in the world of Internet technology, the writing of this trilogy has been a dream come true for Brian and what feels like a return to his roots.

More information at http://BrianRathbone.com

If you enjoyed this book, please consider rating, reviewing, or even just "liking" it on your retailer of choice.

Be sure to grab your copy of Regent - Book one of The Balance of Power trilogy, available now!

Regent on Amazon Kindle
http://www.amazon.com/Regent-Balance-Power-ebook/dp/B005Y6S7RS/

Below is a free sample of Regent. Enjoy!

Chapter 1

Wisdom is the reward for surviving our own stupidity.

--Wendel Volker

* * *

Run!

Instinct and compulsion drove Sinjin's lean, teenage body to greater speed, his shoulder-length, auburn hair streaming behind him. Running was the one thing he did well, and the landscape slid by in a blur punctuated by moments of perfect focus. Leaping over a protruding tree root, his eyes locked on another dark-robed figure moving within the trees. Startled, Sinjin lost his step and nearly went down, but through strength of will, he heeded his father's command and ran.

Faster. Run, Sinjin, run!

Ahead the trail turned sharply upward on a direct course to the top of a steep incline. An unfamiliar pain stabbed Sinjin's side, and he placed a hand over it, hoping it would make the cramp go away. It didn't. The Wood Run was designed to challenge even the best runners, and it succeeded in that, but Sinjin gritted his teeth and persevered. Sweat stung his eyes by the time he crested the steep hill. He wanted to stop and rest, to slow his labored breathing, but knew he could not; something was wrong. There should be

253

no one in these woods, especially not shadowy figures in black hooded robes, and his father's mental commands reinforced his fears. It was unusual for Prios to speak with Sinjin over such distance, and Sinjin knew it must have required a great deal of energy and effort. It was equally unusual for Sinjin to be competing in the Spring Challenges, something that had been expressly forbidden.

Stop!

It took a moment for Sinjin to react to the abrupt command, and his momentum carried him forward. The air sang a sharp note, and a dark flash crossed the trail only a hand's width in front of Sinjin's unprotected abdomen. Thrown from his balance, he lost control of his limbs, and a loose rock turned his ankle. Using his next off-kilter step to hurl himself upward, he tucked and rolled, just as Uncle Chase had taught him. The air sang once again, and a slender bolt struck a nearby tree, giving Sinjin a clear view of the deadly implement. It was not like the thick, stubby bolts used to hunt game; this was delicate and precise and seemed a much more frightening weapon.

Cut the course! Turn left ahead!

More shadowy figures moved within the trees. Sinjin started to turn but caught sight of the next ribbon on his right. Tied around the trunk of an elm, it was the last of seven ribbons he needed to collect. Each was signed by Master Edling, and all were required as proof of staying on the Wood Run course. The thought of facing Master Edling

254

and his father made Sinjin want to quit the race and get home, but he could win this race; he knew it. He'd allowed Durin to talk him into it because he'd secretly desired it. Things were not going to go well for him when he got home--if he got home--and he knew this might be his only chance to win. It wasn't the prize he sought; it was the chance to prove that he was good at something--the best, even. Youthful desire overwhelmed sense and his father's command, and Sinjin turned sharply to the right.

Barely slowing, he grabbed the long end of the slipknot and charged toward the clearing, but just as the lush grasses of the Challenge fields came into view, a dark-robed figured stepped onto the trail and raised his arms before him. Sinjin could not see what weapons threatened from within the folds of the overlong sleeves, but he felt the danger.

His blood froze and he nearly ran headlong into death's embrace, but his training was not so far from his mind. Without slowing, he ran up the trunk of a nearby oak and flipped himself backward over the stunned assassin. Using the longest stride he'd ever attempted, Sinjin propelled himself into the clearing. A roar erupted from the gathered crowd, and Sinjin knew he must be running a faster time than Hester had. All he had to do was finish the race to defeat a living legend. Bolstered by this thought and the sight of the exuberant crowd, Sinjin ran. His shoulders itched, almost expecting a bolt to strike and demanding he at least turn his head and look back, but the pain never came.

Durin stood at the head of the crowd, jumping, shouting, and pointing at the sand clocks.

Sinjin suppressed a smile. Then he lowered his head and poured all the energy he had left into a final sprint. At the finish line, he stuffed his seven ribbons into Master Edling's hands. The crowd erupted. Edling, who normally wore a haughty and sour look, could not keep the surprise from his face.

Get home. Now!

Sinjin barely heard his father's voice in his mind, and that worried him more than anything else. Durin's dumbstruck gaze followed Sinjin as he ran past, not even bothering to accept his prize. Sinjin just placed a hand on his aching side and kept moving.

Durin ran up alongside. "What are you doing? You won! You beat Hester's record! You have to stop and accept your prize. You're supposed to get a wreath of vespa and a kiss from Alissa. I can't wait until Kendra hears about this."

"My dad already knows," Sinjin said between sucking in breaths. He couldn't even think about Kendra; she was an unsolvable problem.

Durin's look was apologetic, as it often was, his expressive face and liquid-brown eyes almost comical. "I didn't think he would find out--at least not this soon. Sorry."

"And there are people trying to kill me."

"What? Really?" Durin asked, stumbling as he tried to keep up.

Sinjin just grunted and jogged north toward his home, and for once, Durin matched his pace.

* * *

By the varying light of five herald globes, Catrin hunched over a crumbling scroll, trying to unlock its secrets before time rendered it back into dust. Her translucent hair fell to one side, a constant reminder of the consequences of power. Four more herald globes rested in small iron pedestals, which currently held down the corners of the ancient vellum. Each globe cast its unique glow over the surface of the scroll accompanied by muted reflections from the polished stone table on which they rested. Catrin didn't notice the white and blue filaments that arched from her delicate fingers to the table.

She sighed and closed her eyes. Vast amounts of knowledge had been uncovered in the past decade, much as a result of the ancient cache Catrin herself had found at Ohmahold, but little had been deciphered and even less truly understood. So many of the things they found seemed meaningless and out of context. Each discovery brought more mystery than certainty. The scroll that currently held Catrin's interest discussed the principles and behaviors of energy. It had been found deep within Dragonhold.

That name still made Catrin shiver. She had proposed Volkerhold as the name of her keep, but the instant Chase

257

had suggested Dragonhold, people latched on to it. Leave it to her cousin to come up with a name irresistible to most yet made Catrin very uncomfortable. She'd seen the true majesty of dragons, and it seemed an impossible name to live up to, especially since her relationship with Kyrien was in question. He was a free beast, and nothing bound him to her. After the war with the Zjhon, he had come to her once every year for eight years straight. For the past two years, though, he'd been absent.

For months Catrin had been trying to make contact with him, but he was distant, and what little communication they managed was garbled and only served to worry and confuse her. It disgusted her that deep down she also wanted more dragon ore. Kyrien was far more to her than just a source of the precious stone, but she was suffering without it. Working the stone into herald globes, though tedious, calmed her nerves and filled the hold's coffers. Truly, a visit from her dragon would do her good. With another sigh, she pushed the scroll aside, unable to achieve the level of focus needed for translation, and a sloppy translation would do her no good at all.

Other papers and scrolls awaited her attention, but she returned to one she'd read a dozen times before. It was from her cousin's husband--a man she had nearly married, a man who might have wished he'd married her instead of her acerbic cousin Lissa. While the letter was polite enough and the words themselves gave no real reason for alarm, the letter's presence alone was cause for concern, and Catrin couldn't help feeling that there was a cry for help hidden beneath the bare words. The messenger had refused to tell exactly how he had come into possession of the letter, but he had said that it hadn't come directly from Wolfhold or Ravenhold, and he had no way to guarantee its providence.

Once again, Catrin's thoughts wandered to Thorakis the Builder, the man said to have saved the Greatland from starvation by building massive fisheries. Much of Jharmin's letter told of Thorakis's achievements, including a huge network of man-made rivers within walls of stone. It was almost too much to believe, and though Jharmin spoke well of Thorakis, there was something else, but Millie's sudden arrival and the worried look on her face brought Catrin to her feet.

"Come quick," Millie said as she pulled Catrin from the room, her breathing heavy. "It's Prios, m'lady, he's taken ill."

"Where?"

"In the viewing chamber, m'lady."

Catrin charged ahead, her lithe form moving easily, leaving Millie to shuffle along behind her, the older and heavier woman's joints allowing for only so much speed.

Though Prios was Catrin's first concern, she also worried that this would cause undo anxiety over the safety of the as of yet untested viewing chambers. Catrin knew the perils of improper astral travel, but she also knew the chambers would be safe. Still, she felt like less of a person for having those thoughts. Any right-minded person would be thinking of her spouse.

When Catrin turned the corner, she found Prios supine on the rough stone floor of the first viewing chamber, his head in Brother Vaughn's lap. Though he was breathing, his pale complexion and trembling hands troubled Catrin. Even in his current state, he looked beautiful to her. The kindness in his eyes offset the hard lines of his regal visage. Even staring into empty air, his expression was locked into a look of compassion.

Seeing her dragon ore carving, Koe, lying beside him, chalky and depleted, Catrin was shocked. Even in its most inert state, the carving had an imposing feline form. Koe had been fully charged, glossy and slick, and had been resting in their bedchamber. Prios would not have taken the carving without very good reason; he knew how important it was to her. She'd never been able to carve another like piece; no other dragon ore had ever revealed its true form to her. A sick feeling clutched Catrin's gut, and she asked, "Where's Sinjin?"

Brother Vaughn, his long gray hair pulled back into a braid, looked up with an apology in his eyes. "Prios charged in here, saying he had a bad feeling about Sinjin and that he needed to use the viewing chamber. I tried to stop him, but he just stared out the opening and fell to the floor. He'll be back. I just know it. He's strong."

Catrin slapped Prios hard across the face. Millie sucked air through her teeth, but Catrin knew he would feel only the most intense sensations while out of his body. Shouting in his ear, just as Mother Gwendolin had once done for her, Catrin told him he was going to die. She scanned the painful memories, hoping to recall something that would help save Prios. Without the grounding effect provided by the chairs of stone and metal, he would have nothing to guide him back to his body. He would be lost.

Lost.

Whether the thought came from Prios or from Catrin's subconscious, the effect was the same, and it drove Catrin to reckless action. Without the aid of the stone chairs to anchor her or the monks' chanting to shake loose her spirit, Catrin gazed out of the viewing portal, pulled deeply on the energy around her, and wrenched her soul free from its mortal trappings. Though she left most of her physical senses behind, she did not miss Millie gasping, "By the Gods! She's gone too. It's like they're trying to kill me!"

Unlike Catrin's previous experiences with astral travel, movement was anything but effortless. Just staying whole required most of her concentration. The world seemed to pull at her spirit from a thousand directions, slowly tearing her apart. What movement she did manage was clumsy and out of control, but her son's life and that of her husband were at stake, and nothing would deter her. Driven by a mother's instinct, her spirit flowed down the Pinook Valley, over Edling's Wall, and into the lands that had once been her home. An almost irresistible urge to visit what had been her family's farm tugged at her. Painful memories rose unbidden, the dull ache of loss all too familiar. With extreme mental effort, she focused her energy and thrust those feelings aside. Nothing mattered more than finding Sinjin and Prios.

The world moved wildly beneath her, bucking and lurching as she cast out her senses, searching for familiar patterns of energy.

Go back.

Catrin barely heard Prios in her mind, but his words struck like thunder. She could feel his pain and the effort it had taken to communicate with her. His essence was nearly depleted, and someone interfered with his attempts to return to his body. Feeling helpless, Catrin reeled with fury. Never before had she tried to influence the world around her when traveling outside her body; always before she had been but an observer. Now though, she sensed an enemy approaching her son and another slowly killing her husband.

Dark energies swirled around her as Sinjin and Durin half limped and half jogged into view. The pain in Sinjin's eyes made it clear that he was in no condition to outrun anyone. The darkness coalesced into two figures that materialized as if made from nothing but shadow.

Durin saw them first and shouted, "Run!"

"I can't," Sinjin said, but he picked up his pace as much as he could. It would do no good. Both assassins raised their arms and aimed at Sinjin.

Though they could not hear her, Catrin screamed and thrust herself into the face of one of the men, feeling for his eyes with her energy. A sound like a sizzling pop split the air, and the assassin fell to the ground, screaming and clutching his still-hooded face. The second assassin seemed frozen in time, yet Catrin watched in silent horror as a slender bolt sliced the air on its way to Sinjin's heart. Leaves rustled as what felt like a tornadic wind rushed past Catrin, and she recognized Prios's spirit. Emotion overwhelmed her as she watched him alter the flight path of the bolt so it soared harmlessly over Sinjin's shoulder. A moment later a wall of malicious intent slammed into her like a wave of fire and nausea. Catrin struggled to hold herself together as her unidentified adversary tried to help the world tear her spirit apart. Everything turned a shade darker, and Catrin knew she would soon succumb. As the assassin aimed once again, she made one last desperate attempt to communicate with Sinjin: *"Run!"*

* * *

Never before had Sinjin heard his mother's voice in his mind, and the sound of it terrified him. It felt as if those words might be her last. Screaming, he ducked under the

263

next bolt loosed by the assassin. Behind him he heard a wet *thunk* and a grunt. Turning to look, he saw Durin drop to one knee, his face pale and drawn. Anger welled up in Sinjin and would not be denied. Howling, he turned and ran toward the assassin, who seemed surprised and momentarily stunned. Using what Uncle Chase had taught him, Sinjin coiled his muscles and focused his core strength to launch his attack. He struck with more force than he could naturally muster, and he felt tingling hands assisting him and reinforcing his strike. The assassin went down and did not rise.

With a lump in his throat, Sinjin turned to Durin, who was now on his side, one leg trapped beneath his body at an awkward angle. It looked to Sinjin as if he were already dead. Tears filled his eyes, but he forced them back. When he pulled Durin from the ground and wrestled his limp body over one shoulder, the boy moaned and Sinjin risked a moment of hope--it was a brief moment. The assassin, too, moaned, and Sinjin moved off as fast as he could while carrying Durin. Once again his shoulders itched, waiting for the next deadly bolt to strike. He nearly dropped Durin at the sound of a snapping branch, but it was Uncle Chase and five of his best men who approached.

Chase rushed forward when he saw the boys and charged past them, looking for their assailants, his soldier's body rippling with intent. Sinjin turned to watch his uncle go, terrified by Chase's deadly charge but also by the thought of losing him. The valley behind was now empty, though, and nothing of the two assassins remained. It was as if they had been taken by the wind. Only the still form of Durin and the deadly bolt protruding from his shoulder gave evidence that they had ever existed.

"What happened?" Chase asked. "Never mind. It doesn't matter. We need to get you back to Dragonhold. Bradley, Simms, you carry Durin. Jorge and Morif, grab Sinjin." Words of protest were cut short as Sinjin suddenly found himself slung over the shoulders of two men who immediately began to run. The desire to run on his own two legs was nearly overwhelming, despite knowing his energy was already spent.

About the Author

Born in Salem, New Jersey, Brian spent much of his childhood on the family farm, where his family raised and trained Standardbred racehorses. Brian lives with his wife, Tracey, in the foothills of the Blue Ridge Mountains. After years in the world of Internet technology, the writing of this trilogy has been a dream come true for Brian and what feels like a return to his roots.

For more information, visit http://BrianRathbone.com

If you enjoyed this book, please consider leaving a review, rating, or even just "liking" it on the retailer of your choice or on Goodreads. Thanks!

Made in the USA
Columbia, SC
09 December 2017